The Call

The Call

Cathy Schieffelin

atmosphere press

For Anna, Caroline and Sam
You inspire me every day.
For John
My grace and happy place.

Part I

The Comoros Islands,
June 6, 2003 – 5:30 a.m.

Chapter 1
Call to Prayer

Nate:

Allahu akbar, Allahu akbar, Allahu akbar, Allahu akbar. Ashhadu anna la ila ill Allah...

Deep voices, chanting, resonate around me. It's musical and familiar, yet jarring in Arabic, a language I don't understand. Webs of mist cloud my vision, foggy and disorienting. Where the Hell am I?

I crack open my eyes. Sun has broken on the horizon, rays warming the sky to colors of peaches and roses. My head pounds, making me wonder if I have a wallop of a headache or if I'm part of the crashing waves in the background.

Waves? We aren't near water. What is that?

I blink, hoping the claustrophobia subsides. The chemical smell of pyrethrum and the grit of salt on my lips brings me back. Rolling to my side, I gaze through the musty mosquito netting. Anjouan—a tropical speck floating in the Indian Ocean, part of the Comoro Archipelago. My work takes me to many far-flung places, but this, by far, is the most remote. *That's right, we left Morocco yesterday.*

Early morning is my favorite—the calm before reality stirs. The reality that my relationship with Emma is over and I'm alone again. The reality that there's more to these tiny islands than meets the eye. Hard to imagine Al-Qaeda has infiltrated this pristine paradise. I'm also grappling with the realization that my team, sleeping nearby, is here at my request.

Gavin didn't bat an eye even though Dani gave birth last week to their first child, Sam. Gavin would have missed the delivery anyway, I tell myself. But I convinced him and the others to fly here to root out a possible terrorist cell incubating in this Eden.

There must be half a dozen mosques within earshot, as the muezzins' voices rise and fall in dissonance and harmony. Despite the cacophony of voices projecting from loudspeakers, there's something soothing about the call—it slows my racing heart and clears my mind. It must be near six a.m. because in this part of the world, balanced delicately on the equator, the sun always rises and sets at the same time. Soon it'll be too hot to lie on this roof.

I push up off the dingy mattress and disentangle from the clammy netting, my limbs stiff and achy. I'm too young to be feeling this geriatric. I miss my regular runs and trips to New River. My last big climb was in Yosemite with Emma...a lifetime ago. I shake my head to dislodge her face from my mind. I need to get back to it; when I don't climb or train, I lose the finger strength needed for tackling harder pitches. Climbing helped me move past that breakup.

Breathing deep, jasmine and vanilla bean permeate the air. The team sleeps nearby, encased in bed nets. An empty bottle of Johnnie Walker rests next to Jorge. *How can they sleep through these prayers?* An Arabic symphony resonates deep inside me. Growing up in rural Kentucky, home to Baptist preachers selling snake oil and salvation, there's something familiar about this place. It's a different kind of spiritual awakening.

I walk to Sara. I need her help this morning with camera angles and lighting. She's on her side, lying awkwardly, mouth agape, eyes partly open. I move the flimsy netting aside.

My heart pounds as I reach for her. Is she even breathing? Blonde hair, tangled and matted; her face, a sickly gray.

My ear to her mouth, no breath. Taking her wrist, I pray for a pulse. Nothing. *Holy shit...*

I shake her. *Come on, Sara, wake the hell up!*

Nothing. She's limp, but warm.

I run to Gavin to demand his help. I pull up short as I reach his mattress. He's in the same condition.

All three of my colleagues are dead.

Chapter 2
Flic-en-Flac, Mauritius, June 6, 2003

Juliette:

He chased me again last night. Is it considered a nightmare if I relive it every few months, waking with a racing heart and a knot in my stomach? Ice-blue eyes, laughing. Later he acted like it was an innocent prank. Pranks don't leave scars.

The raucous cries of common mynas and white-tailed tropicbirds startle me awake and away from my dark thoughts. Below their piercing calls are the melodious songs of Mauritius fodies and yellow-fronted canaries enjoying the bounty of my little garden. And deeper still, in the understory of sound, are the tenor coos of pink pigeons and zebra doves. I can identify many birds by call alone, but I struggle with the variety of bulbuls. Though not native to Mauritius, I enjoy their colorful plumage and gorgeous songs.

I wonder if I'll see Kaulia on my sunrise swim. She's a beauty, tortoiseshell scutes undulating gold and copper under the sun's rays, shining through iridescent waters. Darrien and Claire scold me for swimming alone, but this is my time. Rip currents are a threat. I had a scare last year and stopped swimming for a few months, but I'm back at it now. I've learned to read the tides and weather after spending time with Manu. He's been teaching me to surf when he's not working at the coffee shop.

Yesterday I glimpsed a pod of dusky dolphins. Two years

ago, I joined a group in a playful swim. I couldn't believe they allowed me into their circle. When I treaded water to watch, one nudged me. I followed. When I stopped again, a different dolphin with a scarred fin jostled me. I spent nearly two hours with them, imagining myself a trainer at SeaWorld. But these were wild dolphins, which makes it a serious no-no. In most places I could be fined or even jailed for harassment of marine mammals. I tried to keep a respectful distance, but the dolphins approached me.

I should have pursued marine biology. I'd have stayed clear of Bogota and the mess my life became there.

I struggle out of bed, untwisting from the bedsheets. I'm grateful for the fine mesh screening Darrien installed a few months back. No need for stifling bed nets now. A plumeria breeze blows my gauzy curtains around, ushering a wave of goosebumps up my arms. My damp bikini hangs on the chair and I grab my last clean towel. Need to do laundry.

This colorful Creole cottage sits on the beachside road in a grove of casuarina, ficus, and palm trees. Windows facing the ocean make up its back, shaded by cobalt-hued Bahama shutters that contrast with the mango-yellow bungalow. Climbing bougainvillea vines in vibrant fuchsia creep up my walls, reminding me of home. It's hard to believe I haven't been back in seven years. My parents come here for visits and I'm not sure they understand my reluctance to return home, though I wish we could be closer. I miss them.

My feet sink into the cool, damp sand as I make my way down the beach. The water is a mirror. I take stock in its glassy ripples. Sometimes another woman stares back—someone confident who knows her own mind. Was she always here, hidden beneath complicated layers? This place and this job are peeling away my tough outer shell. Darrien may not know it, but he saved me. He and Claire both.

My morning meditation and swim keep me sane. Once I get to the lab, my world will shrink dramatically. No vast swells of seawater, no great gray herons squawking in the shallows. Only the silence of a microcosm: parasites, bacteria, and protozoa squiggling under a lens.

Chapter 3
Sudden Death

Nate:

Am I having a heart attack? I can't breathe—chest hurts. I remember my Uncle Teddy's face when he had one. Gray—cement gray, the color of locker room walls. He gasped, unable to get oxygen. That's how this feels.

The gold minaret of a nearby mosque warps and blurs. I plunk down, putting my head between my knees. Every part of me feels like a contradiction.

Whom do I call? Local gendarmes? I can't speak French to save my life.

Campbell...I gotta call Campbell. He'll know what to do. I glance across the rooftops. Anyone else out there in a similar predicament? The sun rises. Heat waves create distortion.

I gotta move their bodies from this hot roof.

I start with Gavin—he's the heaviest. I leave him on the mattress and pull it down the narrow stairwell. I reposition him a few times when his arm flops off the mattress and bangs the wall. This is no way to treat a friend. Sweat drips down my back and into my eyes, tearing and stinging. This is the only way. My body knows what to do, even if my mind can't comprehend this fucked-up reality. Back muscles and calves scream as I drag him down the stairs. I've been part of climbing rescue missions before—but this is different. My friends won't be waking up...won't be treated in a hospital in hopes of recovery. They're dead.

Gavin and I worked together for years. He and Dani are family to me. I've spent holidays in their home, eating Dani's lasagna and drinking Gavin's whiskey. How do I tell her the father of their newborn is no longer breathing? I lurch to the edge of the rooftop and gag. *Shit, don't fall off. I can't be another casualty.*

Next, I move Jorge. He's smaller and easier to maneuver. I get him down without mishap. Sara's the easiest. I stare at the flowery tattoo running up her left forearm, remembering when she got it. I should carry her; she's light. But I'm afraid to touch them. Could whatever got them, get me?

I line them up on their mattresses, like a horror scene from a Stephen King novel. Their bodies are still warm, but otherwise, no signs of life. How long does it take for rigor mortis to set in? Thank God they're not stiff. I pull sheets over them, unable to look into their graying faces another minute. I stagger to the kitchen for the satellite phone. It's 7:30. It took an hour and a half to move them. I grab a water bottle from the fridge, chugging. My inner voice tells me to slow down...take a breath...and another breath. I collapse into a chair.

"Campbell, it's Nate. I'm in trouble here."

A groggy grunt is the only reply. I have no idea what time it is there. Don't care.

"Nate, that you?"

I scream—hysterical, but it makes me feel better. Eventually I run out of breath. He's annoyed—thinks I'm pulling a prank. When I lose it a second time, my panic crosses the phone lines and Campbell's voice sharpens and slows.

"Easy, Nate. Slow down. What happened?" He struggles to process the insanity I projectile-vomit at him. "What time is it there?" He curses when he thumps into something. Think he's trying to let Charlie sleep, while I throw him into my maelstrom. He tells me he'll call back after he finds out who's nearby.

My stomach pitches and I run to the bathroom to purge

last night's dinner of goat kebabs. My throat burns from the chile pepper sauce the meat was basted in. The sour taste of Johnnie Walker takes me back to sitting on the roof, passing the bottle around while we ate as the evening call to prayer echoed around us.

I know no one in this tiny country and speak deplorable French, let alone the Swahili dialect most people speak. Looking around, the guest house is sparse—decorated with silver frames of artist-inspired mosques in cheesy pastels and the requisite, austere black and white photo of Comorian president Abdallah Hashim.

Taking a deep breath in, I will myself to calmness. The scent of ylang-ylang hangs heavy in the air. The flower put the Comoros on the aromatic map charted by Chanel No. 5. Its cloying and overly sweet scent turns my stomach again.

The phone rings. *Let this be some wild practical joke. Please.*

Campbell calmly says he has a medical team arriving from Mauritius in the afternoon.

"Please keep this quiet until we know what's going on. I don't want to alert families until we have something to tell them."

The thought of calling families never occurred to me. That's the last call I want to make.

He asks if the bodies are in a cool, dark place. I glance at the shrouded figures, aware of the sun blazing in.

"I'll drag them to a back bedroom. Maybe I can find fans around here."

"Good. Do that. I'll instruct the team to pick up supplies and food. Can you sit tight until they arrive this afternoon?"

No!

Chapter 4

SOS

I stop by L'Igloo on my way into the lab. Need a shot of caffeine.

Mani smiles, handing me my coffee as I dig rupees from my tattered rucksack. "Morning *Juli.*" He's always called me that. "How are things at the lab?"

"Great. How are things here? Keeping everyone suitably caffeinated?"

"You know it. Think you're ready for another board meeting? Or have you mastered pipe, and find my lessons unnecessary?" His eyes dance, flirting. He *is* cute, but that's about all there is to him. There's something else that bothers me, but I can't think of what it might be.

I return his smile. "I've got that pipe thing down—nothing like riding the tube. Thanks for the latte." I swing out the door with a wave before he can press further about surfing lessons.

I didn't expect to see him, since he's usually off Tuesdays. But he was at the register in his customary uniform - a white tank top showcasing impressive biceps and rock-hard abs. I've been dodging him since we hooked up a couple weeks ago, after a night out drinking with the research team. Not sure why, but that night at Enigma, I got wasted. Woke up the next day with him in my bed.

His moto was parked outside my bungalow that morning.

I remember its sputtering as he rode away. I'm not sure anything happened. When I woke, he was beside me, fully clothed. I was not. I found my dress later, balled in the corner, covered in vomit. He treated me like a wounded puppy before he left.

I'm embarrassed because I never returned his calls. I'm not the best at breaking things off gently. In my mind, there wasn't anything to break off since we only hooked up once. I wanted to celebrate catching my first wave that day. Mani made fun because, although I've lived here for three years, I just learned to surf.

I'm a quick study. Years of dance help with the balance thing, the toughest aspect to master when surfing. The other vital skill is letting go—releasing to the energy and motion of the wave, finding the sweet spot between dubious control and utter chaos. That takes longer to learn. It doesn't hurt that my instructor is a hot Brazilian beach bum and surfing fanatic. Up until that night, we were squarely in the friend zone. Surfing lessons, iced lattes, nothing more.

I love surfing now. It's addicting. When I first arrived, Claire warned me about the tight-knit surfing community. I stayed clear as I had no desire to get tangled in anything new, particularly an activity requiring so little clothing. Lab work suited me—just me and the parasites.

Then I sat on the beach one morning and watched as sunbleached ninjas performed crazy acrobatics on raggedy wood boards, tossed about by wind and waves. I witnessed a few impressive wipe-outs but I was transfixed. On lunch breaks I'd zip back to watch. Mani was one of the guys out there. Later we ran into each other at the coffee shop and he offered to teach me.

At the lab, when I observe wriggling *falciparum* malaria parasites dancing across the slide, I remember Mani's fatal flaw. He's a terrible dancer. For his studly good looks and impressive pecs, he's a menace on the dance floor. I woke with bruises all over my feet. His kisses...those weren't so bad. My cheeks heat up just as Darrien pokes his head into my office.

"Jules, we've an emergency. Can you be ready in thirty minutes?"

I push back from my desk, stretching my neck. "What's going on?"

"Think we have more cases in the Comoros." He stands in the doorway, staring out the window behind my head. His hands twist in front of him. When he catches me looking, he stuffs them in his pockets.

I met Darrien three years ago. He wanted someone proficient in French with an interest in tropical medicine. When he learned I'd served in Madagascar as a Peace Corps volunteer, he interviewed me in *Malagasy*. The man's multilingual abilities still astound me. Good thing I was fluent enough. He hired me on the spot. Mom and Dad were less thrilled I was flying back to the far reaches of the planet. I was happy to lose myself in the Oceanic tropics again.

More cases? He's talking about RESV—a new virus we're tracking.

"How many?" I ask. This outbreak has been simmering for a few years, but sometimes we get a clump.

"Four. Americans."

Ahh...that explains it.

"I'll be ready. Let me zip back to the house and pack. The specimen kit should be ready to go."

"I'll pick you up there."

Chapter 5
Killing Time

Nate:

It's too quiet. I nearly jump out of my skin when people walk by the house, talking. I can't do this. I'll go nuts in this steaming house all day.

What if I left? Just packed my bags and got outta here. Tempting. I could be on a flight to...well...anywhere. I'd first have to get on a boat, then a rinky-dink Russian plane, shaped like a school bus with wings. It's called *AeroFlop* for good reason.

I glance back at my friends, their outlines on the mattresses. I can't do that to them and their families. I'd never be able to look Dani in the eye. But the thought of sitting in this stifling house, waiting, is unthinkable.

Maybe I don't have to.

I have a meeting scheduled with an informant. I was going to cancel, but maybe I'll sneak out for a bit. I can meet Ali and do a little work to pass the time. Anything's better than festering here. Nur's Biryani isn't far—maybe a ten-minute walk. There's nothing to do until the medical team arrives anyway, right?

I find a table in the back of the restaurant and watch for Ali. Does he know what transpired this morning? I order hot mint tea to settle my stomach.

My mind drifts to last night. We arrived after sunset and, knowing the house would be hot, dragged mattresses to the roof as we'd done in Morocco. We brought mosquito nets, as the Comoros is rife with malaria and dengue.

We picked up street food; bought out the woman's entire grill. She squatted next to the mini hibachi, basting meat in a hot chile and garlic sauce. Her deep red and white *shiromani* covered her from head to toe, displaying her innate beauty and angular grace as she served us. When Sara spoke French with impressive fluency, the woman offered a special treat—a bit slimy, but not bad. Later we sat on the roof, eating and passing around a bottle of Johnnie Walker as bats carried out their nightly acrobatic display.

I look up when a man in a red *kofia* propped neatly atop his head comes into the restaurant. He wears a long white *bubu*, as if he's just come from mosque. I raise a hand.

"Nate? *As-salamu alaikum.*"

"*Alaikum salam,*" I reply, the Arabic greeting of *Peace be upon you.*

Ali is young—fresh-faced and eager. He has dark, expressive eyes and an easy smile. He's tall and lean and floats through space in his long white robe. He asks about my journey.

"Came on the ferry last night from the capital. It was calm, so that was appreciated. Do you live here in Domoni?"

"*Oui,* but I'm from Moheli, the smallest island. My parents live there, in the mountains. They grow star fruit and watercress." The server brings tea and Ali sips, unflustered. Maybe he doesn't know what happened.

"Watercress? I didn't know it grew here. Comorians like it?" I struggle to keep my knees from bouncing the table.

"No, we don't eat that *mzungu* food. We grow for export." *Mzungu* is Swahili, referring to people who run around in circles, recounting early white foreigners. It's used somewhat pejoratively to describe tourists. "Have you tried our Comorian food?"

"We ate goat kebabs with grilled cassava last night. It was great." *Not so great coming back up this morning, though.*

"You've met Madame Sokaina then. She's famous for her *mshakiki mbuzi*—goat-on-a-stick. You'll have to try *mataba*, made with cassava leaves, crushed and cooked all day in coconut milk. It's a specialty."

"Sounds lovely," I say, grimacing as the sour remnants of yesterday's dinner layer the back of my throat. "Tell me, Ali, are you affiliated with Al-Qaeda? Is there an Al-Qaeda presence here?"

"I never said that. I do *not* work for Al-Qaeda." He frowns. "They don't have a presence anymore. But there've been a few enrollees—uh, trainees who've gone on to unfortunate fame," he says, lowering his voice.

"Like Fazul Abdullah Mohammed of the 1998 Nairobi Embassy bombing?"

His eyes flatten. "You've done your homework. *Oui*, Monsieur Mohammed was the famous Comorian in that attack."

"Are there others like him? In training camps? Does Al-Qaeda recruit here?"

He blanches, eyes darting. "No, no, nothing like that," he whispers. "Sometimes someone will get entrapped in the extremist movement, but Les Comores—we are peaceful. We're poor and need money for better schools and roads. Why would we engage with these tyrants?" His hands rub the tabletop like he's polishing it.

"Maybe, just as you said, this country is poor and needs help. Maybe Al-Qaeda offered to help in exchange for something else."

His eyes burn into mine. "No, *Bwana* Nate, that's not true. We do not interact with terrorists," he says with finality.

"Why'd you tell me there were recruitment basecamps here? Was that a lie?" My earlier nausea is gone—something else fills my belly.

"Shh, *Bwana*, not so loud." Ali presses his hands down as if patting a child's head. "Let's walk; that would be better, yes?"

"Unless you're willing to give me more than this..." I motion to the server.

"*Oui*, there's more. Just not here. We'll talk near the port—more private," he whispers.

I steal glances around the nearly empty restaurant, wondering whom he's afraid of. I leave a few crumpled francs and we walk into the glaring sunlight. Ali's *bubu* billows and gussets as the wind swirls sand and dust in the streets. His *kofia* stays atop his head, as if glued there. He leads me to a secluded bench near the impressive gold-minareted Chirazi Mosque.

Keeping his voice low, he tells me about the most recent Al-Qaeda activity and recruitment camps in the mountains. He recounts a story about his cousin who got caught up in the movement and was never seen again, after attempting to escape from a training site in Saudi Arabia. He speaks with no emotion, like it happened to someone he didn't know. I'm not sure whether to believe him.

I learn these incidences occurred over three years ago. Things have been quiet since. I seethe as he rattles on.

"Comorians aren't built to be extremists. We may be poor and uneducated, but we love Allah and our families. We don't want to kill our brothers, even for the promise of new shoes."

I'd never have made this trip unless I thought there was something worth writing about. I wouldn't have kept Gavin from seeing his newborn child. A nagging headache keeps me from lashing out. I check my watch and make a hasty exit before the medical team arrives.

As I trudge back to the house, grotesque images flood my mind. I open the door and walk to the back bedroom, palms sweating and heart pounding. The silence is eerie. The bed sheets dance, fluttering around the room, as the box fans bring them to life.

It's macabre.

Gavin, Jorge, and Sara are gone.

Chapter 6
Domoni — Comoros Islands

Juliette:

I stare out the window as the small plane dives toward the tiny dots where we'll land. The Comoros are a lovely chain of four islands, volcanic like Mauritius, primarily Muslim. I've vacationed here a few times.

In Madagascar, my Peace Corps job was to lead visitors around Ranomafana National Park, informing them of the biodiversity and how to protect the flora and fauna. For vacation, the other volunteers wanted to go on safari to Kenya or Tanzania. Not me. I wanted an out-of-the-way place to get lost, where I could avoid tourists. The Comoros was perfect.

I met other expats stationed there. We spent days snorkeling with sea turtles, camping on the beach, and grilling fresh tuna.

While camped out, I woke in the middle of the night and walked along the beach. The Southern Cross hung overhead, with the constellations Sagittarius and Carina twinkling on the horizon. Then I saw her—ginormous and rounded, low to the ground, lumbering ashore. In water, sea turtles are effortless swimmers, but on land, they struggle under the weight of their cumbersome bodies and ancient DNA. She breast-stroked deliberately up the beach. I followed from a distance, listening to the rhythmic sound of flippers flinging sand. Once she found an ideal spot, she spent twenty minutes digging a hole deep enough to lay her eggs. I crept closer. She paused and looked right at me. I shrank back, upset I interrupted her work. After another twenty minutes, she trudged back to the ocean, disappearing into the salty foam.

I never mentioned my sighting the next morning, as I was ashamed I hadn't woken anyone. I selfishly wanted to keep the experience to myself. Couldn't chance the others harassing her, snapping pictures or, worse, riding on her back.

Another volunteer invited me to climb Mount Karthala, an inactive volcano on the mainland. I declined. I still had scars from my last hiking adventure. It's a shame one bad experience can ruin something so entirely.

I loved exploring mountains and volcanoes as a kid. I spent my childhood wandering the hills and valleys surrounding our home on the outskirts of Santa Marta in northern Colombia. I had no fear then. I didn't mind getting lost. Sounds of animals in the forest rarely spooked me, and I never feared bad weather.

So many things terrify me now—unexpected and violent. I never know what will set me off or how long the panic will last.

I stick to swimming. Riptides are preferable to jagged rocks, steep mountain passes and unpredictable angry men.

We have a journey before arriving in Domoni. There's no airstrip on the side of the island where we're headed—just long twisting, mountain roads.

Darrien's quiet. I'm not sure who called this morning, but he hasn't told me much besides there's a sole survivor—a journalist from the States. If he's truly the only survivor, this will be a first for us.

Darrien's packed our PPE. This new virus is strange. I double-check the bags to be sure we have all the equipment needed.

Darrien's head doesn't seem to be in the game today. Maybe he and Claire had a fight. I rarely see them argue, but it's tough juggling an investigative medical research program while raising a small child as your wife travels the globe as chief epidemiologist.

Chapter 7
OGRE

Nate:

Voices, laughing and familiar.

What the fuck?

No one was breathing. How's this possible?

I look back into the room with the now-empty mattresses and the sheets billowing. *No, I moved these this morning.* Aching shoulders and quads are physical reminders of what transpired.

I squeeze my eyes shut. *Did I dream this?* Opening them again, I look out the window.

Jorge smiles at Sara while Gavin laughs, his blonde head thrown back. They don't look like graying corpses on the verge of desiccation.

I stumble towards the living room, thumbs pressing into my eyeballs. I want to run to them, to touch them... How are they alive? *Thank God they're alive.*

"Nate—there you are," Sara calls as they come inside. "Wondered where you were. Good prank, by the way."

"Were we snoring too loudly?" Gavin jokes.

"Uhh..." Then it hits me. They woke in that back bedroom, covered in sheets. That would be weird. "Where'd you guys come from?" I will my voice not to crack.

"The Indian restaurant down the street—great chicken kebabs there," Gavin says as he thumps into the kitchen, carrying bags from the market. "Feel a bit hungover from last night's Walker binge. Atrocious headache," he says, pulling Advil from his backpack. "Why do all Francophone countries drink that stuff? They need to import something better."

The kitchen is claustrophobic. I back out, feeling Sara's eyes on me as I drag myself to a chair at the dining table.

Gavin rubs his arm, wincing. There's a bruise on his bicep. *Shit, I did that to him.*

"You okay? You don't look so good." Jorge sits across from me.

I don't know what to say. Visions of my dead friends and the call to prayer swirl in my mind as Jorge's eyes probe. "I'm okay..."

A loud knock at the door jolts me from the table. I lurch to open it to find a man decked head to toe in white biohazard protective gear. *This isn't good.* He's tall and lean and carries a medical bag with a large red crescent stitched into the center.

"Nate? *Bonjour.* I'm Doctor Derriere Gauche."

Derriere? Really?

He has a thick French accent and I picture his masked face as an ass. My addled brain finds this funny and I suppress a laugh, though I should worry someone will see this Storm Trooper at our door. I expect him to introduce himself as Inspector Clouseau.

No, this isn't a joke.

"Hi, uhh, I..." The sun blazes as sweat drips down my back. "I, uh, may have been wrong. But no...they were dead. I thought they were dead..." I step outside and shut the door behind me. Jorge cannot see this guy.

Things go sideways. Masked Clouseau grabs my arm.

"*Facilement*, Nate. We're here to help."

I lean against the white cement pillar. Bright green and blue splotches cover the inside of my lids.

He mumbles something about a global emergency organization and he's with a colleague. Then he shouts something in French. I'm in no shape to translate. I grip the pillar, listening to Gavin and Sara laughing in the kitchen.

The doctor peels off his face shield and head covering. I'm surprised by the mop of damp black hair and deep blue eyes. Those PPE coverings are hot as hell. He's drenched, but looks like he could have stepped from the pages of French Vogue, the rugged doctor edition.

"They're no longer dead? That what you want to say?" He is French, but now I understand him.

A young woman materializes in green scrubs and baseball cap. She glances at me. *Wow.*

"Darrien, do we need the specimen kit too?" she asks. American, I think. *Darrien, not Derriere. Whew.*

"*Oui.* Juliette, come meet Nate."

She smiles, then grabs my arm. "You okay? Sit down."

Her face blurs as tiny constellations explode behind my eyes. Hands push my head forward.

"Breathe slowly. It's okay," she says as she kneads the back of my skull.

Things must not be so dire if they don't need the biohazard suits.

"You aren't the first to experience this. Have you spoken to your friends yet?" Darrien asks.

What? He crouches before me, face level with mine when I glance up.

"This has happened before?" I blink, hoping the large spots will clear. The woman—Juliette—sits. I look back and forth between them. She has extraordinary eyes – a green-eyed goddess. "How can this happen? How can someone die, then come back to life? They don't look sick. They aren't zombies, are they?" I laugh. I haven't taken Malarone in years, but this is one effed-up dream.

Darrien sits too. "This may sound crazy, but we're here to help. It's a new virus we're tracking." He pauses, calm. Too calm.

I want to run inside and slam the door.

"In truth, it's not that new. It's just new to humans," he clarifies.

I look to the green-eyed goddess, who smiles and nods like this is *so* everyday for them. "It causes its victims to go into an unusual state—like hibernation. But it can look like death," she explains.

What the hell are they talking about?

"We just need samples," Darrien adds.

My head swivels between these two remarkable creatures. This can't be real. "Hibernation? Like bears?" I repeat, unsure what I'm asking. "Samples of what?"

Darrien puts a hand on my shoulder. "We'll take blood, saliva, urine, and sweat samples. We'd like to observe them a bit before telling them anything. Have you mentioned what happened yet?"

He's mad—a mad scientist. A striking mad scientist and his gorgeous assistant. Maybe it's the accent.

"No, I just found them..." *How do I put this?* "...revived moments ago. You want me to keep quiet about... everything? These are my friends...my colleagues... How can I *not* tell them?"

Darrien's dark blue eyes betray nothing. He holds my gaze, unblinking. *How many of these cases has he really seen?*

Juliette takes my wrist, drawing my attention. I want to rip my arm from her. "Just taking your pulse. Don't get up right away," she says quietly. "We need to test everyone but it's best if they don't know about the virus just yet. Can you introduce us to them?"

She smiles benignly, keeping a hand on my wrist. Her touch is gentle. She has lovely hands—smooth and tan. I avoid looking into her sea glass eyes. Those eyes will turn me to stone or render me incapable of rational thought.

"This doesn't make sense. We just got here. How can they have gotten sick with something so fast? Don't viruses need days to show symptoms?" My brain turned back on, thank God.

"It has a quick onset. Campbell said you arrived yesterday evening?"

Campbell knows these two? He sent them?

"We flew into the capital, then caught the ferry. We arrived at sunset last night. How's it contracted?"

They exchange a look. I wish I could translate their secret code.

"What did you have for dinner last night?"

It takes me a moment to recall. "I think goat kebabs, with grilled cassava and..." I gag and shake my head to dispel the reminder of last night's dinner.

Darrien waits, patient.

"Green papaya salad too. Why?"

"You sure it was goat meat?"

That stops me. "What are you saying? What else would it have been?"

Raised eyebrows now and nods. "Your friends weren't dead—just in a hibernating state, like bears." He's unflustered, even with sweat dripping down his face. " Nate, the good news is everyone we've encountered recovers. They typically have no idea what occurred. Frankly the news of their condition is more upsetting than the physical aspects of the virus."

He holds out a hand and helps me stand. I have more questions, but we can't stay out baking in the sun all day.

"Let's meet your colleagues, okay? Then we can better assess what's going on." Darrien quickly peels off his PPE and shoves it in his medical bag.

I step inside as Jorge emerges from the kitchen with a green coconut.

"Jorge, this is Doctor Darrien Gauche and Doctor...?" I pause, wedged between them.

"Just Juliette—Juliette Fernandez. I'm a virologist with OGRE."

Jorge's eyes narrow, but smiles reluctantly. "OGRE? Where'd you guys come from?" He's standoffish which doesn't surprise me.

Darrien grins. "*Oui*, our founder has an unusual sense

of humor. We're with the Organisation Globale Response Emergence, based in Mauritius. We met Nate earlier, near the port. Please, call me Darrien." He offers his hand.

"Heard it's beautiful there. What brings you to this tropical paradise?"

"We're conducting a disease surveillance study. Nate mentioned you might be willing to participate?"

Jorge's eyes meet mine for a moment then back and forth between me and the OGRES. "Is there a reason you're coming to see us?"

"We're collecting samples from tourists and expats. When we ran into Nate, we knew he wasn't local."

I glance behind Jorge, hoping Gavin and Sara will appear. They'll be less suspicious.

"What kind of study?" Jorge sits. It's awkward, as he doesn't invite them to join him at the table. I'm too dizzy to risk leaving their sides.

"We're investigating a virus found in Mauritius. It's cropped up here too." Darrien rifles through his medical bag after moving to the table. I'm grateful Juliette stays at my side, a stable presence.

"We only just got here, so I doubt we'd have been exposed. Is it dangerous? Nasty side effects?"

Juliette takes my elbow and guides me to the table.

"It has a quick onset—eight to ten hours. You came by ferry from the capital?" Darrien pulls out documents, unbothered by Jorge's tone.

Gavin and Sara wander from the back room, with camera equipment. Sara's wiping lenses.

Gavin takes in the visitors with ease. "We flew from Rabat two days ago, then hopped on the ferry from Moroni last night. I'm Gavin and this is Sara." He strides over to shake Darrien's hand. *Thank you, Gav.*

"Nice to meet you. There's just the four of you?" Darrien asks, glancing around.

"Yup, we're on assignment for the next week. What about a virus?" Sara asks, sitting next to Juliette.

"It's impacting a few expats in the area. We're collecting blood, urine, saliva, and sweat samples from anyone willing to participate. How about it?" Darrien pulls out consent forms and pens.

"Happy to help. Anything to further the science. What do you think, Nate?" I must not look too good, as he stares at me for a moment.

"I think we should do it. Good with you, Sara? Jorge?"

Sara nods as Jorge puts up a hand. "I need to hear more about this thing. Not gonna throw my DNA around to complete strangers—no offense."

"*D'accord, d'accord.*" Darrien laughs, his deep voice echoes off the cement walls. He digs into his bag and pulls out more papers. "*Regarde,* these are our credentials. OGRE's been around for two decades. I'm the lead physician and have worked with them for the past seven years. Juliette's been with us for three years. We collaborate with the CDC and the NIH." He hands the papers to Jorge.

Jorge shifts in his seat, scanning the pages. An uncomfortable silence settles in the room.

"We'll answer any questions you have."

The evening call to prayer begins, haunting me again. A flashback to the morning drops a cold stone in my belly. I shake my head to dislodge the images of my friends dead on their mattresses. Juliette gives me a sympathetic smile.

"I tell you what." Darrien clears his throat. "We can do the sample collection first and then chat more over dinner. There's a lovely spot nearby that specializes in vanilla lobster. It's a Comorian delicacy. Our treat ... and there's a decent bar. How does an ice-cold beer sound?" Darrien knows his expats; a cold beer is serious currency in the Muslim world.

Jorge doesn't look convinced.

"I think we should do this, especially if it's impacting

tourists. You need blood, sweat, and tears?" I interject.

"*Oui, fantastique.* And urine, please." Darrien motions for Juliette to set up. She labels specimen cups and hands them out.

When they've collected everything, Darrien requests a safe place to stow things while we go out for dinner. I lead him down the hall to the back bedroom.

"This is where I pulled them this morning," I whisper.

"Any chance you can get away later tonight? I have more questions." He tucks the medical bag and sample kits into the corner of the room.

"It'll be late."

"I'll pick you up at one a.m., on the corner. We have a house nearby."

Chapter 8

Impressions

Juliette:

"You live in Mauritius? Are you from there?" Sara asks. I feel she's sizing me up. She disassembles a large, complicated camera, clearly knowledgeable of the workings. A thousand black pieces scatter across the table.

"Yes, but I grew up in Colombia."

She tucks a strand of blonde hair behind her ear as she glances up - light blue eyes meet mine.

"The country—not the city. My parents run a horse trekking business outside Santa Marta," I clarify.

"Very cool," Gavin pauses from cleaning the lenses. "Colombian or American?"

"Both—my dad's American and my mom's Colombian. I grew up in Colombia except for a couple years finishing university in New Orleans. Where are you guys from?" My eyes follow the delicate, floral vine tattoo trailing up Sara's left arm—sweet pea, I think.

"I live in Philly. Jorge's from Newark and Gav and Nate live in Bethesda. How'd you get connected with Darrien?"

I've learned to answer these questions better. Americans are the most curious about origin stories.

"At a job fair when I finished my master's at Tulane. I think he hired me because I could speak Malagasy."

Gavin and Sara nod, smiling. Even Jorge takes notice.

I wish Darrien would get back here—he draws attention

with his thick French accent and striking looks. I hate being the center of attention. Thankfully Nate and Darrien return and we head to the restaurant.

Nate looks like a deer in the headlights. I feel for him. One minute he thought his friends were dead, the next they're walking around like nothing happened. Earlier he stared at Darrien like he was a cult leader. I tried to assure him with a smile, but I don't think it landed.

His team looks up to him, even if they don't quite under-stand what's going on—everyone but Jorge. He thinks we're not to be trusted. I tried to convince Darrien to change the name of the organization, especially when we encounter native English-speakers. Local Mauritians and Comorians don't find the name OGRE off-putting.

At least Gavin and Sara don't seem jarred by our arrival. Are Sara and Nate together? I don't think so; I overheard her mention a Tom. The way she said his name... he's her boy-friend.

Nate's quiet and seems spooked. Gavin and Sara rely on him for answers, but he doesn't give them much. Jorge shoots sideways glances at everyone – particularly Darrien.

As we walk to the restaurant, Nate's wobbly. I bet he hasn't eaten today. I'm tempted to hold his arm – give him some-thing to lean on, but that would be weird. Maybe a cold beer and food will help. Even I could use a cold one, and I'm not much of a beer drinker.

Just wait until they hear how this thing spreads. It's gonna be a long night, even with vanilla lobster and cold beers.

Chapter 9
The Wadzi Nadzi

Nate:

My head pounds as we walk to the *Wadzi Nadzi*, meaning Naked Coconut—a funky beach shack with tables under a bright blue awning. Night-blooming jasmine and frangipani linger in the air, leading my fuzzy mind to an earlier time - my last vacation with Emma in Hawaii, two years ago. *Goddamn, I've gotta get that woman out of my head.* I need a drink.

Spending time in far-flung Islamic villages usually means no alcohol. Sometimes we'll come across a local moonshiner distilling cassava or banana hooch— but it's terrible stuff and not always safe. Darrien promised a cold beer and that's what I look forward to, despite the blinding headache.

I sink into a hard plastic chair at the long table. Buzzing in my ears makes me wonder if I'm still in shock. I have no desire to talk or even find out more about this virus. I focus on the lapping of waves as seabirds dip and dive around us. The sun makes its slow descent, dissolving into the ocean, painting a gorgeous blaze of orange and purple across the night sky. A server brings beers—cold cans of South African Castle Lager, waking me from my meditation.

"Tell us about the virus. What are the symptoms?" Jorge pounces. He's not one to let things go, particularly when he suspects something going on.

I attempt to tune him out as I savor the bitter hops sliding down my throat. Darrien lifts his can before answering, in no rush to respond.

"Symptoms are unusual. Most don't realize they've been exposed."

"No symptoms, then?" He ignores his beer.

"I didn't say that. There are varied responses to the virus." Darrien catches the server's attention and speaks quickly in French. I catch a word—*langouste.*

"*Pardonez, mais...*" he stutters. "This place is famous for their vanilla lobster. I put in an order for us. I should have asked—any seafood allergies or dislike of lobster?"

I expect Jorge to come up with a reason not to eat, but even he is eager for a lobster dinner, fresh from the sea.

"*Tres bien.*" Darrien smiles, taking another sip of beer.

"What are these symptoms?" Jorge continues.

Darrien nods to Juliette, passing her the baton. She clears her throat and speaks quietly, her voice competing with the cacophony of shrieking gulls and waves.

"Patients appear to be dead. But just briefly. A few hours later, they revive." It sounds so benign.

A fruit bat flits into the fading light, catching my attention.

Jorge continues his cross-examination. A server appears with plates of lobster coated in a white vanilla and spice sauce. I'm famished. We dig in and there's silence.

But not for long.

"You're saying people appear dead—not breathing, no pulse, etcetera, and somehow come back to life? *Are* they dead?"

Gavin chokes on his lobster and Sara pounds his back.

"They're not dead. The virus lowers the heart rate and slows metabolism—like a form of hibernation. It's hard to detect a pulse," Darrien says.

Could I have missed their lowered pulses?

"How long's it been around? And how many people have been exposed? Has anyone been carted off to the morgue because it's assumed they've died?"

I look around, thankful the restaurant is empty. Darrien keeps his cool as Jorge floods him with questions like driving rain. He sits back with his beer, measured and calm.

"Nothing happens quickly in this part of the world, so no one's been buried. We've studied it for a few years, but it's been around a long time. Only recently has it impacted humans. Patients we've seen have made a full recovery and not passed it to others. It's not communicable. You must eat contaminated meat."

"What kind of contaminated meat?" Jorge is quick to ask.

"It's been found in lemur tissue."

We all stop eating. Darrien swallows a sip of his beer and rests his hands on the table.

"People eat lemurs here?" I ask. *Why am I only hearing of this now?* They didn't mention this tidbit earlier. Why the secrecy? I finish my beer, still thirsty.

"Not usually. But when there's an epidemic of chicken malaria, people dispose of their chickens. When they aren't available or there's a reduction in goat meat, the bush meat trade takes off."

"Chickens get malaria?" Gavin asks and smirks.

"Yup, there's all kinds of malaria."

I swig from my empty beer can, wishing for more. The heaviness of the meal I've consumed too fast, sits in the pit of my stomach, a lump. Should have eaten slower. I ask for water. Everyone else wants another round. My pounding head keeps me from adding alcohol to the mix churning in my belly.

"Are certain people getting sick while others don't?" Sara asks.

Darrien smiles. "We're looking at that. Studies are a moving target. Oddly, local Comorians and Mauritians aren't as impacted as expats or tourists. Our assumption is they have antibodies to the virus. That's not to say it doesn't happen to them. It's not reported as often."

"Wouldn't they likely be the ones eating lemur meat?" I inquire.

"Yes, but tourists don't always know the provenance of their food. When you order the goat kebab at Ali Baba's, you could be getting lemur instead of goat. How would you know?"

"Are you also testing Mauritians and Comorians?" Gavin asks. He stretches, pushing away his empty plate.

Everyone's plates are squeaky clean.

"Yes. Most are Mauritians we work with. It's harder to convince people on the street to agree to a blood draw if they aren't sick. There's distrust of the medical community—especially foreign physicians. Sometimes we include it in a panel if they come in for something else. Consent is tricky."

"I'm sure," Jorge says, rolling his eyes.

I rub my temples, fighting to relieve the pressure building. I catch Juliette's eye.

"It's late and I could use some sleep. Let's meet tomorrow and talk more," she says, rising.

When my watch vibrates, I'm eager to escape the guest house. Despite my exhaustion, I can't sleep - my mind won't turn off. Jorge is sleeping a few feet away. I tiptoe, tucking the mosquito net under the mattress, and walk to the street corner, where I find Darrien on a Kawasaki. A few minutes later we pull up to a white-board cottage with a screened-in porch, out of place among the cement block houses. A small brown dog bounds from the bushes, barking and wagging his tail.

"That's *Kafiri*, our house pup. He's lucky they don't eat dog here." Darrien reaches down to pet him. The dog cowers from me. I crouch and wait. He sniffs in my direction, keeping his distance.

"That's the downside to this work," I say. "No pets. I'm glad they don't eat dogs here, though. Can't say the same for Mali. I've been served dog heart, and as much as I try to live by the mantra '*When in Rome*,' I can't eat any part of man's best friend."

The pup inches closer.

"He likes you. He's not one to suffer strangers. Let's sit on the back porch and you can tell me what happened. Get you anything? Beer, whiskey?"

"Water'd be great."

"Sure."

I admire the quaint hillside cottage in a grove of citrus and flowering trees. The porch overlooks a picturesque garden, butting up to tropical forest beyond. In the distance an animal screams. There aren't many mammal species on these islands, but whatever I'm hearing, sends chills up my spine. The dog sniffs my legs, unbothered.

Darrien reappears with two bottles of water and a bowl of pretzels as the dog settles on the floor between us.

"Tell me more about this morning."

I relate waking to the call to prayer and finding everyone under their nets, having died in the night.

"You never heard anything? You woke and found your friends in their vegetative state?"

"Nothing vegetative about it. I was sure they were dead. I know CPR."

Someone walks around in the house. Juliette? Are she and Darrien a thing? He's a little old for her, but who knows.

"Know how long they were unconscious?"

"I left the house to meet a research contact. Maybe two hours. When I returned, the bedroom was empty. A minute later they showed up, laughing like nothing happened. Thought I was losing my mind."

Darrien's eyebrows jump. " You left?"

I nod.

"Did they seem okay? Any signs something was off?"

"Gavin complained of a headache, but felt better after eating. Sara and Jorge agreed. They thought it was a hangover from the Johnnie Walker. They've all drunk more and not complained. We passed it around while eating goat kebabs for dinner."

"Madame Sokaina's kebabs are magnifique. You try that *putu*? *Tres chaud*—the best hot sauce ever. Think she uses Scotch bonnets. She give you anything else?"

"Well..." I forgot to mention the slimy treat. When I tell him, he nods.

"What was it? I assumed goat liver."

Darrien's smile makes my skin crawl. "Think she gave you lemur liver. It's a delicacy here. And likely the goat kebabs were not goat. Goat's expensive. Lemurs—not so much. They practically fall out of the trees."

"You kidding? Why didn't you say something earlier?"

"I'll visit her tomorrow. It's just a hunch. I didn't want to upset your team, especially Jorge. How've you been today, aside from the stress?"

"I'm fine... just exhausted and a headache." The pounding is worse. I hoped the water would help.

Another scream pierces the night. Darrien doesn't notice.

"Have any meetings tomorrow?"

"No. I need to talk with Campbell to see what he wants to do. He may scrap the whole story."

"What's it about? Not many journalists here."

We talk longer and I ask him if and when I should let the others know what happened.

"If they think they've been exposed to a weird virus, their behavior could change. Let's wait a few days. Campbell will want to keep quiet until we look at labs. We'll send the samples to our facility in Geneva tomorrow and will know something soon. Anyone have health issues or take medications I should know about?"

"No, all very fit and healthy." I look down when Kafiri rests his head on my foot. Guess I passed the sniff test.

"Everyone taking antimalarials?"

"The others take Malarone. It gives me horrible nightmares and paranoia. I sleep under a bed net, drink tonic water, and bathe in DEET. I've had malaria a few times, but nothing too serious."

Darrien gives me a sharp look. "Hmmm. Let me get you back before anyone notices you're gone. We're staying in Domoni until we know what's happening with your team. I'll drop by in the morning to grab my bag."

After Darrien leaves me at the corner, I sneak into the house.

"Where were you?" Jorge's voice startles me, from the darkened room.

Chapter 10
Don't Need a Dog

Juliette:

Darrien pulls up on the Kawasaki, late. I think he wants to chat with Nate privately. Fine by me. Being grilled by Jorge and watching Nate fall apart was stressful.

I'm curious why they're here. Not much happens in this corner of the world. Are they chasing a story? Most journalists come to report on the Livingston bats or other unique fauna. It must be something pressing as Gavin's wife gave birth to their first child a week ago. And he's here? I wouldn't be as tolerant. I overheard him on the phone, making jokes and gurgling to the baby. Seems they've got a rock-solid thing. I was reminded of my own parents in how they tease each other. He showed me her picture that he keeps in his wallet. She's beautiful: long, dark hair and dancing brown eyes.... hoisting a kayak over her head. She works for an outdoor adventure company.

Goran pops into my mind. How would he have handled waking to find his friends dead? He'd have hightailed it elsewhere. Goran didn't have friends; he had *associates*. I wasn't exactly a friend either, even in the beginning. His interest in me was something else, entirely.

Even distressed, there's something captivating about Nate. Wavy, dark hair, blue-gray eyes flecked with flint, fit and lean... He has no idea how hot he is. If it weren't for the stress of the virus, I imagine he'd be easygoing. Tonight, at dinner, he was mute. When I tried to draw him out, asking about work, he didn't say much. Usually I can get guys to talk.

It's a shame Nate lives halfway around the world. When this is all through, I can't entertain thoughts of running into him at the local coffee shop in Port Louis. Maybe I wouldn't get stupid drunk if we went out one night. He's nothing like Mani, either. Mani's obsessed with the perfect swell... waves and otherwise. That and comic strips. Nate's deeper.

But can he dance?

Hell, I'd tolerate two left feet if he talked to me the way Gavin talks to his wife.

Where are the decent men? Are there only Gorans and Manis—or Tonios? Tonio was my cadaver buddy from anatomy class at Los Andes. We'd go dancing on weekends. He was sweet but a little too devoted, like a dog, always coming back for a pat on the head.

I don't need a dog.

Chapter 11

Parasites and Protozoa

Nate:

Jorge sits in the dark. His questioning eyes bore through me.

"I was out... getting air. I had weird dreams...can't sleep. What are you doin' up?"

"Cut the shit, man. Talk. Where were you?" He turns on the light.

God, that's bright. He's not gonna let me blow this off.

I rub my eyes, wishing for darkness. "I can't do this now. Can we talk tomorrow?"

"Shit, Nate... you're not telling me something—something important."

"I promise we'll talk tomorrow." I wince, leaning against the table.

Jorge hands me Advil. "Sorry you feel shitty. You think we can trust that guy? A resurrecting virus... it's crazy. And OGRE? What kind of medical team is called that?"

I take the pills, grateful. "We'll talk in the morning, I promise."

3 Days Later...

Someone pushes on my neck, another hand on my head. It's the mad Frenchman.

"Welcome back. How're you feeling?"

I try to speak but can't. My throat burns, scalded. Blinking to clear my vision, I struggle to remember what's happened and why I feel so wretched. I roll to my side. "Shit."

"Malaria wreaks havoc with the liver. It'll get better. Just move slowly."

Hands help me sit up. Things are spinning. *Malaria, again?* Stomach cramps.

"Bathroom," I grumble.

"Take it slowly," Clouseau says. He helps me limp to the bathroom. "Put this on the sink." He hands me a plastic bag of clear fluid ...it's attached ...an IV.

Darrien—that's his name.

Jorge hands me a glass of cloudy liquid when I come out of the bathroom. "Want some coconut water?"

I nod, hoping he isn't poisoning me.

"Look who's risen from the dead. Mr. Malaria Man!" Gavin's voice bounces off the walls like a boomerang.

I take a sip of the cloudy water. It's nectar, sweet and soothing. I want to gulp but know that's a bad idea.

"Jorge found you three days ago. We've been trying to get your temp down. I've got you on fluids and malaria meds that are finally taking effect. How're you feeling?" Darrien says as he rehangs my IV.

"Three days?" I cover my eyes, shielding them from the sunlight blazing in. What day is it? *Shit, I gotta call Campbell.*

"Uh-huh. You've had this before."

"This feels worse," I croak.

"Don't talk too much. Let's see what your temp is now." Darrien pulls out an infrared thermometer.

Chapter 12

Waste Away

Three days is a long time to be out of it, not eating and fever-ish. Nate didn't have spare weight to lose. It's hard to watch someone waste away.

Sara and I managed kitchen duty. We found chicken bouillon to make broth. I picked up young coconuts, great for rehydrating and replacing electrolytes—not that he could eat or drink, but we wanted to be prepared. Jorge and Gavin helped Darrien with the heavy lifting, dousing Nate in the shower when his fever spiked and running IV fluids and meds into him once the malaria diagnosis was confirmed.

Early on, I sat with him, cooling him with cold compresses and chilled water bottles. He mumbled, twisting to avoid my touch, his skin searing. He thrashed, delirious, his voice raspy as he cried out for Emma. Girlfriend? I'm not sure if he thought I was her, but at one point, he glared at me like I'd betrayed him. Thankfully, Gavin took over.

When his fever broke, he went from Dante's *Inferno* to Siberian winter, teeth chattering so hard I feared he'd break a tooth. With the chills came headaches and violent retching. I held the dead weight of him as he vomited into a bucket, groaning and shaking. Normally I can't handle throw-up, but I managed. He grew accustomed to my touch, allowing me to soothe his burning skin or wrap him in sun-warmed blankets.

Sometimes he'd gaze at me, eyes glassy, like he could see

me. He gave me a goofy smile and held my hand, mumbling unintelligibly. Did he think I was the mysterious Emma? Later Darrien used antibacterial wipes to wash him; as he was ripe after three days of fevers and chills.

The smell of antiseptic and constant drip of an IV jolted me back. Sallow skin stretched across bone and sinew, no fat to speak of...

There was a time when my own appearance wasn't too different.

...woke from a nightmare...wedged in the periphery of my mind... sunlight fading, chilling wind and the smell of smoke. Itchy blankets around me, I shivered on the hard ground. My mouth tasted like something died in it. Desperate thirst—could think of nothing else. Wearing tattered jeans and a faded T-shirt...feet bare and scratched.

I touched my swollen lip, throbbing and tender. My left eye blurred and achy. I reached my fingers around the base of my neck, where the loss hit like a sledgehammer. Where's my hair?

Rays of dying light glittered with dust flecks beamed through the dirty windows of the old shed. The metallic stink of used car oil and freshly rolled hay layered the air.

Peering out the window, a wall of green, multi-hued—trees and more trees, towering and lush. Evening fell as the temperature dropped. I must have slept all day. I looked around for anything to eat or drink. Only broken-down car parts and rusted tools filled the cramped space. I opened the door slowly, listening.

Insects buzzing, frogs chirping, and primates barking filled the night air. I recognized the flora—trees and plants, familiar. Palo Santo and the ever-invasive Ojo de Poeta, whose vibrant orange flowering vines wrap around native trees and plants, suffocating and deadly. A beautiful menace...

As darkness draped like a shroud over the forest, I sought refuge in the shed for the night.

A cold nose on my leg startles me from my dark thoughts. Kafiri. I reach down and pet him.

"It's okay, boy." I get up and refill his water bowl.

How much longer will we be here? I'm relieved Nate's on the mend. Three days is a long time. Now we're waiting on results from the lab in Geneva. We suspect everyone's been exposed to the virus.

This isn't a bad place to be stuck. I've been in far worse places.

44

Chapter 13
Village Visit

Nate:

After conferring with Darrien, we're encouraged to visit an old Al-Qaeda recruitment site. I'm surprised Campbell wants to pursue the story—I assumed he'd want us to get the hell outta here—but I don't argue. I'm curious about what lies beyond the town of Domoni. I'm eager to get back to work and away from the claustrophobic confines of the guest house.

"Nate, you need to come clean." Jorge corners me as I'm packing for the trip. He pulls me outside.

"Nate, I had the virus."

"You did?"

He cocks his head, almost angry. "Yes, we all did. That's why we woke in that bedroom. It wasn't a prank. Remember?"

"Who told you?"

"Darrien ... when you were sick, I confronted him. I suspected something that night you snuck in late. No one knows... Not Sara. Not Gavin. You think it's a good idea to traipse off to some remote village right now?"

He's not wrong but I recall Campbell's instructions. "Campbell wants to keep us here until the lab results are back. Darrien wants to observe us a bit longer. That's why we're going. There might be something worth writing about, to justify this trip, " I reason. "It'll be fine. Darrien wouldn't let us go if he thought it was a bad idea, right?"

Jorge shakes his head, frowning.

Gavin and I prepare to meet Ali in a remote village, high in the mountains, while the others get footage around Domoni. I'm exhausted but don't want the team to think we're wasting time. Ousini is a tiny village, isolated during the monsoons. It's renowned for being home to the Livingston bat, the world's largest bat species with a wingspan of over five feet.

The bush taxi is rough. Poor Gavin squeezes his six-foot-two-inch frame into the back of a pickup, crammed onto a bench seat with fifteen other Comorians half his size. The roof is stacked with gas cans, cages of live chickens, and huge bundles of sticks and stalks of green bananas. The stench of sunburnt dirt, unwashed bodies, and chicken shit permeate the air.

Many families have *shambas*—plots of farmland they cultivate around the island. Families are complex; one man may have multiple wives in different villages. They spend their days traversing the mountains to visit families while harvesting subsistence crops to barter for goods. It's primitive, but I see a guy trading spices for fresh tuna—not a bad trade.

The view out the back of the bush taxi is enchanting: lush green mountains, men and women carrying unfathomable loads balanced on their heads, walking miles. And children—dust-covered and laughing, run alongside the taxi as we pull into villages. Old men sit on the roadside in fours, playing heated games of dominoes.

Ali meets us in the forest of a midsized village. Low clouds hover, giving the place a dreamy, mystical feel. We need to hire a motorcycle to get to Ousini since bush taxis can't navigate the treacherous road.

"How do people get around out here if they can't afford a taxi or moto ride?" Gavin asks.

"They walk," Ali says, matter-of-factly. "Most of these tiny villages are so secluded, people must walk everywhere."

I've seen remote villages in India and other places, but this feels more extreme.

"Are there schools or health clinics? What if someone is deathly ill? What happens during the rainy season when roads are impassable?" My recent health crisis makes me worry.

Ali replies, "When the road is impassable, they walk. The sick find a healer with herbal medicines. Some of the bigger villages have their own health clinics."

Gavin and I look at each other, grateful I hadn't been here a few days ago. Ali flags down a man on a moto. He agrees to transport me for a few hundred Comorian francs—about two US dollars. I climb aboard and follow Ali and Gavin. The road is steep and jutted—the mini moto sputters and bounces along, spewing smoke from the exhaust. It's bone-jarring. *What the hell am I doing?*

Ousini has about a dozen mud huts spread in a small clearing. Towering mahogany trees dangle delicate, colorful orchids like ornaments. Each hut is surrounded by a tiny courtyard where the occasional chicken struts and clucks. An outdoor cooking shed where young children are charged with lighting the fires, bustles with activity.

Ali leads us on foot, up a tight trail behind the village. It winds for about a mile before arriving at an austere cement block building.

"How the hell did they get these cement blocks here?" Gavin asks.

"They hired Comorians to haul them, one at a time. Young boys were happy to make a few francs. The *terrorists* also imported vehicles that could manage these twisting roads. There's an old Humvee on the other side of the village. I'll show you later."

I chuckle at his benign use of the word *terrorist*.

We follow him into the cement building, where a long, rough-hewn wood table sags, abandoned. "This is where they recruited young men." There's no other furniture. It's windowless. Dark. Bleak.

"What ages were they recruiting?" I ask.

"As young as twelve and up. Anyone willing was welcome, even some of the older men. They had to pass a certain level of physical fitness to be promoted to official trainee. Ousini is poor and many suffer malnutrition. Al-Qaeda brought vitamins and food. They also brought medicines hard to come by. People thought they were Allah's missionaries. They were considered heroes."

I snap pictures inside the building, needing a flash. We spend the rest of the afternoon looking at places Al-Qaeda worked. Ali tells stories and interprets when we speak with families. He shows us a mosque used by the Al-Qaeda training team. I photograph a discarded prayer mat in the corner.

Ali suggests we head back to M'Remani if we don't want to spend the night in a hut. I consider it but Gavin isn't keen. We return to the lower village as the sun sets and the evening call to prayer begins. Ali bids us farewell after securing us a room. We stay with a family who feeds us dinner of rice and greens cooked in coconut milk. There's no furniture aside from a straw mat, and we hang our mosquito nets. I'm wiped from the day and fall asleep as soon as my head hits the ground.

Chapter 14

Jamilla's

I spot Sara and Jorge on my way to the post office. They're shooting footage of the port and the many mosques. Sara juggles multiple cameras, decked out in a long, flowy skirt, shoulders covered with a colorful *kanga*. She knows how to dress in a Muslim country. A *kanga* is a piece of light cotton, worn as wraps by women. These kangas are covered in vibrant motifs and Swahili proverbs. I learned my favorite proverb from a kanga—*Haraka Haraka, Haina Baraka*—*Hurry Hurry has no Blessings*.

Mauritius isn't as conservative. I wear whatever I want there, usually decked out in scrubs or a swimsuit. Different rules apply in the Comoros. I learned my lesson the hard way when I first visited. My usual getup—sundress and flip-flops, bare shoulders, naked knees, was not appreciated the first time I visited. Men *and* women stared as if I were strutting around naked. Another volunteer kindly offered her kanga. I never made that mistake again.

"Hey Juliette, what are you up to?" Sara asks.

"Running to the post office. How about you guys? Getting anything good?"

"These old mosques are gorgeous. And the *dhows* floating in the port—we got terrific footage of fishermen hauling in their catch. So much tuna!" Her eyes light up, breezy and happier than a day ago when we worked around the clock to care for Nate.

"If you haven't had tuna pilau here, you gotta try it. Jamilla's is terrific, tucked into the *medina*. They make gorgeous rice dishes and Tunisian tagines. Tell them I sent you."

Sara and Jorge grin at each other.

"We got lost in the *medina* this morning," Sara admits. "Those narrow streets are a hellish labyrinth .... lots of wrong turns. We found a restaurant owner to guide us out—lovely man. Is their place the pretty blue building with the yellow awning?"

"That's it. Moncef rescued you and if you find your way there again, enjoy their spicy harissa crusted tuna...unforgettable." I smile to myself. Even during a viral outbreak on tiny islands in the Indian Ocean, there are people who'll look out for you. Moncef and Jamilla were priceless to me a few years back when I, too, was lost.

"Any more viral outbreaks?" Jorge asks. He's far more relaxed than the night of the vanilla lobsters.

I'm unsure how to answer. I don't think Nate mentioned their exposure before he left with Gavin. I fuss with my rucksack, stalling.

"Uh, not so far. How about Nate and Gavin—heard anything from them?"

Sara puts down the heavy camera bag for a moment, stretching her back. "No, we won't hear from them 'til tomorrow when they're due back. Just hope there's something worth shooting up there." She stares past me. I follow her eyes to Madame Sokaina setting up her hibachi across the street. "Would you and Darrien like to join us for dinner tonight? Thought we'd pick up more brochettes."

I nearly blow it, telling them not to eat from the street corner again. Goat kebabs are fine. "Sure, that'd be great. Tell you what, I'll pick them up on the way over."

"We'll provide the Johnnie Walker."

Chapter 15

Side Effects

Nate:

I'm roused from sleep roughly. Gavin's agitated, mumbling about being hunted. Think he's having a bad dream. When his raving reaches a fever pitch, I grab his shoulders and shake him.

"Gavin, wake up! You're having a nightmare."

After a few hard shakes, he pushes me off. "They take us?"

"What are you talking about?" I stare into the crow blackness, looking for the shine of his eyes.

"We're taken yesterday," he whispers.

"Taken? By whom? What are you talking about?" I ask, annoyed.

"Extremists."

"Extremists? Gavin, we're in that little village where we met Ali. We're heading back to Jorge and Sara this morning." I keep my voice slow and even, the voice I use when I'm helping a terrified climber out of a tough spot.

Gavin's eyes flare like glowing charcoal about to burst into flame. "You're one of them, aren't you? Why are you feeding me lies?" Standing over me, he's massive and menacing.

"Gavin, look at me. We spent last night in a guest house. We're catching a ride back to be with Jorge and Sara. Any of this ring a bell? Do I look like I've been taken hostage? We've got all our things. Here's the sat phone." I wave it in front of him.

"Stop fucking with me! Who are you really?" he roars, knocking the phone from my hand.

"Gavin," I plead. "Stop. It's just me, Nate. Only the two of us here."

Seething, it occurs to me how much larger he is and that if he wanted to kill me, he probably could. I've never been afraid of my friend—that is, until now.

"If you aren't with them, why do you have a sat phone? Who are you reporting to?"

Where the Hell is the door? A sliver of light to my left guides me. I make a mad dash, feeling Gavin on my heels. I burst into the blistering courtyard, where a headless chicken dances, spurting blood. A small child and woman squat in the dust. They stare at me with blank eyes. I turn to find Gavin on his knees, holding his head in his hands, groaning.

I touch his shoulder. "Gav, you okay?" He jerks away. "Easy, Gav—it's just me. Your head hurt?"

He grunts, unwilling to look up. Sunlight bothers him.

"Hold on a minute. I've got Advil." I pull out my water bottle and the pills and put them in his hand. He flinches again but takes them. I hand him a baseball cap and leave him under the cooking shed, while I find a bush taxi.

The drive downhill is twisty. Gavin is hunched next to me, silent aside from the occasional moan when we hit a pothole or the truck lurches. Back at the house, I leave him in the back room and call Darrien. Something's not right. I wonder if Gavin's behavior is related to the virus.

Gavin suffers another episode. He's convinced we've locked him up and are using him in some kind of experiment. Darkness makes his delusions worse. In daylight, the old Gavin returns, but with a horrible headache and nausea. His eyes dart around the room.

Juliette takes his face in her hands and talks quietly. I worry he'll attack her, but he remains calm.

"Breathe with me, Gavin." She inhales slowly, holding his

attention with her gaze. After a few moments, his eyes settle and he's calmer. We leave him to rest in the bright bedroom with the fans whirring.

Darrien tells us more about the virus and that our test results came back positive. He relates that Mme. Sokaina's kebabs were goat meat, and not lemur. *Whew.* However, the raw bits *were* lemur liver.

"What the fuck? How does everyone here know about this, but me?" Sara spits.

I try to appease her, but she's livid and feels betrayed.

Even Jorge steps in. "You didn't have any symptoms. Neither did I."

Sara glares at me again.

"I asked Nate to keep quiet. You weren't the only one unaware. Gavin didn't know either," Darrien intervenes.

"I died? And you never told me? I thought we were a team. Is that why we woke up in the bedroom the morning after our arrival? We all died? Is that why you dragged us off the roof?"

My face burns. "I'm sorry... I was gonna tell you, but things were complicated, and then I got sick. I should have said something before Gav and I left for Ousini."

I tell her about moving everyone from the roof and calling Campbell. Her expression softens when she hears the rest of the story.

"Why didn't you also 'die' like the rest of us?"

"I have a theory," Darrien offers. "Nate doesn't take anti-malarials. His chronic malaria exposure may have had an inverse effect. Malaria causes temperature spikes, blood cells burst, leading to crushing headaches. They also allow your cells to reboot, which may have made it difficult for the virus to invade them. But, he may have more dramatic bouts of malaria."

"What about Gavin?" I ask. "Are these delusions a permanent concern? Are there other side effects we should be aware of?"

We learn about the possible side effects: delusions and paranoia. It's unsettling that we could become raving mad out of the blue.

"Most unusual behavior occurs within the first seven days, post-exposure. After that window, it's much less likely. Gavin's symptoms should wear off in a few days' time," Juliette says calmly. I hope she's right.

We're advised to find infectious disease specialists and to keep track of one another. It's suggested we stay together for a few days before reuniting with our families. Campbell agrees to host us at his apartment in New York.

One week later we depart the Comoros, saying goodbye to Darrien and Juliette. After two long flights and a stopover in Paris, we arrive at JFK.

Chapter 16
Hunger — Port Louis, Mauritius

Juliette:

It's good to be back in the water, even on this chilly morning. A rainstorm moved through last night, dropping the water temperature significantly. I've missed this...cool sand, pearl-white, flecked with pink, squishing between my toes. Goosebumps rise on my arms as I swim out to the reef.

My backyard in Flic-en-Flac is world-famous for its pristine beaches and crystalline waters. Surfers and tourists flock here but today is Ashadha Purnima, a Hindu holy day, and I have the entire place to myself.

My arms stretched overhead, I pull myself through the swirling water. Swimming against the current is a workout, like a challenging run uphill. I don't run anymore but I'll never tire of ocean swims, despite the risks. This helps keep my head on straight in a topsy-turvy world.

I spotted a pod of orcas earlier from my back deck. They swam into the shallows, allowing me a glimpse of their pack dynamics: fierce hunters using coordinated tactics to corral and trap prey. But they're playful too. One breached, leaping out of the water, while others flipper-slapped and spy-hopped, like boasting teenage boys showing off for a cute girl. Sometimes I'll spot dusky dolphins, but the orcas thrill me with their shiny black and white bodies, sleek and powerful, shearing the water like knives.

A mother with her calf demonstrated strong maternal instincts when another orca swam too close. Makes me wonder about my own maternal instincts—not sure I have any.

Months ago, I watched a young mother and her daughter playing on the beach. The little girl clung to her mother, afraid of the ocean – a foaming mouth trying to eat her. Mom sat in the shallows with the child tucked between her legs, letting the water lap their feet. The little girl giggled as the water tickled her toes – no longer afraid. Mom knew how to make the vastness of the ocean feel a little smaller. Would I think to do that if she were mine? Would I have that kind of wisdom or patience? I'd like to think so. I just don't know.

It wasn't always like this. Growing up, I babysat my cousins: playing games, taking them on treasure hunts, and encouraging them to get dirty to annoy my judgmental aunties. Did my time in Bogota ruin me for anything else besides solitude and lab work?

Mani stopped by the lab a couple days ago. He wants to take me out. I put him off, making excuses about a heavy workload. It's not a good idea to get involved with him...especially when I can't get Nate off my mind.

Nate...that wavy hair, startling blue eyes, and cute smile. He kept his team calm and admitted his mistakes, even when Sara was raving mad at him. He never lost his cool with her and she was *pissed*. I wish we'd had more time together—more time when he wasn't sick...more time when he wasn't dealing with Gavin's symptoms. Damn virus.

Wish I had his contact info. I bet Darrien has a way to get in touch with the team. He's good about checking up on his patients. Not sure how to ask for that without arousing suspicion. What would I do with it anyway? I live on a tiny island in the Indian Ocean and he's back in the States. Not ideal for any kind of relationship.

Oddly, I've never tested positive for the virus since moving here. I know not to eat slimy organ meats. The World Health Organization advises travelers not to eat bush meat, but how would you know if you're served bush meat versus goat? Lemurs are abundant and easy to hunt, as they're practically domesticated here.

Early cousins to primates, lemurs are comical to watch bounding through the forest, tree to tree or on all fours. Unlike siamangs or gibbons, they don't brachiate but cover vast territory quickly. On Mauritius we have crab-eating monkeys and long-tailed macaques. No lemurs or other prosimians. I miss my Peace Corps days watching lemur antics from my back porch in Madagascar.

I've eaten lots of weird things overseas, but never anything that felt like kin. Lemurs are too closely related. I'd rather go hungry than eat cousins – even distant cousins. I've never been that hungry... except that one time...

Chapter 17

Return

Nate:

We arrive at Dulles after a long weekend in New York. The Comoros feels far away. Gavin and Dani's reunion is sweet. I'm relieved they're back together to start their new life as parents. I feel a pang of envy for what they have. Dani's radiant, carrying baby Sam in an infant car seat. He's the spitting image of Gav with dark blue eyes and blonde peach fuzz covering his noggin. I miss Emma...or the idea of Emma. As I say my goodbyes, my parents make their way to me.

Mom grins ear to ear. Dad's harder to read, his forehead scrunched when he sees me. I'm gaunt, my clothes hang off me. I'll rebound after a few home-cooked meals and a return to the gym. Right now, I look like a famine victim. My parents don't usually come into town when I return from trips but news of my illness changed their plans.

"Surprise! We missed you, honey. How was your flight?" Mom hugs me, smelling of apples and cinnamon. Bet she was baking.

"Good, just a bit bumpy coming in. I missed you too. Thanks for coming. How long're you in town?"

"Just a few days to be sure you're healthy. Looks like we need to fatten you up," she jokes, pinching my sunken cheeks.

"Trying to get rid of us already, huh?" Dad grumbles, smiling.

I hug him and laugh. "Yeah, I'm already sick of you."

There are grocery bags in the back seat of their car.

"You shopped already? Thanks."

Mom is pleased. She always loved welcoming me home, cooking my favorite meals—stewed chicken and biscuits, sauteed collards, circle pie. I wish any of that sounded appealing.

"Looks like you could use a hearty meal. Thought I'd whip up beef stew. How's that sound?"

The headaches since the malaria aren't letting up and I'm nauseated most of the day. Nibbling crackers is all I can handle, but I don't want to disappoint her.

"Sounds great."

We arrive at my apartment and I put away groceries. Dad perches on a barstool at the kitchen island. From his expression, I know what's coming and brace myself.

"Nate, you've been evasive about this virus. How'd you know the others were infected?"

My father doesn't like to feel out of the loop. He's an electrical engineer and is all about the hard science of things. He hoped I'd work with him one day, but I had other ideas. In his mind, writing isn't a real job, at least not a well-paying one. He doesn't quite believe I can afford to live in D.C.

I tell them about the Comoros and attempt to assuage their worries about my bout of malaria. My work takes me to unusual places. I've seen things I'd never share with them. It was hard to tell them I accidentally ate lemur liver and contracted this bizarre resurrecting virus. They aren't globe-trotting people. They live in rural, eastern Kentucky, where I grew up.

"Mom, how's the pottery?"

"Great. I have some new commissions and may be doing a show in the next few months," she says as she chops up hunks of bloody meat. I turn away, trying not to gag.

I hand Dad vegetables to chop. He's her sous chef.

"That's great news. Hope I can make it this time." I grab a bottle of ibuprofen and take three.

"Nate, back to the virus. What happens if you have a weird

episode like Gavin? You live alone. No one would know." He finishes chopping the onions and garlic and passes them to Mom, who's browning the meat. The smell is nauseating.

"Gavin lives nearby. Even Jorge isn't far. We'll check in with each other. I feel fine and I'll call if something seems off. Be right back, need to check the mail." I lurch outside for a breath of fresh air as my mother sings out they've already brought it in. I open windows to air the place out.

At dinner I choke down a few bites of stew. The apple pie goes down easier.

My parents aren't too happy I only have two weeks off before our next assignment. Mom wishes I'd meet a nice girl and settle down. She still bugs me about Emma.

I think about Emma too, though I shouldn't be thinking about her at all.

Chapter 18

Listless in Mauritius

The reef is full of activity this morning. No sea turtles, but lots of other colorful creatures: parrotfish, wrasse, triggerfish, pufferfish, and angelfish. I even spotted a rare sea cucumber. It's nice to be back to my routine, but after spending time with Nate and the others, I'm lonelier here. I'm close to Darrien and Claire and other OGRE staff, but something's missing. I don't get a thrill like I did when I'd find myself standing next to Nate in the kitchen, making tea or helping prep dinner.

Mani pops by my cottage as I'm coming in from a swim. I'm shaking out my hair and wrapping myself in a towel when he appears from behind one of the fig trees in my yard.

"Juli, sorry—didn't mean to scare you."

I trip over my feet, nearly landing flat on my face. "Mani—what are you doing here? Not stalking me?" I stutter, righting myself.

He laughs, his eyes dart. "No, I just...I, uh...get the feeling you're avoiding me."

"I'm not avoiding you, I'm really busy with work stuff."

He moves out from under the tree and cocks his head.

He's calling my bluff.

He's never given me a reason to lie or be afraid. He's a decent guy.

"Yes, I'm avoiding you. Sorry. I don't want you to think

there's more to this than there is." I press my toes into the sugary sand.

"I like you, Juli. I like spending time with you. That's all. No expectations here...just a bit of fun. Is that too much to ask?"

Fun with a guy like Mani is quicksand. Easy to dive into but hard as hell to get out of.

"Mani, I'm not up for dating right now...even for fun."

"Is it because of what happened that night? You know..." The bronzed skin of his cheeks reddens. "We never talked about it."

"Talked about what? I got drunk and tried to hook up with you. I'm sorry if I led you on. Not sure why I got so fucked up." I feel naked in my bikini, even though I'm wrapped in a towel.

His dark, expressive eyes hold mine. "You tried to hook up with me?" A sly smile emerges, tipping the corners of his mouth.

How's that?

"Ummm...let me get changed. Meet at the coffee shop later?"

"Sure." He nods, still smiling. It's a smile that makes me nervous. *What am I not remembering?*

I watch his retreating back as he glides down the beach. I head inside, locking my doors, which I never do. He's not Goran. But I learned my lesson. Getting lusty with the wrong man is dangerous.

Chapter 19
Lab Rat

Nate:

Jorge calls a few days after my parents return to Kentucky. We catch up on things. His wife Bea is unhappy with his travel schedule. She wants to start a family, but Jorge's not sure he's ready. He likes the nomadic lifestyle and chance to see the world. Bea's a choreographer and dance instructor. She's a lot of fun, but intense. This last trip was hard on her—especially learning about Jorge's exposure to the resurrecting virus. News of this virus, thankfully, has not hit the mainstream. But all our families are concerned about any future travel.

Mom would like me to settle down too. She's worried I'll never give her grandchildren. She liked Emma when they visited us in Yosemite.

My mind goes to the last image of Emma climbing in Hawaii—silky blonde hair with a dyed lavender stripe, tucked under a trucker's cap while we scaled Haleakala over four days. Sex under a sky of stars, swathed in the heady scent of tuberose and pikake, had me thinking she was the one. Later, it was clear she never felt the same.

I shake my head to jar loose those confusing images and share with Jorge my concern over my headaches and lack of appetite since returning.

"Have you seen your doc yet, with that file?" he asks.

"No, that file makes me nervous. My cousin's a surgeon and when she gets patients with weird health issues, she marks their file with a big red circle. That file's gonna get me referred to the psych ward, not an infectious disease specialist."

Jorge laughs. "Get checked anyway. Could be related to the malaria—you had horrible headaches then."

I see my internist, Dr. Tim Hanson, a few days later. I tell him about the headaches but keep the file tucked away.

"Blood pressure's a little high. We should check that. And your LDL's higher than usual too. That's new for you. We'll need to keep an eye on that. Are you depressed?" he asks, looking through the chart.

"No, I'm just tired and sleeping more than usual."

He looks up. "Do you feel like you want to hurt yourself or others?"

"No. Why would you ask that?"

The exam room is icy and smells of antiseptic. Dr. Hanson sits on his rolling stool, glasses low on his nose, reminding me of Anthony Edwards from *ER* with his receding hairline.

"Not sleeping and lack of appetite," his eyes graze over me, "are classic signs of depression. Do you want to talk to someone?"

"I'm not eating because I'm nauseated most of the day. And I'm nauseated because I have blinding headaches. This isn't because I'm sad or feeling hopeless."

He nods, writing in my chart. "Sounds like your body needs to recover from that bout of malaria. Tell me about your appetite."

"I'm forcing myself to eat. I need to show you something, but..." I stare at my bare feet.

"But what? Something related to your last assignment?" He tears his eyes from my chart.

Tim's seen me through a few incidences of malaria and other tropical diseases. I trust him, but this file has me on edge.

"Nate, I can't help you if you don't tell me what's going on."

I hop off the table and grab the file from my bag, handing it over. He reads slowly, silently, then looks back at me, eyebrows furrowed.

"I wish you'd shown me this sooner. I want to refer you to my colleague at Thompkins. He's head of Infectious Disease and will want to do testing. Nate, are you okay?"

Whew, doesn't think I'm a nut job.

"I'm not great. I don't know what to do."

"Let me call Doctor Bradley to see if he can get you in today. Be right back."

I dress and pace the small room. He returns ten minutes later in a face mask and latex gloves. *Shit.*

"He wants to see you. Now. I've arranged transportation."

My ears prickle and burn. "Tim, come on. You read the file? The virus isn't contagious. I ate something I shouldn't have. I can get over to Doctor Bradley's on my own." I lurch upright, aiming for the door.

Tim grabs a prescription pad from his desk. "Sorry, Nate, this is a new virus and you may be the first case we've seen in the US. We can't take any chances. It's my responsibility to transport you, especially with this file in my possession."

The room shrinks. I back toward the door. A large male nurse in a face shield comes up from behind, scaring the shit out of me.

Tim continues jotting things in my chart. "It's going to be fine. Doctor Bradley's excellent. He's one of the best."

I dodge the nurse, trying to steady my breath. I look at Tim again. He wants to seem nonchalant—he's anything but, taking sideways glances at me while scribbling furiously.

"Look, I drove here. I'll wear a face mask if that makes you more comfortable."

He shakes his head. "Wish that were possible...now it's a liability issue. Joe can take you for a quick ride up to Baltimore and bring you right back."

I was terrified of shots as a kid. My parents had to trick me, saying we were going to the toy store. I'd wind up being held down by a burly nurse trying to cajole me into taking my shots like a big boy. Humiliating. I don't want to relive that, especially as a twenty-seven-year-old grown-ass man.

As I'm coming up with a plan of escape, I feel a jab in my arm...

Blurry figures hover, muffled voices garbled. I try to move but can't. My brain buzzes and crackles. Everyone's dressed like Storm Troopers with face shields and what I recognize as bio-terrorism-grade PPE.

"Where's Doctor...?" I croak, wanting to sound firm but forgetting the name of Tim's colleague.

"Mr. Fisher, you're awake. Doctor Bradley," one of the masked men says. He reaches out to shake my hand, then quickly drops it. "How're you feeling?" I imagine he's smiling but can't see his face.

"Like a hostage. On the set of *Star Wars*. How'd you feel if someone drugged you and transported you without permission? Is that even legal?" I strain against the straps.

"I apologize, Nate. I asked Doctor Hanson to have you transported. We've recently learned of the virus and you're one of a select few who've been exposed. We're being cautious as we don't want another SARS outbreak. I'm sure you understand." His voice is muffled behind the face-mask. It brings me back to the Comoros when I first met Darrien. This Thompkins joker is less trustworthy than Darrien and the OGRE medical team.

"I was assured I wasn't a public health risk when I left the Comoros. I came to Tim for headaches and lack of appetite... not to be turned into a lab rat. Undo these straps, or do I need a lawyer?"

At the mention of a lawyer, the other masked figures dissolve.

"Of course—we didn't want you thrashing about." The doctor releases the restraining bands from my arms and chest. "Better?"

I reach to pull my cell from my pocket but they've stripped me of my clothes. "Where are my things? I need to make a call."

"Yes, in a minute. Just have a few questions."

Really? Who does this guy think he is?

"I'm not answering anything without my cell," I say slowly, enunciating as clearly as I can.

A place like Thompkins, with its research and cutting-edge reputation, is too excited to see their first Resurrecting Virus victim. These guys are eager to make a name for themselves as proclaimed virus hunters. I've met gung-ho researchers in the field with no quandary about breaking the law for a chance to claim they've cured Ebola or SARS. They lose sight of the big picture fast when notoriety and grant funding are on the line. I don't intend to be their guinea pig, helping them to get published in the esteemed *New England Journal of Medicine*.

Dr. Bradley hesitates. After a moment he lowers the plastic face shield, but keeps on the N-95. His skin is pinched and sallow, his scalp sporting an unfortunate comb-over. He's clearly spent a lot of time under these fluorescent lights.

An hour later, I'm in a Starbucks waiting for Gavin to pick me up.

Chapter 20
Unreliable Narrator

Juliette:

I meet Mani and we grab coffees and wander down the beach to worn wooden benches with a view of the sea.

"What were you saying about that night?" I ask quickly. It's better to get to it—the sooner, the better.

He sips his latte and stares at the water. I follow his gaze. Tide's coming in. Stormy weather's expected this afternoon.

"I'm surprised you think you were the first one to make a move. Not sure that's what really happened." His ears burn bright red as he looks at his feet. I look at them too, tanned and sand-buffed.

I think back to that night. We were dancing and I felt the pleasant buzz of one too many margaritas. Tequila's my down-fall. Despite his terrible footwork, I held him close, enjoying his muscly mass pressed to me. He ran his hands from the base of my spine up to my neck, tilting my head back. I remember the warmth of his hands on my skin. It had been a long time since I'd let a man hold me like that. It felt good. Reckless, but good.

"Then what happened? Since I'm clearly an unreliable narrator."

He smirks, making him cuter. *Geez.*

"Juli, I've had a crush on you since we met. I've been work-ing up the courage to ask you out. That night you weren't the only one drinking too much." He pauses, waiting for a reac-tion. What can I say to that?

"Go on." I hold his gaze.

"After we'd had such a great afternoon surfing and then dancing..." He pauses, brown eyes boring into mine. "...you were beautiful...dancing circles around me..." He blushes, looking away.

What the hell did I do?

"I kissed you. You didn't mind. You kissed back, you know. But later at your house, you, uh...well, you got sick when we were... Uh...you know." His face is beet-red now.

Heat rises to my cheeks too. "I'm sorry, Mani—that was uncool."

"No, I don't care about that. But you started talking—and crying...and kind of lost it. You talked about some guy with a weird name—Gor-something. I couldn't figure out what you were going on about. But you showed me scars..."

Oh fuck.

"I shouldn't have gotten so wasted and thrown that on you," I interrupt him, not wanting him to continue.

He wrings his hands in his lap. "Juli, you were terrified. You thought you were being chased by that guy. Are you?"

"What? No. I promise, I'm fine. I'm sorry you had to deal with that. I don't remember much."

"So, you're not hiding in Mauritius, away from him?"

Geezus, what the hell did I tell him?

"No, he was a guy from a long time ago. He was bad news, but I left. I'm fine now."

Mani smiles and takes my hands. I want to pull away, but he's too nice to be a jerk. He must have cared for me that night.

He clears his throat, his expression hopeful. "Can we try again? Another date?"

What'll it hurt?

"Sure, but let's not call it a date, okay?"

His eyes drop, studying the sand around our feet. His shoulders slump.

"I gotta be honest. I'm not looking to get involved with anyone right now. It's not you. I like you. I like surfing with you—but I can't be with anyone like that."

He releases my hands and takes a deep breath. "Is it because of that guy? The one who hurt you?"

I take a deep breath. "Partially. Can you be okay with being friends? I need friends more than I need a boyfriend. And I love surfing with you and hanging out on the beach. Can we do that?"

He nods, but keeps his eyes out to sea. "Yeah, we can do that. How about Friday afternoon—another surf lesson?" Hope in his voice, he glances at me.

"Perfect. Need to show off my pipe skills," I joke.

He leans in and kisses my cheek. He's too sweet. I wish I felt something for him because it would be easy. But I know myself. He's too nice a guy to lure in and then dump. I've kept my life here complication-free. And he makes a mean latte. I'd hate to jeopardize that.

At work the next day, Darrien's got a bunch of samples for me to run. There are more outbreaks of the virus in Mauritius and Madagascar which means long hours in the lab. Oddly, local islanders don't exhibit symptoms like expats. Darrien suspects it has something to do with prior exposure to malaria. Seems chronic malaria is protective against the virus.

I think about Nate, imagining him in Washington, D.C. I wonder what he's doing now. It's three a.m. there—so likely sleeping. Wish I slept better.

Mani and I surf again together. I'm improving and he's good about keeping things in the friend zone, though I catch him staring on occasion. It's a little creepy, but I think with time he'll see me as a buddy. Maybe I should find him a girl. That would take the pressure off.

Chapter 21

Paranoia

Nate:

"You look terrible," Gavin says as I climb into his old green Jeep Cherokee.

"Thanks. Can we get outta here?" I look around.

"What the hell happened?" He stares at me, idling the car.

"Overzealous doctors worried I was contagious. Decked out in hazmat bioterrorist garb. I just wanted relief for these headaches."

"Stay with Dani and me. Sam's a good sleeper." He puts the car in gear and I breathe a sigh of relief. Before donning aviators, I notice dark circles under his eyes. He's not sleeping well either. That's from caring for an infant. I notice something else...fatherhood agrees with him.

"I don't know what else to do. Can we swing by my place?" I ask, looking in the rearview mirror.

"Sure. What happened after they drugged you?" He maneuvers into traffic.

A silver sedan trails behind us. I'm sure it's following until it turns. *Need to get a grip.*

I fill him in on my Thompkins adventures and that my threatening a lawsuit eventually led them to release me.

He shakes his head as we pull up to my apartment. "What should we do if we can't find reasonable doctors?"

"Let's call Campbell when we get back. Maybe he has an idea. We need to warn Sara and Jorge too."

"Bea's not gonna like that call."

Dani meets us, cradling baby Sam in her arms. She kisses me on the cheek.

"Good to see you. You okay?" I hate that she looks at me with such pity. Do I look that bad?

"Better now that I'm not being used as a pin cushion. Thanks for letting me crash. I'll stay out of your hair. You two deserve time alone with that gorgeous baby. Can I see him or are you worried I'll infect him?"

Dani laughs. "No, if Gavin hasn't infected him, you won't. Here."

Sam is tiny with Gavin's dark blue eyes and Dani's chin.

Gavin watches, smiling. "We were talking. How would you feel about being the godfather?"

"Really? You trust me with that?"

Gavin gives Dani a look and they both laugh.

"I'd love that. He's perfect." I pass him back, fighting to keep it together. "At this rate, Sam will be the closest thing to having a child of my own. Can't wait to teach him to tie knots and pee in the woods."

Gavin cuffs my shoulder as Sam fusses.

"Should I take my stuff to the guest room?"

"Yup—you know where it is. Gonna put this bugger down for a nap and we'll call Campbell. Dani's heading out to meet friends for a drink. It'll be just us on baby duty."

"Sounds good." In the back bedroom, I sit on the bed. I kick off my shoes and lay down. Why am I so exhausted?

I wake with a throbbing headache. It's dark outside. I check my watch and realize I've slept two hours. I pop two Tylenol and find Gavin on the couch with Sam. He's making googly eyes and the baby is smitten.

"Evening, sleepy head." He looks at me. "You gotta be

hungry. How about some lasagna Dani made before she left? It's delicious."

"Thanks, but I'm not hungry...just took something." I plop down beside him. "My head's ringing again. Water for now."

Gavin frowns. "Campbell's chicken noodle? You gotta eat. You look like that kid from *Into the Wild*, who starved in the Alaskan wilderness." He hands me Sam as he gets up.

"I know. Soup sounds good." I don't have the energy to argue.

Sam squirms, then settles. He's dang cute, big blue eyes looking around.

Later we call Campbell.

"I've good news. Darrien's coming to town in a few days. He wants to see everyone. Sara and Jorge'll come to you. I'm sending another team to Edmonton but I've got a new project. I'll fill you in after we've seen Darrien."

Chapter 22

Reunion

Juliette:

Darrien asks me to meet him in D.C. to see the team again. He tells me about Nate's unfortunate experience at Thompkins. His symptoms remind me of Liam, the UNICEF worker we treated months ago. Some people, like Gavin, experience weird psychotic episodes while others have more physical manifestations. Others, nothing at all.

Liam was a guy who kept dropping weight. We nearly hospitalized him before we were able to disrupt things. The virus mucked with his metabolism—as if he were running a marathon every day. His heart rate was erratic and he complained of terrible headaches. Darrien suspects that's what's happening with Nate. I'm just glad for the excuse to see him again.

I've done my research—guess that makes me the stalker. I read Nate's piece for *Cascadia Magazine* on the use of primordial tools among the Nunavut. He won the 2001 CPJ Cultural Heritage Journalism Award two years ago and the story was later picked up by *Outside Magazine*. I remember the striking close-up photo of an elder's gnarly hands gripping a battered, oily ulu knife for skinning seal fur... I could practically smell the seal oil and rendered fat from his words. He's a talented writer.

The flight to D.C. is long but I get in some good reading... more of Nate's articles. The man's been everywhere—a remote village in the Amazon rainforest, tracking caribou with reindeer herders in Finland, near the Arctic Circle.

Speaking of Arctic conditions, when I walk into the conference room, I regret not wearing a ski parka. It's an icebox. Wish I had more layers with me. I make my way to the empty seat next to Nate, hoping I won't trip in my flip-flops. Even he looks chilled…and thin. His face is more chiseled.

"We want to do work-ups. Then we'll send your samples to our lab in Geneva. Nate, we'd like you to come with us for a few days. We can do more extensive testing. OGRE funding will finance it and you won't be treated like a lab rat," Darrien says.

"Sure. I'd love relief from these headaches. No hazmat suits, right?"

Darrien laughs.

"You won't be in the high-level containment lab, so no PPE necessary," I offer.

He smiles, relief written in the released crease over his gorgeous blue eyes.

Chapter 23
Liquid Courage

Nate:

Darrien and Campbell have arranged for the team to dine together at the Hilton's restaurant this evening. Juliette walks into the dining room as everyone is getting seated. She's in a simple black sundress. Think it's the same dress she wore earlier. Only now there's something more alluring about it. I study her secretly. No jewelry, no makeup—just her. She sits next to me, golden hair falling across her face. Was she always this gorgeous? Those eyes—I've only seen that color in the Aegean—like sea glass. I offer her water as she settles... We talk about the Comoros and her work in Mauritius. She tells me about a guy they treated with symptoms similar to mine. She wants to meet later to talk more.

After dinner I head back to my room to brush my teeth and wash my face. I don't want to go to her room smelling of garlic and onions. She answers barefoot. She invites me in and offers a drink from the mini bar. I ask for whiskey.

Barefoot and golden-skinned, floating through the room in her sundress, she's one of the most beautiful women I've ever seen. She hands me a glass and opens a mini red wine for herself. She grimaces but keeps sipping. Maybe she needs liquid courage too. She sits on the couch, tucking her feet beneath her.

After we clink glasses, I ask about the UNICEF guy. She describes his symptoms, which sound like mine. I'm distracted, gazing at her in the garish light of the hotel room. She's luminous, like she's just walked out of the sea.

She braves a few glances at me, but her eyes dart, avoiding mine. People aren't usually nervous around me. She moves around, stretching, exhaling excess energy. She must be an athlete—toned arms and, from what I see of her legs...well, they're gorgeous. She's lean and light, moves like a dancer. I wonder if she's ever climbed. She's got the body type for it. Strong upper body with a light frame.

But something about me, clearly has her unsettled.

Chapter 24
Biology

Juliette:

His arm drapes along the back of the couch. I have the urge to nestle into it. His clavicle peeks from the deep blue of his shirt. What is it about that particular anatomical feature I find so damn alluring? He catches me staring. I cough to clear my throat and tell him about the treatment we gave the aid worker. When I glance up, lapis-eyes level mine.

Words tumble from my mouth. I don't know what I'm saying. I lay a hand on his forehead, sliding along the planes of his face. Heat flushes beneath my fingertips.

His eyes darken, onyx marbles. I'm pulled by some invisible force... praying for collision ...

Hands on the back of my neck, lips on mine... this can't be real.

He pulls back first, holding my face. He asks if I'm seeing anyone or married. I giggle at the thought, not the mood I'm going for. He's not bothered by my nervousness. When I confirm I'm truly single, he grabs me.

I've been starved too long – ravenous. I want his clothes off, skin on mine. After flipping the light switch, I push him against the wall and unbutton his shirt, taking my time. The hotel AC blows across his chest and goosebumps erupt. His eyes glitter like chips of coal in the darkened room. I think we need the sturdiness of the wall, but he surprises me.

He's strong and I recognize his urge to rip the dress from

my body. He stares after deftly stripping me naked. A shard of streetlight cuts across the room exposing my left breast. He tells me I'm beautiful, his voice gruff. He runs a hand roughly through my hair and slides it over my shoulder. I want to hide, despite feeling like the most desirable woman on the planet.

His fingers find the thin, white scar at my collarbone...a scar that's been numb since it was inflicted.

My skin burns, searing.

An explosion of memory rockets me out of my body. Lapis eyes turn ice-blue. Dark, wavy hair shapeshifts to blonde, sleek and gelled. Gasping, I push away, covering myself with my arms as the stench of Aquavit and fennel assails my senses. I crouch to grab my dress.

"Gor—uh... Shit." *I can't do this. Fuck.* I scramble from him, crawling to a corner.

"Juliette?"

I'm afraid to look - but steal a glance anyway. He transforms again. He grabs his shirt from the floor and offers it to me. I shrink from his outstretched hand, curling into a ball, trying to make myself as small as possible.

I sneak another peak at him. His eyes are kind, concerned. Not cold. Not cruel. *What am I doing? I need to get out from under this rock.*

"I'm sorry. I'm so sorry."

He's on the floor with me. "Are you okay? Did I do something wrong?"

"No, you didn't do anything. I...uh, just..." I shiver, shutting my eyes, afraid he might transform again. Buzzing fills my ears, like I'm deep in a hive. Terrifying fragments of my past cover the inside of my eyelids. I open them to dispel the shards. Huddled, naked in a corner, I use my scanty dress as a blanket.

He talks quietly, helping to diminish the buzzing. I don't understand anything he says. He may as well be speaking Swedish. I'm startled when he wraps me in a blanket. He holds me gently, still talking. There's a cadence to his voice, like a song or a poem... He's reciting something. It lulls me...

Who is this man?

I wake in the bed alone, in his shirt, buried under the covers. He must have carried me here. Now he's gone. It's probably for the best. I'm so embarrassed. Same thing happened with Mani. Did I call out Goran's name? That's never good.

My mind's fuzzy with images from last night. Kissing and the way he looked at me, all of me. Was that the trigger? Goran's eyes on me usually spelled trouble. Nate didn't look at me like something to exploit or break. But his fingertips on my neck, lightly traced my lines... So many lines now.

But he didn't run. He stuck around—at least last night—grounding me with his voice. I crouched in the crook of his arm. I usually hate being touched; the thought of a hug—particularly a friendly, platonic hug—can throw me into blind rage. I've had to squash that instinct many times in the past six years.

But Nate's arms around me weren't those of a lover or someone with ulterior motives. His voice helped me find the floor beneath me. His pine and citrus aftershave was refreshing—nothing like the poison I inhaled around Goran.

Is that water running?

Chapter 25
Sea Nymph

Nate:

She walks in, wearing my blue button-down, Aegean eyes on mine. She flicks off the lights, strips off the shirt, and joins me. She says nothing but takes the soap from me. She stands behind and soaps my chest. The feel of her naked skin against my back, warm and wet, wakes me—wakes every part of me. She lets me know what she has in mind. I oblige despite the questions running through my mind. She's of the sea...nymphlike. I should be careful, as nymphs are tricky.

Hours Later...

Sunlight streams across the bed, casting dust-dancing rays across Juliette's bronzed back. Her honeyed hair's a wild tangle. We're late to our morning session. Don't care. I roll to her, wrapping my arms around her. She stiffens a moment, then relaxes. Does she think I'll hurt her?

"Morning. It's late, I'm afraid," I whisper into her neck.

She turns to me, squinting at the light spilling into the room. "What time is it?" She lifts an elegant arm to look at a watch that's not there.

"Nearly nine." I run my fingers down her arm. She shivers,

nestling into me. I kiss the top of her head as she lays on my chest.

Her breath on my skin reminds me how much I've missed being with someone like this. I don't want to let her go. I could fall asleep with her here as my eyes droop. *Need more sleep.* But my watch buzzes, waking me. She shifts her weight too.

I think about last night. We should talk about it, but I don't know how to do that without being nosy. Whatever happened wasn't something she could control. She had a panic attack—no question. I just wish I knew what caused it. She saw me as someone else for a moment.

Her stomach rumbles, making her laugh, dragging me back to the present.

"Hungry? There should be breakfast at the meeting."

"Yeah, I'm hungry. Guess we should get going," she says.

I untangle from her with reluctance and perch on the edge of the bed. After pulling on boxers and jeans, I look over. She's on her side, watching me.

I hope she doesn't have regrets. I'm self-conscious without my shirt. I'm too bony, but maybe she doesn't mind scrawny guys.

"Are you okay?" I ask after a long silence.

She sits up, gripping the sheet to her chest. "What? Yeah, I'm fine. Sorry about last night." She pauses and I wait, wondering if she'll say more.

Uncomfortable silence urges me to fill the space.

"You don't need to apologize. Just don't want you thinking I took advantage of you."

She laughs. God, she's a knockout—draped in a sheet, smiling, golden hair a curtain, covering her mysterious eyes. *Let time stand still, just for now.*

"I'm not sure who took advantage of whom, but I did invite you to my room."

Chapter 26
Composed

Juliette:

I managed to keep my cool while getting everyone's samples. I even kept them straight, although I nearly mislabeled Jorge's. My hands shook when I took Gavin's blood. He was kind enough to look away while I jabbed him. I'm usually very good at blood draws. Not today.

Nate asked for a ride back to his apartment. I should have said no. Bad idea. This little love fest isn't going to last long—and the end will be harder if we hook up again.

Despite knowing better, I want him. We've got chemistry. He's one of the good guys. I'm usually attracted to the bad ones—lured in by their mystery and sexy scowl. That's never a good combination. And if things don't pan out, he lives halfway around the world from me. Maybe that's for the best.

I think back to Javier, the boy I dated in high school. He had a wild side – the kind of wild side that terrified my parents. I'd bring him out to the ranch and we'd ride on the beach. He was pretty good on a horse, unlike the other boys, but his passion was motorcycles. I'd sneak off after school to meet up with him and we'd zip around the mountain roads, looking for places to make out. We did that until he decided he wanted more.

I wasn't ready. The teenage male sex drive was unfathomable and confusing. I knew Javier liked me and liked riding with me. He was finally taller and had filled out from football workouts. My Tia Esperanza warned me I'd be a heart-breaker. Never knew what she meant exactly...until the afternoon when Javier decided we needed to seal the bond of our love for each other—out in the middle of a field with no one around. He wouldn't take no for an answer.

When it was over and I was left crying in a heap, as he stood over me, scowling and angry. That was the first time I saw the male temper and what came with it. He blamed me for leading him on—for making him do it. He stormed off, leaving me with my dress torn and body bruised. I walked home three miles, limping and humiliated. I hid out in the barn with the horses, cleaning up. Javier never came by the farm again and he avoided me at school. Instead, he spread rumors. That's when I decided to get out of Santa Marta once and for all.

For the first time in my life, I'm attracted to someone who isn't an asshole or a playboy. He's the boy next door...kind of irresistible.

If only we didn't live on opposite sides of the world...

Chapter 27

Lighting the Ember

Nate

I throw my bag in the back seat of Juliette's rental. On the drive, she talks a mile a minute about the medical facilities in Geneva. I have a hard time following. Something about the clinic being a few miles from the house they rent. After parking, she falls silent. She looks at the apartment building, then back to me.

"Want to come in?"

More silence.

I take her hand. It's clammy. "No pressure."

Her silence unsettles me.

"We can meet at the airport tomorrow or you're welcome to come in," I say to fill the void.

She looks at my hand holding hers. My hands are veiny and thin. Doubt creeps in. Maybe last night's ghost still haunts her.

"I'll come in, for a moment," she whispers.

I walk to her side and open the door. I glance at her tanned legs beneath a light blue shirtdress. The delicate scent of almond oil scrambles my brain.

Once inside, she sags against the door. Not sure what she expected. My apartment is not a wonder of high style or modernity. Rock-climbing gear, ropes, carbiners, and a mountain bike cramp the space.

She walks in, looking around, but stops when she sees

the ropes piled in a corner. She looks back at me, question-ing. Surely, she knows they're for climbing. Then she sees the enlarged photograph of the Tetons I took years ago over my desk. I captured the sun setting behind the mountains in the west, with a loop of the Snake River in the foreground. Dark clouds hang suspended over the tallest peak as rays of sun-light squeeze through the mist and fog.

"Did you take this?"

I stand behind her, resisting the urge to wrap my arms around her. "Yeah, it's near Yellowstone. Was there a couple summers ago. Ever been?"

She backs into me. I grab her waist to steady her. One touch and the ember from last night catches. She's as strong as I remember. And God, she smells good.

She pulls away. "I'm not sure this is a good idea..." Her eyes dart.

"Juliette, I like you. I want to get to know you better."

She looks down, shaking her head. I'm not sure what she's gonna do. I want her body pressed to mine, but maybe she's not ready for that. It happens in slow motion – the feeling before a wipe-out when skiing. Ever so slowly she migrates closer ... eyes on my face... She's shy, holding herself back? It takes every ounce of restraint for me not to grab her. But I wait. And then she's flush against me – lips on mine – our bodies pulsing and magnetic... all restraint and good inten-tions gone. I tangle my fingers in her hair. She tastes of Tic Tacs.

She tugs my sweatshirt over my head and pulls my face down to hers. Urgent. Her shirtdress falls to the floor after I've unbuttoned her. I nuzzle her neck and work my way across silky, toned shoulders and collarbone.

Over the next day and a half, I struggle to wash laundry and pack, as we can't keep our hands off each other. I learn more of her story. She's lived in Mauritius for the past three years, working with Darrien. Before that, she did the Peace

Corps in Madagascar. She's a virologist and a specialist in vector studies. The only thing she doesn't talk about is the elephant in the room. And I'm not brave enough to bring it up.

Her smile makes my heart thunder. She listens with her eyes—a range of emotions in those sea-glass pools. I'm falling off a cliff. I don't care that I'm headed for a rocky landing when our time in Geneva is through.

We meet Darrien at the airport in the afternoon. When I help Juliette with her bag, Darrien gives us a curious glance. It's hard to fake nothing going on between us.

Part II

Two Months Later
Port Louis, Mauritius

Chapter 28

Buen Viaje

Kaulia's back. These last few weeks are my final swims with her. I'll miss my work with Darrien and Claire and the rest of the OGRE team. I wonder what this next phase will bring. I hope I'm doing the right thing.

I sat out on the beach earlier, watching the waves crash in, thinking about my new reality. This move *is* impulsive, but there hasn't been a day I haven't thought about Nate. I ache for him. We talk daily and it's never enough.

Our brief time in Geneva was incredible. We were like a newlywed couple, although we both worried about what was coming.

I take my time packing up my beach cottage. I've shipped some boxes already but I need to send another two this morning before my flight. Darrien's been kind to lend me a staff vehicle. I have yet to tell my parents of my move. I'm afraid to tell them. They'd probably show up and drag me back to Santa Marta if they knew I was moving for a guy.

At the post office, I run into Mani.

"Juli, welcome home. Or should I wish you *Buen Viaje*?"

Shit, I've been avoiding him. Again. But Port Louis is small and word gets around. And here I am with two large boxes.

"Hey Mani..."

"Heard you're moving. Were you gonna tell me?" Veins

pulse from his temple as he drums his fingers on one of the boxes.

"Mani, I'm sorry. I'm not great with goodbyes."

He cocks his head, the way he does when he thinks I'm full of shit. "You've been back for weeks and never came by. You're not sorry. You're running. Again." His dark brown eyes bore into me.

We're making a scene as he's blocks me from getting to the counter. I look down at the boxes at my feet.

"Let me help you." He picks up one and places it on the counter. "Have a nice life, Julieta ." And with that, he's out the door.

I want to crumble. This is not how I wanted to leave him. I hadn't figured out what to do exactly, but I *was* planning to see him—to tell him a proper goodbye. I chickened out each day I thought about swinging by the coffee shop or the beach where he surfs.

I pick up my second box and push it across the counter.

Darrien and Claire bring me to the airport.

"We're gonna miss you, Jules, but you always have a home here." Claire pulls me into a hug.

I try not to cry but the tears flow anyway.

"That's right. If things don't work out in D.C. for whatever reason, know you can always come back. But I get the feeling we won't see you anytime soon. My colleague Mark at the NIH is thrilled to be getting someone with your experience." Darrien kisses the top of my head.

"I already miss you guys," I sob, clinging to them, then feel tiny arms wrap around my legs. Sidique.

"Don't go *Judi*."

I crouch down so I'm level with the curly-haired toddler. "Sidi, I'll be back. I promise—and maybe you can visit sometime. Would you like that?"

He bounces up and down, smiling and laughing. I give them all a final hug and turn to make my way onto the plane.

"Juli! Juli! Stop."

I spin around to find Mani running up, out of breath. Darrien and Claire glance at us and then take Sidique by the hand to leave.

"Mani..."

He grabs me in a hug before I can say anything. "I'm sorry I was mad at you this morning. And, well, since you came back."

"It's okay... I wanted to say goodbye—I just didn't know how." I return his embrace.

He hands me an envelope. "Don't read this until you're on the plane. But I hope you'll come back to visit. Don't forget – *Pvendza dudja, pvendza mlango.*"

I stare at him a minute. He's never been one to spout proverbs before and this one's Swahili. *Where there's a wave, there's a door.* All the surfers love this saying.

I smile. "I'm going to miss you, Mani. Don't kill yourself out there, okay? You should ask Celeste out. She likes you." I give him a wink.

He blushes and pulls me into another hug. "Oh, Juli, why can't I be the man you want?"

I kiss him on the cheek, and turn on my heel.

Chapter 29
New Beginnings

Nate:

I spent the last few weeks reviewing the team's footage from Hudson's Bay. They did an impressive job capturing the region's unique ecosystem of boreal spruce forests and Arctic tundra to the north. Sara's photos show mats of vibrant purple saxifrage bursting through barren, exposed rock as the first plant to flower after a long, harsh winter. Hundreds of species of plants are found in the refuge and Jorge provided an exhaustive list of lichens and mosses alone. Caribou, muskox, grizzly, polar, and black bears, walrus, orcas—it kills me I missed the migrating narwals and belugas. Damn virus. I'm bummed I couldn't be with them but I'm relieved to have been treated in Geneva. And a week with Juliette - that was better than I ever expected.

Gavin and I are at the gym, getting in a quick workout before everyone shows up tonight.

He finds me at the shoulder press machine, on my third rep. "How far'd you run this morning?"

"Maybe four or five miles. Not sure. Why?"

He glances at the weight I'm lifting, making me self-conscious. Gavin's a big guy—not big in an overweight kind of way, but tall and thick, like a lumberjack. I've always felt puny next to him.

"Don't overdo it. Hate for Juliette to show up to a broken Romeo."

He teases that I'm using exercise as an outlet for missing her. He's not wrong. Long runs and bicep curls keep my mind from overthinking things. I feel good and the *statins* have knocked my metabolism back into balance.

"Talk to her lately?" He picks up free weights and lays on a bench, doing overhead presses.

"Yup, early this morning. Though the eight-hour time difference is tough."

"I bet. How's she doing? When's her big move?" Something in his voice makes me look at him.

"Not for a couple more weeks. She's finishing OGRE's disease surveillance maps before she can leave. She sounds good. Busy, but good." I'm not interested in telling him about the intimate details of our conversations.

It's hard to be away from her. I see her in my mind when we parted at the airport—her hair tied at the nape of her neck, her shy smile. I miss the feel of her next to me.

"Jorge and Sara get in this afternoon. Want to pick them up with me?" he asks, grunting on his last reps.

"Sure."

"Cool, then I thought we'd hit Clyde's for drinks."

"May pass. Got to get through more of the editing before tomorrow's meeting."

Gavin stands over me, as I'm doing shoulder flies on the bench.

"Uh, 'fraid not. Your presence is requested this evening. Besides, your big day's tomorrow. Can't disappoint Jorge and Sara being lame. You'll just be all sad and sappy missing Juliette."

I put the weights down and sit up. "Gav—you guys won't miss me. Come on. Tomorrow's the day—not tonight. Let me get my shit done."

He shakes his head adamantly. When Gavin decides something, it's hard to dissuade him.

"Fine. I'll go. Just not staying out all night."

He grins, cuffing my shoulder. "Gonna hit the showers.

Wear the blue shirt—brings out your eyes."

What the hell's he talking about?

"Pick you up at 6:30."

We arrive at the airport just in time to get Jorge. He and Sara arrive within minutes of each other. Jorge comes out with a shit-eating grin on his face and grabs my arms, telling me to flex my new guns. He looks around, certain Juliette must be nearby.

"No," I laugh. "She's still in Mauritius. She'll be here in a couple weeks."

"She might not recognize you." He's animated—for Jorge, that is. He pulls out a black and white photo from his pocket.

Gavin grabs it. We both do a double-take.

"Congrats, you devil! Guess the virus didn't muck things up—your boys swam," Gavin jokes.

"Yup, they swam. Didn't think I was ready, but no time like the present."

"When's Baby Garcia due?" Gavin stares at the photo. I think he's trying to see if he can tell whether it's a boy or a girl.

"Not for seven months," Jorge says sheepishly.

"Feeling okay?" I ask.

"She's great. Me, not so much. Hmmph." He frowns.

"Sympathy symptoms, huh? Aching back? Nausea?" Gavin teases.

"That's a thing. I'm a wreck...glued to *Consumer Reports*. Need to find the safest car seat and crib. Those things can be death traps, you know."

We laugh, but he's not joking.

I put an arm over his shoulders, guiding him to the C terminal where we'll meet Sara. "It's gonna be fine. Gav's managed to keep Sam alive. Can't be *that* hard."

Gavin shoots me a dirty look. "Dani's sisters set us up, so we've got everything you could possibly need. We'll take care of Baby Garcia—not to worry. Got down to business after that last trip, huh?" he teases.

We find Sara who runs to us, happy to be reunited. A new tattoo on her forearm looks like a maze. She tells us about taking her niece skydiving as a graduation present. Although she peppers us with questions and tells us the latest from her end, dark circles under her eyes and lines across her face tell me something's going on. Whatever it is, she keeps mum.

We find a table at Clyde's, a popular hang-out in Georgetown. The place is packed, full of twenty-somethings meeting for drinks with colleagues. As I sip my gin and tonic, I spy Dani walking across the restaurant. I don't realize who's behind her until they're practically next to the table. I nearly choke on an olive I just popped in my mouth.

Juliette...she's here? In the flesh...wearing a nervous smile and the most alluring silky green shirtdress. It's the color of feather moss, like the photos Jorge took in Manitoba, matching her stunning eyes.

I can't speak. I stare. *Please don't be a delusion.*

"You should see your face." Jorge and Gavin laugh and pound me on the back, snapping pictures.

The noise in the restaurant was deafening, but now I'm underwater, eardrums popping. Her dress accentuates so many of the things I've missed. In the dim lighting, her eyes glow golden-green, like an exotic cat. Her glistening hair is shorter, just reaching her shoulders in gentle, honeyed waves. She's a goddess.

"Happy birthday, Nate! Like your surprise?"

I'm speechless. I struggle to swim upstream, clumsy. There

are too many bodies to navigate. I pull her to me. She takes my breath away.

I feel her eyes on me, taking me in. I look different from the last time we were together. She squeezes my hand and nuzzles my neck like she's scenting me out to be sure I'm really me. *God*, I want to drag her back to my room.

Waiters appear with heavy trays of drinks. Gavin offers the first of many toasts. My mind wanders back to that dinner months ago in the Comoros, when we dined on vanilla lobster, having just learned about the virus. A lifetime ago.

I press my thigh to hers, keeping an arm around her. If she were any closer, she'd be in my lap. She smells of the ocean and sunshine, salty and floral. She laughs at Gavin's jokes while her foot works its way up my pant leg. Not sure how long I'm gonna last.

Hours later, we stumble from the restaurant, sated and a little drunk. Gavin and Dani invite everyone to their room for a nightcap. Juliette and I have no intention of going. I grab her hand and lead her to my room. We're barely through the door when we pull off each other's clothes. Fighting to get Juliette's shirtdress unbuttoned is torture. There are a thousand tiny black stone buttons. I don't know if she wore this intentionally, but I curse as I fight the blasted things. By the time I get them undone, she laughs and shows me the invisible zipper on the side.

I worried that once she returned to the islands, she might change her mind. Why would she leave a good job she loves? I run my hands across her bronzed skin, down her back, her silky hair against my cheek...this is too good. I cup her hip, fingers gliding over a ridge of raised skin. She moves her hand down, distracting, until I can't think straight. We're a mess of limbs, muscle, and flesh, entwined.

Chapter 30
Flashback

Juliette:

He comes out of the shower, a towel slung low on his hips. I can't believe his transformation - deltoids, biceps, pecs, glutes and a six pack - all the major food groups. I don't want to stare - but it's hard not to. His eyes find mine as the sheet slips down. I'm less shy after last night. We did things I haven't done with another man since I fled Bogota. And I was only slightly tipsy.

"How'd you keep this a secret? Are you a Soviet spy?"

I respond in a terrible Russian accent, batting my eyes. It's fun to flirt with him.

"Guess I better keep an eye on you. Can't have you running amuck, causing madness and mayhem. May hide you in my mountain lair, so I can have you all to myself," he teases.

I laugh, but a prickling from the top of my head creeps down my spine, slowly, painfully.

I can't breathe. Where'd all the air go?

It's happening again.

His mouth moves, but the sound is garbled - nothing makes sense. I curl up - the safest position I can find.

"Hey, what is it?" His voice is gentle.

I rock in a ball. He's at my side. When he touches me, I flinch.

"Juliette, hey. Look at me."

I understand what he's trying to do but there's no way I'm

looking at him. I stay curled. *Please leave.*

"What'd I say?" He tries to sit next to me, and put his arms around me. I nearly jolt out of bed. Thankfully he pulls back and gives me space. Maybe I'm insane.

"Jules, you okay?" He takes my hand again, and this time I let him. He gives me a gentle squeeze.

"No, sorry. I'm...I..." I rock more, unable to stop the motion. Maybe I should be in a looney bin. Goran claimed that's where I belonged.

"Talk to me, Jules. Is this like the last time?"

Oh God, there was a last time. I've done this before.

I glance at him. He's worried. Goran never looked at me like that. He could have cared less if I was afraid or hurt.

"I just remembered something. It's okay. I'm fine." I pull myself out of bed, away from him.

"Juliette, come on. Tell me what's going on." He follows, trying to take my arm. Not happening. I know what happens after they catch you.

"Nate, it's nothing. Really. Just a weird flashback from a long time ago. Please don't worry." I escape into the bathroom.

I struggle to keep from hyperventilating, I try to remember the breathing exercises he did with me that first time.

Maybe this isn't going to work. Maybe I'll never be normal enough to be with someone like Nate.

A flash from the past reminds me why I've been so careful.

He wanted to do lines of coke after a tense day at work. I said no and he backhanded me so fast I didn't see it coming. His eyes were black. I lay on the floor, holding my head, hoping he didn't break my cheekbone. I nearly collided with the white marble coffee tabletop. He grabbed the mirror shard and stormed out. I hid in a spare bedroom for the night.

The next morning, he found me. He touched my face gently as I pretended to sleep. I wanted to smack his hand away but knew better.

"I'm sorry about last night. I don't know what got into me," he cooed softly, a whisper. He caressed my face, his fingers like worms squirming over me. It took all my willpower not to push him away. I reluctantly

opened my good eye and squinted. His hand trailed down my face to my throat. I wondered if he might strangle me.

My past won't release me. The fear has never left. Even in Madagascar I had night terrors. I tried to keep them secret but that was impossible. I remember volunteer decompression sessions when we'd come for a weekend to the director's house. Jaime was great—always thoughtful of our need for connection with each other. At some point you crave a familiar meal and the opportunity to express things without filtering through others' expectations of you in an unfamiliar tongue. Jaime understood this and made sure his volunteers got a break. But those were also the times when I'd wake screaming. Eventually I chose to camp solo or got juiced up on caffeine to keep from sleeping.

Compared to where I'd been, my time in Madagascar was a dream. A few sleepless nights or solo campouts near Jaime's house was fine.

Now I have to face this again. It happened that night with Mani too. How am I going to deal with this? At least I haven't woken Nate screaming.

Not yet.

Chapter 31
Sara's Heartbreak

Nate:

This morning I watched her sleep, curled on her side. I noticed a scar where the sheet draped, exposing her lower back. There were other faint lines. I assumed she was a kid like me, falling out of trees or getting scraped up hiking in the woods. Now I wonder if those marks are the result of something else...something not as innocent as signs of an active childhood.

I wait around, hoping she'll come out and we can talk. But she stays in the shower and yells for me to head to the meeting.

Before my mind spirals into the never-ending cycle of what-ifs, I walk into the conference room to find Jorge and Gavin consoling Sara.

"What's going on?"

Jorge smiles. "Good to see you this morning. Not sure you were going to make it."

I smirk, lightly punching him in the shoulder. I turn to Sara, who's trying to smile through tears. "You okay?"

"Tom's being transferred to London. We're at an impasse," she says, wiping her face on her sleeve. "How's Juliette? You guys were so cute last night...the look on your face when she walked in. I'd give anything for Tom to look at me like that," she mumbles, trying not to sob.

I pull her into a hug. Sara and Tom were hot and heavy early on, but Tom's a machine. He travels for work even more than we do. Sara loves her job, but it isn't the only thing important to her.

"If he doesn't know what he's got, then he's a fool. Is his transfer definite?" I ask.

"I think so. He dropped the bombshell as he was leaving me at the airport. I didn't want to rain on your parade with Juliette. Where is she, by the way?" Sara glances behind me.

"She's headed to the NIH. I'm not sure how all this came about, as I knew nothing of her arrival." I shoot a look at Gavin.

"Did she tell you about the new apartment?" Gavin asks.

"What? Uh, no. We, uh..." I stammer.

"Guess there wasn't much talking last night, huh?" Gavin's enjoying this too much. I want to wring his neck.

Sara and I walk to the deli to bring sandwiches back for the team.

"He waited 'til I was about to get on a plane to tell me about London. You and Juliette are still new to each other. Tom and I've been together three years. I thought he was the one. Have I wasted three years of my life with his guy?" She looks dejected.

I put an arm around her as we walk. "I get it. Emma was my last long-term relationship—let's just say she left a bad taste in my mouth. I haven't been with anyone I could imagine building a future with until Juliette. Now I'm terrified." I look down and realize my socks don't match.

"You guys have something. It's like no one else is in the room. Most people don't get that, but when you see it, it's blinding. I'm happy for you." She squeezes my arm.

"Thanks. Hope you and Tom figure it out. He may have pulled the cheap trick of telling you as you were getting on a plane 'cause he wasn't sure what he wanted to do. Guys have no idea how their poor timing can fuck with someone. Talk to him. He's career-driven, but he's crazy about you. Remember when he rescheduled his two weeks last summer to whisk you away to wine country?"

She kicks a rock down the street as we walk. "I know. Sometimes I get in my head too much. How did you and Juliette get so lucky?"

"Truthfully, we have work to do. Our thing *is* new—it's dawning on me how little we know about each other. We spoke regularly these last two months. Still, I didn't know she'd gotten an apartment. Last night we didn't really say much of anything, you know."

Sara laughs and winks at me. "Yeah, I know. Thought you two weren't going to make it to the hotel room. You guys are good together." She grabs my arm to keep me from walking into traffic.

"But are we? Yeah, we have chemistry. I have this fear that may be all we have. I don't know anything about her family. I only know what she does for a living because I went to Geneva and saw her at the lab. At some point the sex isn't going to be the only thing to keep us together. I've never been one of those guys driven by his dick. Sorry." My face heats up as the words pop out.

Sara laughs, throwing her head back. She sees my tormented look and takes my arm again. "Oh, Nate, you'll never be one of those assholes. That's not you. You just need to find a way to keep your hands to yourself tonight and talk to her— just like you're telling me. I saw her in Domoni—she's quiet and unassuming, like you. But she's strong. She's seen some things."

Chapter 32
The NIH

Juliette:

Darrien and Claire surprised me at the hotel this morning. They arranged to come in for a few days to help me get settled. They pick me up and we head into the offices.

Claire knows something's up. She takes my hand in the car, using her thumb to soothe my racing pulse. She doesn't ask anything, but after years working together, she knows my history.

I don't know why I felt comfortable telling her about Goran. It just came out one afternoon when we were at the beach swimming. She noticed a scar and asked. I revealed my reasons for wanting to work in a place as remote as Mauritius. She understood. It never felt scary or weird to tell her. She didn't try to fix me. She listened as she held my hand.

I'm reluctant to tell Nate. I don't want him to think I'm damaged goods—that I need his pity or, worse, his saving. I need to move past this. I'm not sure it's something that will ever leave me.

I worry there's more to come with Goran. When I left, I took things...although nothing has come of it in the past six years. My strategy of moving to a distant corner of the globe kept me safe. It also kept me blissfully unaware of Goran's whereabouts and activities. It's possible my double-crossing him will bite me in the ass sometime in the future and I don't want Nate to get caught up in that. The less he knows, the better.

I need this fresh start and the NIH is a place I've dreamt of since I started down this road.

I meet Mark, my new boss. He's in his mid-forties, ruggedly handsome with light brown hair and dark eyes. Despite his weathered persona, he's wearing neatly pressed khakis and a button-down. I get the feeling he'd be more comfortable in trail pants and a flannel. His gold wedding band glistens as the sun hits it. Behind his desk are family photos: a pretty redhead and two boys. He catches me staring.

"That's my wife Lydia and our boys, Justin and Jake."

I nod, embarrassed I've been caught snooping. "Beautiful family. How old are your boys?"

"Justin's nine and Jake's twelve. How about you? Any family?"

"My parents and extended family are back in Colombia." My relationship with Nate isn't definable in any kind of way, though I'm sure Darrien has mentioned my reason for moving here.

Mark doesn't press. We talk work. I'll create infection control education modules and train research teams how to gather specimens in a hot zone.

I'm relieved to focus on other things besides Nate and the weirdness this morning.

Chapter 33

Who Are You?

Nate:

I glance up when I hear her keycard at the door. Her scrunched eyebrows and frown give me pause. She wears green scrubs with her hair tied up. She manages a smile when she sees me. Sara's voice in my head tells me to take it slowly.

"Jules, can we talk?"

Green eyes widen as the frown deepens.

"Hey, it's not like that," I say gently.

She pulls the ponytail from her hair, shaking it out. "Sorry about earlier," she says, not looking at me.

"Sorry about what? You didn't do anything wrong. What happened?"

Her eyes flare, jaw clenches. "I'm not sure what you want me to say. I overreacted. It was nothing. Don't worry about it." She kicks off her shoes. "Let me change."

She pulls jeans from her duffel but gives me a blank look when I follow her towards the bathroom.

"I'll be out here." Things feel topsy-turvy.

She comes out in ripped jeans, low on her hips and a fitted T-shirt, no bra. She could be in a rock music video, draped over a muscle car. I stare a moment too long, then look at her tanned bare feet. Did she just arrive a day ago?

"What do you want to talk about?" Her question digs my mind out of the gutter.

"I hear you got an apartment."

"I found a place with Gav and Dani's help. You didn't expect me to move in with you?" Challenge fills her eyes.

Sheez, this isn't what I intended. "No, I just figured you'd have told me when we were talking these last few weeks."

Blue veins, forked like a raging river, pop from her neck. "I asked Gav and Dani for help so I wouldn't be dependent on you." She rolls her shoulders. "Sorry, I'm kind of touchy."

"Why?" I move to the sofa, hoping she'll sit next to me. "Anything I can do?"

"Not sure... Guess I'm adjusting to a new life. I haven't been here twenty-four hours yet..." Her voice drifts off. She comes up from behind and rubs my shoulders.

She has strong hands. It feels good, *sort of.* I'm glad she wants to connect with me, even if just physically right now.

"Will you tell me what scared you this morning?"

She digs her fingers deep into the fascia between my shoulder blades. It aches. I don't know if she's trying to hurt me, but I squirm away.

She drops her hands. "Sorry... Shit. I like you. I *like* you a lot. Guess you figured that since I moved halfway around the world. I don't want to ruin things by diving into ancient history," she says almost under her breath as she walks around and sits on the couch. That's better.

"I want to know you, Jules. Even stuff that's hard to talk about. Otherwise, what do we have? Great sex isn't the only thing that keeps people together, right?"

She laughs, that deep sultry laugh of hers. "Nothing wrong with great sex." She moves closer. "Don't you have things in your past you're not proud of...things you'd rather not talk about?"

It feels like the most honest thing she's ever said.

"I was going to sprinkle those in gradually—so you wouldn't run away screaming."

She barks a laugh. It's unexpected, but I laugh too. "You're no dark horse with a sketchy past," she says, moving closer. I catch a hint of tobacco beneath the honeysuckle and almond shampoo. "You're too wholesome for any of that."

"That may be convenient for you to believe, but I'm not as innocent as you think." I run my fingers down her face.

Her legs press to mine. I trace the gentle swell of her breasts under the flimsy T-shirt with my eyes, wanting to kiss her there.

"We have the physical stuff down," I say gruffly.

"That's the easy part." She shifts, putting her legs in my lap.

I press my fingers under the ripped denim of her jeans, massaging her warm thigh. *Slow down, Nate,* Sara's voice says in my head.

"I haven't dated in...well, a long time," she says as she stretches, cracking her back. "I'm not sure how to do this."

"Maybe we need to back up...you know, recalibrate..." *What am I saying? I want her. Naked.*

"Recalibrate?"

"Tell me about Colombia, your childhood..."

She looks past me out the window, smiling. The setting sun's gilded rays warm her face. "I always wanted to work in medicine, even as a little girl. My Tia Esperanza was a pediatrician. I dreamed of being like her. She worked in villages along the Rio Negro and everyone adored her."

"Is that what you studied at school?" I run my hand through her hair, sliding it over her shoulder so she can't hide behind it like a curtain.

She looks down. "Yes, I started pre-med classes in Bogota, at Los Andes University, before coming to the States."

"Bogota? You grew up there?"

She shakes her head. "No, I grew up on the northern coast, near Santa Marta, but went to Bogota for university. It was quite a change, but I loved it there."

That's right. She told me about living near the beach and working horses for her parents' business. I think about my own journey from rural Kentucky to Columbia's School of

Journalism. I hated New York when I first arrived. Too much concrete.

"That must have been jarring after your upbringing. You didn't mind the big city?" I ask.

Her eyes light up. "I could be anyone I wanted to be in Bogota. It was magical..." Her bright eyes suddenly go dark, like she's just remembered something.

"Did you graduate from Los Andes or transfer to Tulane?"

Blue veins pulse again. "I failed out of Los Andes...never finished my pre-med classes." She looks away, pulling her legs from my lap. I miss the warmth of her.

"What happened?"

She considers me a moment. "I got in over my head with some guy and spent all my time with him instead of studying. It was stupid." She shakes her head, moving back.

"Who was he?"

She takes a deep breath like this will cost her all the air in the room. "His name was Goran. I met him out dancing one night." She turns away, shoulders hunched like a turtle wanting to retreat into its shell.

"And then what?" I ask gently, wishing she would look at me.

She bolts off the sofa, stung. "He beat the shit out of me. That's what happened. I had to leave."

"What? Jules..." I don't know what to say. "I'm sorry. I..."

She stalks to the kitchenette and finds a glass, filling it with water. "He was a psychopath. And I was an idiot, thinking I could manage him." She stands over me, gulping. Her hands shake as she splashes water on her T-shirt—her very thin T-shirt. "Can we please talk about anything but this?"

I take the glass from her, afraid she'll drop it.

"It's just..." I'm treading in the deep end. We've been sharing bits of our lives over the past two months, but this never came up. "How'd you get away?"

"Why? Why do you want to know?" Her face burns red.

I struggle to keep my eyes on her face, not her nipples stretching the translucent material of her shirt.

"I made bad choices years ago. I don't want to be that person anymore. I don't want to relive it—ever."

"Don't you think this is something we should work on together, if we're going to try and be..."

"Really? I have to tell you all my dark secrets? I just got here. Can't we just have great sex and worry about this shit later?"

Yeah, I'd like to have great sex right now, damn it. She has no idea how turned on I am by her.

I can't be that guy.

"No," I say softly. "That's not how it works." A smooth expanse of belly, reminding me of the Kalahari, taunts me. I want to run my fingers across that desert. "There are things that upset you and I don't want to do that to you. You don't have to tell me right now. I just want to know you."

She collapses on the bed, staring out the window, her back to me. I wrangle my courage, hoping she won't lash out again, and crawl onto the bed and lay my head in her lap. In this prone position, maybe she'll be less likely to see me as a threat. *Or she could just go for the jugular.*

She runs her hands through my hair, looking down. "Nate, I'm probably not the right girl for you. I've got baggage. I should have revealed that before moving here." She traces my cheekbones, goosebumps erupt in the wake of her touch.

"Then why did you move here?" From this angle I see all the colors in her eyes: olive, moss, hazel and honey, too many to fathom.

"Because I couldn't stop thinking about you." She kisses my forehead.

"I couldn't stop thinking about you either. That's where we start."

Chapter 34
Deluge

Juliette:

I should tell him about Goran...even Lukas Enterprises. I've kept quiet since I left years ago. Nothing good can come from diving into that hot mess. Once I open the dam, there's no going back. I'm afraid of the deluge.

I avoided romantic liaisons in Mauritius. Though there were plenty of options for something meaningless, I chose to steer clear. Too much risk. After escaping Goran, I had no interest in climbing into anyone else's bed.

Mani was a one-off, although he hoped for more. My past snuck in and Mani was too much of a gentleman to take advantage. Unlike my days with Goran, I woke with only one sign of our time together—bruised feet from dancing. Those scars I can live with.

Now I'm with Nate. Could I be any more impulsive after being careful the past six years? I expected to come to my senses before moving, but I couldn't stop thinking about him—wavy, dark hair and lapis-lazuli eyes...the way he leans in to kiss my neck. We've got chemistry. In fact, we excel in all the high school sciences. He can talk about anything and isn't someone who agrees for the sake of keeping the peace. We spent hours arguing conservation theory, and why certain species behave the way they do. I like a man who challenges me.

Now he's challenging me in ways that scare the shit out of me.

I wish we could go back to those days in Geneva where it felt like we were on a honeymoon, without the hassle of a wedding. Crazy to think I only knew him a few weeks before deciding to move 10,000 miles. I tell myself it was for the opportunity to work at the NIH, and it's true. But since meeting Nate, I can imagine something more—something I wasn't sure would ever be possible. It's like I've known him all my life.

Mauritius was an antique photo: sepia-toned. Burnt yellow corners and blurry. Each day like the one before...morning swims with turtles or dolphins, hours behind a microscope or computer, an occasional surfing lesson with Mani. A good life...fulfilling. But in Geneva I rediscovered colors again—vibrancy I only see with Nate. Flowers smell more pungent, coffee richer. All my senses have woken since colliding with him.

These past two months apart, I planned my days around our long-distance calls, even skipping my morning swim to catch him before his day ended. I wanted his image in my mind and his voice in my head to hold on to for the rest of the day.

Last night's reunion was spectacular and, God, he looks good—no longer skeletal. We gave each other a good workout. There wasn't much room for talk, which I appreciated. I've got stamina. It's the mushy soft stuff, feelings and expectations, I find so terrifying.

Our talk this afternoon...that was miserable. I didn't expect him to pin me down so quickly after arriving. I figured we'd have a few weeks of mind-blowing sex and *then* we'd talk about the "real" stuff—the couply stuff. But no, he got right to the point. Instead of folding and telling him my sob story, I challenged him in a way I know too well.

I ran my fingers through his hair with his head in my lap, gazing up at me, his arousal obvious. I know when a man wants to fuck me. Unlike Goran, Nate's not as driven by lust. He held back, even though my skimpy T-shirt drove him to distraction. I know how to manipulate. I shouldn't pull that with him. He deserves better.

And tonight is his birthday party. Gavin's picking us up in a few. What to wear...

Chapter 35

Overserved

Nate:

Hot water runs over me, washing away last night's decadence—chocolate fondu, a fifteen-year single malt, and Juliette. Not a bad way to spend my birthday.

Despite her unknowns, I'm glad she's here. I should run the other direction but can't. Even after our complicated conversation, I want to hang on to her. My birthday dinner with everyone was memorable. Darrien and Claire joined us at the swanky Sequoia along the Potomac with its floor-to-ceiling windows overlooking a sculpture garden and views of the Roosevelt and Key Bridges. Gavin secured us a table on the terrace, knowing I prefer to eat outside.

Juliette stunned in a deep green sundress with gold leaves, a delicate gold chain at her throat highlighted her honeyed waves and she smelled of wildflowers and rain. It was hard to keep my hands off her. Campbell presented me with a Montblanc Writer's Edition rollerball pen. Darrien and Claire gifted me a bottle of Bordeaux, from his home region. Sara, Gavin, and Jorge gave me a gift-wrapped box of iodine tablets to use with a new water filter. And Juliette's gift...she wasn't kidding when she said, "Dessert's on me."

I leave Juliette sleeping as I make my way to the elevator, where I find Sara, bleary-eyed.

"Sara, you look a little, uhh..." Her face is pale with a hint of seaweed. Dark circles beneath her eyes tell me she didn't sleep well last night. She leans against the wall, waiting on the elevator.

"Rough? Overserved last night. I missed Tom and watching you and Juliette together—kinda painful. Shit, I'm sorry. I'm happy for you two. Just wish I knew where my life was headed."

When the elevator arrives, I take her elbow as I'm not sure she's entirely sober.

"Have you talked to him?" I press the Conference Room level.

"Last night, right before the party. He sounded far away, like he couldn't comprehend I'd be bummed he wants to move to London." She stops talking when another person joins us.

"Why couldn't you go with him?" I ask as we wander into the spacious room. Sara heads for the coffee. "There are film and production jobs in the UK. I'd hate to lose you, but if you want to be with him, why isn't that possible?"

She sips the liquid black, grimacing. "Shit, that's hot. He hasn't asked me to come. That's the hang-up. This is something new for him." Her shoulders slump. "He talks about his move—not *our* move." I think she's going to cry.

I put an arm around her, careful not to jostle her. *Goddamn Tom. What the hell's he thinking?*

I used to have a crush on Sara. She started working with the team as a film editor a few years back. I was drawn to her wicked wit and badass tattoos trailing up her muscled arms. Sara's a creative genius, and a prankster. I remember when she rewrote one of my pieces featured in *Outside* about a remote tribe in the Amazon. I spent weeks researching and writing from a tiny village in the Brazilian rainforest. It was grueling. She created a spoof article and imbedded it in a fake copy of the magazine she ingeniously doctored. I was shocked at the typos. But when she sauntered past my desk, decked out in tribal makeup, eyes dancing, I knew she'd pulled a fast one. She's been a great friend and colleague. Tom's an idiot if he lets her go.

"Sorry. You sure or could you be misunderstanding? Have you asked him outright?"

"Shit, I'm not good at asking this kind of stuff. I'm afraid my little world's gonna crash down around me." She hiccups, trying to mask a sob.

I steer her to a quiet corner. "Just ask him. Do it today, before you leave. If it's bad news, stay with Juliette and me for the weekend. We'll sulk, drink cheap whiskey, and watch sappy movies. We'll help you get over him."

"Are you kidding?" she cry-laughs. "I can't stay with you two, when I'm falling apart. I can't watch your blooming love. Maybe I can crash with Gav and Dani."

"They'll take care of you. Find out what's going on. Not knowing is torture. Don't do that to yourself." I hug her and head to the buffet.

"We've identified lemurs as secondary hosts." Darrien stands in the center of the room, clicking through images on the big screen. "It first infects bats, impacting their feeding behavior. They've been found eating during the day, bringing them into contact with lemurs, that share a similar diet of fruit. Somehow, the virus has jumped to lemurs, causing an amplification of the viral properties. When the lemurs become infected, they demonstrate the 'death and resurrection' symptoms you're familiar with. The good news is we haven't found any dead lemurs. They go into a hibernating state and come back to life and go on with their little lemur lives."

Darrien explains the plan for further research and that funding is available due to the number of European expats and American Peace Corps volunteers who've been infected. We may be requested to spend time in Mauritius to assist their research. Sounds good to me. I'd love to see where Juliette lived these past three years.

I head to the room to pack up. Grabbing Juliette's bag, I hear the unmistakable sound of pills in her satchel. Probably just vitamins.

There's a knock at the door as I'm about to head out. I find Sara, eyes streaky and red.

She sniffles and hiccups. "He's leaving. When we were in Manitoba, he reconnected with an old girlfriend on a business trip to London. I didn't even know he'd gone. Said he'd been thinking about proposing and wanted to take me back to the Comoros...but after seeing Marcie, he realized she was the one. They'd been a hot item years ago and then she'd married some asshole and is now divorced. Shit, Nate, I'm so pissed. I mean, why the hell did he have to tell me he'd planned to propose? That's just cruel. I didn't need that little detail."

She buries her head in my shirt, sobbing. I rub her back, trying to think of something to say. At that moment, Juliette lets herself into the room. Shock registers as she sees me holding Sara.

Sara stumbles back, embarrassed. "Hey Jules, sorry. I just found out Tom's leaving me for an old girlfriend. I'm...oh, shit..."

Juliette crosses the room in three strides and throws her arms around her. "I'm sorry. What can we do?"

Sara snorts as she laughs through tears. "You two..." She grabs us. "I'm staying with Gav and Dani this weekend. You guys better come over tonight to drink. I'm getting wasted and I'll need someone to hold my hair out of the toilet."

Chapter 36
Prowling Lynxes

Juliette:

I dropped Sara at the train station this morning. After her devastation over Tom and drunken night, I invited her to move in. Not sure she was totally on board at first, but we bonded over the weekend. She was grateful not to return to her apartment to watch Tom pack up and leave. I think we'll make good roommates and she was terrific help outfitting the apartment. We found lots of treasures and cool knickknacks at funky consignment stores.

Unpacking my things from Mauritius makes the place feel like home. Sara added plants in the shower and along the edge of the tub to magnify the island vibe. When I got home, I moved the plants to the living room. I want no reminders of my past...especially that damned finca.

The master bedroom was elegant in shades of ecru and khaki with woven sisal rugs. He liked sex on those rough rugs, leaving my backside a map of rope fibers and burns. Later, when sudsing up in the steam shower, he ran his fingers along those marks. I was too mesmerized by his bathroom to notice his interest in my topography. Overhead, exotic plants suspended from an octagonal sunroof, cascading to meet climbing trellises of bougainvillea and plumeria. I felt like I was in a terrarium, minus barking frogs and spiders.

Nope—no plants in the bathroom. Keep it simple. Keep the past in the past.

What to wear today. I'm not sure how patient Nate will be when he learns what I have in mind.

I arrive on his doorstep fifteen minutes late. I'm shameless in an iridescent purple slip dress that shimmers when I move. He leans across the doorway, his lips on my neck, breathing me in, nearly crack my resolve.

"Come with me," I murmur.

"I'd go anywhere with you."

His French blue shirt matches his gorgeous eyes. Maybe we can skip the foreplay and head straight to the main attraction. He pulls a small grocery bag from the counter and we make our way to his car. I've been using it to outfit the apartment. As thank-you, I washed and spritzed it with honeysuckle and rainwater body mist.

"It's early...dinner'll be later," I say. He eyes my legs. "We're not going to the apartment just yet. I thought we'd do something touristy today, just the two of us, and then we'll head there for dinner. How's that sound?"

His head flops back, letting out a sigh. "I was hoping we'd go to your place and I'd help you out of that stunning dress. You're testing my willpower, Juliette."

I sit back, adjusting myself in the seat, crossing my legs. I smile, laying a suggestive hand on his thigh, and tell him to drive to the apartment.

He thinks I've given in, as I rub circles into his khaki-clad leg. He grabs my hand roughly, gripping it, then places it back in my lap. I squirm as the cold zipper on the back of my dress connects with a sensitive bit of skin.

When we arrive, I lead him from the apartment to the Metro station, where we catch the Red Line toward the complex of Smithsonian museums.

We start at the Museum of Natural History. I've never

been. I feel his eyes on me as we wander from one hall to the next, taking in the mastodons and saber-toothed tigers. Fiery currents shoot through me when his fingers graze my neck or lower back. I want him to push me up against the glass enclosures, to inhale me, like the prowling animals surrounding us. The stalking posture of the Canadian lynx teases.

Meandering from hall to hall, I rub up against him when he least expects it. He surprises me when he grabs me and pulls me behind a wall leading to the restroom. He grips my back as his teeth graze my neck. "Juliette, stop tormenting me or I'm gonna haul you into the men's room."

I squeeze his ass and push him off. "One more room. I want to see the bat-eared foxes."

After I've exhausted my willpower, I lead him back to the Metro. I find a seat next to an older gentleman and stare straight ahead on the ride home. Walking back to the apartment in silence, Nate's arm snakes around my waist tightly.

I enter first after unlocking the door. He sucks in a breath as he stands in the doorway, staring.

"Wow—this is something else."

I slide past to open the French doors to a balcony where flaxen linen panels stir seductively in the evening breeze. The room, in shades of mango and emerald, is accented by simple, dark rattan furniture. My ebony-hued dining table is low with colorful floor cushions as chairs. Tropical plants bring the outdoors in. Ficus and elephant ear with large, kale-colored, waxy leaves. It's a sultry island paradise.

I light candles around the room and put on a favorite CD— Baaba Maal. His haunting voice resonates as he sings in both French and Pulaar, provocative and erotic. At my mini bar, I open the whiskey decanter and pour a lowball on the rocks. Standing in the doorway, waiting for an invitation, Nate watches.

"You've good taste, Juliette," he says after taking sip.

Thank you, Sara. She told me his favorite—Blanton's Original Single Barrel Bourbon.

I lead him to a chair and sit in his lap. "What can I get you?"

His aftershave of citrus and pine reminds me of freshly chopped wood and campfires. He doesn't say a word, running his hand up my leg to the short hem, teasing with light finger touches. When he feels me squirm, he stops a moment.

"How's your willpower?" he asks gruffly. His other hand traces my breasts beneath the stretched silken fabric, tormenting. He slides the strap of my dress down, running his lips along my collarbone, sending jolts of electricity everywhere.

He carries me to the low dining table and lays me out like a meal he intends to savor. I kick off my heels, gripping his torso between my thighs, kissing his neck, while struggling to undo the buttons on his shirt. He slides the zipper of my dress down my back, running his hands along the length of me. He pulls back, giving me a suggestive look when he realizes...skin and more skin.

"Had I known...I'm not sure I would have waited until now," he growls in my ear, cupping my ass. His breath on my neck tickles, as I drag my nails across his chest.

I wake to the scent of coriander and braised chicken. I'm famished. My grumbling stomach reminds me we haven't eaten. I've been slow-cooking a Mauritian stew and the apartment smells of toasted spices. I slink out from under his arm and grab a kaftan from the end of the bed. We'd been so caught up in each other, we forgot to eat. As the sun makes its final descent, I put on a Cesária Évora CD, allowing her sultry voice to float on the air.

I head to the kitchen to finish prepping dinner. I lose myself in the music. I miss dancing. I'm startled when I'm hoisted off my feet and spun around.

"You are a dangerous drug. And if I didn't get any words

out earlier, this place is amazing. You've brought Mauritius to Bethesda—it's gorgeous."

I cling to his muscled shoulders. He's wearing one of my colorful kangas. I smack his ass to distract him from the sound of my heart hammering in my chest.

"I'm glad you like it. Believe it or not, you haven't seen the other hidden gems in this place. We'll see if you can find them later."

He reaches his hands under my kaftan, fingers grazing my skin. I push him off, laughing.

"No, they aren't on me. Let's eat. Think we worked up an appetite. Come, sit on the porch. Would you grab the wine?"

My little porch is charming with a bright blue bistro set. I love the idea of grilling outside as the sun sets over the Potomac.

I push him down into one of the chairs. "Please pour the wine and I'll be back with the food."

"Yes, ma'am."

I return with two heaping bowls of chicken stew, cardamom, cloves, and allspice permeating the air. I run back to get the bread and salad.

"So, you didn't tell me you were a four-star chef, on top of your other impressive attributes." The breeze blows my kaftan up. He smiles, admiring my legs. This is nothing like my time with Goran.

"I love to cook. I learned from my mother. She always had a pot of something simmering when I was a kid. I wanted to make something from Mauritius since you've never been. This dish is traditionally made with goat, but that's hard to come by. And after your last goat experience, you may not be interested. Chicken and pork work equally well. The trick is the layering of spices that slowly brings the dish together for its unique flavors."

He takes a bite, his appreciation obvious when he closes his eyes, savoring the bite like it's the best thing he's ever eaten. Not everyone is a fan of earthy stews, but I find this to be a great introduction to Mauritian food, where warm spices and perfectly stewed chicken melt in your mouth. I'm relieved he likes what I've cooked.

"You even talk like a chef. I had no idea." I blush at his compliments and offer him homemade naan. He stares at the bread. "Is there anything you can't do?"

"I can't change a flat tire on a rusted-out Jeep. And believe me, I've tried," I laugh, hoping to mask my fear when I recall that particular incident. "And I can't rock climb. I'm terrified of heights. I probably should have divulged that sooner."

"You haven't climbed with me. I'm good at getting people up a rock face. I know you have the physical strength. Been admiring your athletic abilities these last few days." He puts a possessive hand on my thigh, peeking through the slit of my kaftan.

Just like that, I want his hands off me.

He catches my expression and releases my leg. "Hey, I'm kidding," he says gently. "I'd love to share my love of climbing with you, but it's okay if that's not your thing."

I take a deep breath. He's not Goran. But I have no interest in hiking with him or anyone else.

We eat in silence, watching the sun melt into the horizon. It's warm but not stifling, a soft breeze brings the linen curtains to life.

"More stew? There's plenty. Dessert too."

"Please... Can I get you more?"

I shake my head. I change up the music while he refills his bowl. He comes out humming.

"You know Habib Koité?"

"I saw him in Bamako a few times. I love his Afro-Caribbean drum beats and acoustic guitar."

I'm impressed. He's been around, like me. I put my legs back in his lap. I relax as he draws images on my thigh. We sip our wine, relaxing as the suns sinks from view.

Later, I lead him to the bathroom, where a jacuzzi tub bathed in candlelight awaits. I've thrown in bath salts and dried flowers. I unwrap the kanga he's wearing and he pulls my kaftan over my head as we step into the steaming, fragrant bath. We nearly fall asleep as the fatigue from the day hit us.

The next morning, he treats me to breakfast in bed. It's romantic and sweet. We spend much of the day curled up with each other until I convince him to go on a walk. I need to learn my neighborhood. We stroll through the tree-lined streets, admiring picturesque gardens and quaint houses.

Maybe having a boyfriend—a nice boyfriend—won't be so bad. In the apartment, I worried he'd stumble on something I didn't want him to, though I kept those things locked away. He's not overly nosy and stuck to me like glue, which helped.

He ran his fingers lightly over my scars. Thankfully I didn't relapse into a another PTSD spiral. My body was a book of braille he wanted to read, using his fingertips to decipher the different messages imprinted on my skin. Goran ran his fingers across my scars too, though there was nothing gentle or nuanced in his touches.

I swore I saw him on the Metro yesterday. I nearly jumped off at the wrong stop for fear he'd see me.

Chapter 37

Her Place or Yours?

Nate:

I'm depressed going back to my lonely apartment when Juliette heads to work the next day. My place isn't exactly inspiring—lots of climbing equipment, a mountain bike, and piles of books. I need to up my game. I want her to feel comfortable. When Sara moves in, she may be spending more time with me. I meet Gavin for lunch.

"It's unlike any other apartment I've seen. She's brought the islands to Bethesda. I need to make some improvements to my place."

We're at a quaint French bakery known for their sandwiches and salads. Gavin digs into a triple-layer club sandwich. He has a sleeping Sam in an infant carrier propped on a chair.

"Uh-huh. Worried she'll be less seducible in your rock-climbing gym?"

"Something like that," I mumble. "She wants everyone to come to a house-warming and welcome party for Sara next weekend. Can you guys make it?" I bite into my BLT.

"Absolutely. Chat with Dani if you want to amp up your decorating game. She's good. She did our place. It's a huge improvement over the man cave I lived in."

We stop and stare when an older man walks by with his orange tabby on a leash.

We catch up on work projects and make a tentative plan to

climb one afternoon at New River Gorge.

"I gotta run. Need to pick up something to cook tonight."

"Her place or yours?" he asks, smiling.

"Hers. I'm almost ashamed to have her at my place. She and Sara did that over one weekend. I've had my apartment for three years, and it's not changed since the day I leased it."

"Get with Dani, and if she can't help you, my buddy Kenny's great too. He works for one of the interior decorating firms in town. He was in the running to be one of the guys on *Queer Eye*. He loves a formidable challenge!"

I head back to my apartment and, walking in, imagine it from Juliette's perspective. It's neat and not a true man cave. I'm not sure Dani can help as she's busy with Sam and part-time work at REI. I shoot a text to Gavin asking for Kenny's number. Anyone in the running for *Queer Eye* must have credentials.

At the grocery I pick up ingredients to make tuna and vegetable curry and find a nice rosé and ice cream for dessert. I head to Juliette's, knowing she won't be home yet. She gave me a key, although somewhat reluctantly.

I want to surprise her with an elegant dinner. Not all guys can cook, but this is in my wheelhouse. I marvel how everything came together to make this space seductive and beautiful. I snap pictures for inspiration and bring in her mail. I hunt for paper to leave a note but the desk drawer's locked. Weird.

Her CD collection is impressive—lots of music I've never heard before. I find the Baaba Maal she played the other night. It's mysterious and sensual, like her.

As I'm sweating the shallots and garlic, I hear her key in the lock.

Her eyes narrow, forehead creasing into a sharp line. *May have overstepped.*

"What are you doing here?"

"Sorry, thought I'd whip up dinner for us. It's my turn to woo you."

Her icy expression melts a fraction, but there's something behind those gorgeous green eyes. "Are you wearing my apron?"

I dance over, waving a spatula in the air. I'm a lousy dancer, but my herky-jerky attempt at a salsa has the desired effect. She laughs and allows me to lead her back toward the kitchen. Her eyes warm when I pull her in for a kiss.

"It smells incredible in here. What're you making?"

"Green curry with tuna and veggies. I've got some rosé in the fridge chilling. Like a glass?"

"Sure, let me get out of these scrubs and I'll be right back."

She comes out in a pair of loose sweats hanging low on her hips and a cropped Rolling Stones T-shirt. How can she look so fucking hot in sweats and a T-shirt? I look down so I won't chop off my finger accidentally. She laughs and goes to the fridge for the wine. She pours two glasses and sits across the tiny kitchen island from me.

I finish chopping the vegetables and add oil to a pan. She stares at her phone, frowning.

"How was work?" I ask to draw her out.

"Good," she mumbles, not looking up. "I'm meeting my first group of trainees tomorrow. We'll practice catching insects to demonstrate how to handle a potentially dangerous animal we want to study."

"Where're you doing that?"

"Someplace called the Capital Crescent Trail, I think."

"Great spot—part of a *Rails to Trails* program where old railway lines were converted to biking and walking trails. You'll love it. Need my car to get out there?" I want to make everything okay. I want her to smile. I add coconut milk and curry to the vegetables I've been sautéing.

"I don't think so. The division has arranged transportation for us, so we'll have our specimen collection gear with us.

It'll be a short trip, to familiarize people with how the work is done. Later we'll demonstrate how to collect specimens in a hot zone." She looks at the door.

"I brought your mail in." Her eyebrows jump. "It's on your desk."

She moves stiffly, the forehead crease returning. I focus on cooking, unsure what's making her tense. I sprinkle in turmeric and red pepper flakes and check the rice. When I look up, she's back at the island, watching me.

"Seems you know your way around the kitchen too."

"I'm a recipe nerd. Like to collect 'em. I had a similar dish in Kenya a few years ago." Pulling out a Pyrex dish, I lay a piece of tuna. I season the fish and pour hot curry sauce over it and stick it in the pre-heated oven. I grab raw veggies from the fridge and blue cheese dip we can munch on while the fish cooks.

"It'll be another thirty minutes but snack on these? How do you feel about blue cheese?" I love the stuff but know not everyone's a fan.

"The stinkier the better." She wipes a smudge of blue cheese from my mouth.

"Don't look at me like that," I scold, breaking eye contact. "I gotta keep an eye on the fish."

She laughs and takes another sip of wine. Her cell rings. "Hello?"

I look up when the phone clatters to the hardwood floor.

Chapter 38
Found

Juliette:

Oh God, he's found me.
Everything moves in slow motion.
Aquavit permeates the stifling air.
Maybe that was him on the Metro.
Shit, he can't be here.
Why now?
I did my part. I never reported him.

Chapter 39

The Call

Nate:

"What is it? Jules?"

She holds the counter like she might pass out, her face ashen. She slips past when I reach for her.

"Juliette, talk to me. What's going on?"

She inches to the French doors, peeking through the linen panels, out to the street. She slams the doors, but the fabric panel catches, muffling the sound. She moves through the apartment, a silent tornado, closing things up tight.

"Was it Goran?" His name on my lips startles her.

"No. Umm, I don't know."

"You can tell me."

She stops and stares into space. She sags in on herself, close to collapse. I take her arm and guide her to the sofa. She sinks down, burying her head in her hands.

"I can't. I've said too much."

I pull a blanket around her shoulders. "Why? Why do you think that? Are you in danger?" I ask gently.

Her startled green eyes rim with red. "I don't know. If he's here, it's not good." Her body shudders. When I touch her leg, she flinches.

"Hey, it's just me. When's the last time you saw him?"

She opens her mouth to answer, then clamps it shut. I know he hurt her. But that's all I know.

"If he's here, then we need to come up with a plan, right?" I offer.

"Wrong!" She explodes off the couch, seething. The blanket tangles around her feet, causing her to trip. I catch her arm to keep her from toppling. This pisses her off even more. "This is my problem. Not yours. I'll deal with it."

"Whoa, Jules, I'm not the enemy here..."

"Nate, I can't talk about this right now. You're always here, crowding my space. I need air."

What the fuck? I feel slapped.

"Shit, I don't mean that. I just..." She backpedals.

"What's that supposed to mean?" I spit out. "And for the record, I'm not always here. You just arrived, like, three days ago, to be precise. We haven't been in the same place in two months."

Her face drops. "I'm sorry. I shouldn't have said that. I'm... I'm...."

She glances around the apartment. I'm not sure what she's looking for. Her eyes fall on the table set for two.

"You cooked a nice meal. Let's eat." She spins around to the kitchen and grabs the fish from the oven. I doubt it's done cooking but this is not the time to demonstrate my inner Julia Child.

"Jules, we don't have to eat. Was that him on the phone?"

She ignores me, plating the fish. It's jiggly in the middle. Her nose wrinkles. She brings the plates to the table. How long can she pull off this charade? I sit across from her, not bothering to lift my fork. My stomach's too twisted to eat—particularly undercooked tuna that's not sushi. She takes a bite, then pushes back from the table and runs to the bathroom. I wait a few moments before taking our plates to the sink. I wait until she emerges from the bathroom and try again.

"Juliette, talk to me. What's going on?"

She glares at me. "I can't! Don't you get it?"

I struggle to keep from yelling back. "No, I don't get it,

because you won't tell me anything."

My mind flips to last night...gorgeous, naked Juliette laid out on this very table. Astonishing how quickly things can change. She turns away and I feel even more shut out.

What the hell am I doing? She doesn't want me here. I promised myself I wouldn't let another woman destroy me the way Emma did. She's no different—walled-off and distant. I'm repeating the same mistakes.

Where's my bag? I should leave.

"Nate, don't go. I'm sorry." She's behind me.

"Sorry for what? Moving here? Pushing me away? What exactly are you sorry for?"

"I'm sorry for all of it," she says in a small voice.

"Juliette, I want to be with you. I want to help, but I..."

"I know. I'm sorry for getting you tangled in this." She takes my hand. "I don't want to push you away, but..."

"Then don't." I put her hand on my chest.

"I'm afraid to get you involved with this mess." Tears pool in her glassy eyes.

"What exactly is 'this mess'? You know I'd never hurt you. I'd never do the things Goran did to you. Do you believe that?"

She nods, wiping her face on her sleeve, sniffling.

"If you can't talk to me, then what do we have? I don't want to be with someone who can't share themselves with me. I've been in that relationship before." I tilt her chin up and stare into her fathomless eyes.

"Emma?"

"Yeah, Emma. This feels too much like that, only you haven't cheated on me yet."

She jerks like I've smacked her. I hold on to her.

"I wouldn't do that," she whispers. She nuzzles my neck, sending electrical currents all down my spine. Her tears run down my throat.

"Can you let me in, just a little bit?" I murmur in her ear.

Chapter 40

Imprint

Juliette:

2 a.m.

The moon's nearly full as I shiver on the balcony, swimming in Nate's sweatshirt. This is the best place to think, despite the cold.

I think I'm glad he's here, but I also feel like he's invading my space. Why does this all seem so strange? I told him what I could. I don't know if that was Goran on the phone. But the way he said my name, the sneer in his voice... And he called from an unlisted number. My body reacted the same way it did all those years ago, shutting down, unable to withstand what might be coming. How do you tell someone about that?

I spared him the more graphic details. When I left Goran, my body bore the signs of his imprint. Most of those scars are faded—little white lines, unobtrusive. Could be the scratches of an angry cat, or the stain of an angry man with a penchant for violence.

Was there a time when things were good with Goran? We had a beginning—kind of steamy, fueled by sex and alcohol. Or maybe I was too enamored with having snared him to notice he wasn't all that nice.

He sent flowers. Two dozen roses. White and red ones. Ana was home when they arrived, since I was in class. I'm glad she didn't read the note as it was rather suggestive. We'd slept together for the first time the week before. When I called to thank him for the flowers, he invited me to spend the weekend with him.

He made no illusions about his expectations for our sleepover. In the days leading up to our date, he sent detailed notes, hand-written, of things he wanted to do to me. I was turned on, to say the least.

I remember the slinky underwear and new dress I bought for the occasion. Spent far more than I should have but intended to return it the following week. The dress did the trick, though maybe too well—it was in no shape to be returned.

We spent the first hour on the balcony, where I froze my ass off. He liked to watch me squirm, especially as my body reacted to the cold. Later, back inside, we sat at a long table, each of us on either end. I shivered throughout the meal, not eating much. After dinner he put on music and pulled me in for a dance. He held me tightly, unpinning my hair so it fell around my shoulders. He grabbed a fistful, pulling my head back to expose my neck. I was stunned by his roughness but when his lips and teeth scraped against my throat, a current coursed through me from the base of my spine to the top of my head. It was erotic, although terrifying as I wondered if he might actually bite me.

My body responded to him in a way I'd never felt with other men. I may not have understood a lick of Swedish, but his intent was clear. He fucked me on the dining table and then again in front of the fire. He wanted to take me back out to the balcony but I refused. I was finally warm and wanted to stay that way.

Eventually he dropped me home and I slept for a day and a half. He wanted me to come the following weekend. I made an excuse, as I wasn't sure I could handle another weekend like that.

That was the beginning, when things were somewhat normal. But thinking back, it wasn't about romance or the heart-thumping of new love. It was about power and lust – nothing romantic about that. I forgot about freezing on his balcony, wearing practically nothing so he could gawk and molest me.

Since fleeing Bogota, I haven't heard a word from him or about him. When I arrived in New Orleans, I wanted to forget everything I'd been through. One evening after I'd moved in with my aunt, I overheard Aunt Gigi and Uncle Stefano arguing on the phone. My uncle wanted me to press charges and report the abuse. Every time Gigi would bring it up, I'd come apart. After a few episodes where I'd lock myself away for hours at a time, she stopped bringing it up.

So what's changed? Why would he be looking for me now?

Chapter 41

Degrees

Emma made me leery of secrets. I was scarred by her lies and deception. Juliette's no Emma, but I'm afraid to be hurt like that again.

In high school, my friends Tom and Hobe teased me for being clueless about girls. I was focused on getting a swimming scholarship and keeping my grades up so I could leave east Kentucky. I kept to myself, swimming and weight training in my free time. I didn't want to get stuck and have UK as my only option. I saw too many kids trapped—teen pregnancies being the biggest reason. That and getting lured into working the mines. Cousins on my dad's side were miners. He never wanted that for me. He assumed I'd follow his lead and go into electrical engineering. That never held any appeal, as I hated math. History and English were my favorite subjects.

When I got a full ride to Cornell for swimming, I was ecstatic. I had no idea how lonely and hard it would be. Swimming kept me sane that first year. That and writing for the school newspaper. Thank God for Dr. Littleton, my adviser, who encouraged me. My parents weren't thrilled I was pursuing a career that could take me so far away, but they let me find my way. Dad thought I was particularly delusional. We had some heated discussions.

I dated a little in college but found Cornell girls intimidating. When I discovered rock climbing toward the end of my junior year, I found my tribe. I met Cassie climbing but she had a long-distance boyfriend. We flirted and messed around a bit, but I never felt good about it.

After graduation, I was accepted into Columbia's School of Journalism. Going from quaint Ithaca to living in the bowels of New York City was soul-sucking. I remember Dad's face when they visited my teeny apartment in the city I shared with three other students. Mom smiled and nodded, taking it all in. Dad was sure I'd be on the next train home. I stuck it out and thrived despite the concrete and smog.

Every weekend was spent at a climbing gym. Coming home for holidays was what I looked forward to the most. I missed Mom's cooking, the mountains, and the familiar twang in the singsong way people spoke, though I worked to lose my accent. Dad accused me of putting on airs when I came home talking like a *Yankee*, as he put it. He had no idea how judgmental people could be when I'd open my mouth.

Step by step, degree by degree, I found my way here. Juliette's not that different. She, too, came from an idyllic rural upbringing and wanted to make a splash in the big city. I just wish she'd never met Goran and Bogota hadn't tried to drown her.

I know she doesn't want my help with this. She's fiercely independent, but how can I stand by and not do something? I'm old-fashioned. My southern roots raised me to care for someone I love. And I love her. I wish I were less crazy for her, but it's like she's a part of me. I don't want her to struggle through this alone. And deep down, I don't think she wants to.

Was that Goran on the phone? She's not sure. I'm relieved she told me some of what she lived through. And she let me comfort her last night after all the tension finally evaporated. It was nice to fall asleep with her in my arms.

"Thanks for telling me, you know," I stutter, the next morning when I find her coming out of the bathroom.

Her eyebrows scrunch. When I try to hug her, she dodges me.

"You okay?"

No response.

"You know...the stuff you told me...that's gotta be hard..."

She stares at me like I've grown three heads. "Umm..."

"Goran—you told me about Goran and what happened," I clarify.

She closes her eyes tightly.

"Goran? Uh, right." She shakes her head, avoiding my eyes.

"Jules, I know it wasn't easy telling me about him." I lean in to kiss her naked shoulder. She ducks under my arm, grabbing her clothes. "Let me drive you to work today. You know, just in case. I'd rather you not go on the Metro."

She glares at me before disappearing into the bathroom, shutting the door in my face.

What the hell is going on? I wait outside the bathroom until she emerges. She dodges me again, slippery as an eel.

"I'm fine, Nate. There's nothing to worry about." She heads for the kitchen. She grabs a cup off the counter.

"Jules, he called last night. Come on. Don't mess around with this."

She spins, and yesterday's coffee nearly spills from the cup. "Who called?" She sips, making a face.

"Ummm... Goran."

Her hand, midway to the microwave, stops. All the color drains from her face. I grab the coffee mug from her.

Her eyes glaze over and I'm not sure she can see me. It's like a part of her is paralyzed. I guide her to a chair and sit across from her. She reminds me of climbers realizing they have a fear of heights after looking down for the first time.

She says nothing but some kind of horror reel unspools in her mind.

"Juliette, he called last night. You escaped out a bathroom window. Any of this ring a bell?"

In a flash, her eyes clear. "Who told you that?" she snaps.

"You did." I slide my chair back, her words smack me.

When she bounds up, I nearly topple.

"Fuck you, Nate. Stop playing head games. I'm late for work." She grabs the apartment keys and heads for the door.

I instinctively grab her arm. She reels back like I'm about to attack her.

"Whoa, you think I'm gonna hit you?" I drop her arm. "Can I see your phone?"

"No, please. No," she begs. Tears threaten to spill.

She grabs her purse and is out the door.

I follow her to work. I need to be sure she gets there safely. Then I make my way to Gavin's. Dani opens the door. Her eyes are red as she holds a fussy Sam.

"Dani, I need to talk to Gav."

She looks behind the door briefly.

"Nate, uh, it's not a great time right now," Gavin says, coming around the corner as I push my way inside. "Can..."

Before he gets any further, I babble about the call. I can't contain the diarrhea pouring from my mouth regardless of the marital spat they're having. Dani disappears upstairs as Sam's screams amplify. Gavin stares after them a moment and looks back to me.

"Slow down, start over. Slowly."

I tell him about the phone call – about Goran. I tell him about what Juliette revealed last night and then our interaction this morning.

"She didn't remember the call? Didn't remember that she could be in danger? Just went to work?"

"Yup. She thought I wanted to hit her. That sound like her?"

"Did you?" Gavin glares at me.

"God, no. I grabbed her arm—I wanted to... Oh, shit. I really scared her. I know she's been hurt before... and now she thinks

I'm like that. Fuck." My skin prickles around my neck.

"Why'd you grab her arm?"

"She has a scar – she told me about it. I was trying to jog her memory. I wanted her to... I don't understand what's going on. It's like she's lost her short-term memory...or her mind."

Gavin stares at me.

"What? You think I'm nuts?"

"No," Gavin says, eerily calm. "It's weird, that's all. Talk to Darrien. He knows her well. Maybe he has an explanation."

Dani comes downstairs, bouncing Sam, who continues to holler.

"I interrupted something here," I say. "I'm sorry. Everything okay?"

Gavin puts a comforting arm around her. "Dani's milk's been drying up. Started slacking a week ago and now she's having a hard time feeding Sam. He doesn't like formula. It's stressful."

"I'm sorry, Dan—sorry I butted in here. Have you been to the doctor yet?"

Dani sniffles and shifts Sam to her other hip. He's cried himself to exhaustion and I see the stress his duress is causing his parents.

"Yeah, she says it's weird, as I was producing enough to feed an army of babies. Not anymore. They're running tests and I'll hear later today. Just gotta find a formula he'll take."

I give her a hug. "I'm sorry for barging in. Let me know if you guys need anything."

An hour later, I'm not much clearer on things. Darrien's reluctant to talk to me about Juliette's past. He's protective and says he'll check on her.

I attempt to work on the story I've been editing. It's no use. I can't focus.

Chapter 42
Aftermath

Juliette:

When I close my eyes, I see the office walls, beige and decorated sparsely. Goran's signature style. Simple and soulless. His icy eyes, blank, before he attacked me that afternoon. I shudder, remembering...

After that, I became someone else. I stopped questioning the relationship. I yielded to it. To him. I let him have complete control. I allowed him to make me complicit in his money-making schemes—even justified his abuse as my punishment for not being strong enough to make a stand against him.

Meeting Nate and moving to work at the NIH, I thought maybe I could find myself again—the real me. But that other Juliette never left. She's still here...hidden in the shadows...

I leave the office after a day of complete non-productivity. Mark's going to fire me if I don't find a way to manage this.

Nate's green Subaru is parked in the lot, waiting. Although I don't want to, I get in the car. His expression is hopeful, conciliatory.

"How was work?"

"Fine." I sit as close to the door as I can. If I need to bolt, I want an escape. My heart pounds when the automatic door locks click into place.

I sneak peaks at him as he drives. Why's he here?

When he passes my exit, I panic. "Where are we going?"

"My place. Hope that's okay. Thought I'd cook for you tonight. How's that sound?"

I can't do this. I shift closer to the door, eyeing the door latch. "Just take me home. It's been a long day."

His hand reaches for mine. I stare at it like it's grown hideous tentacles...inching towards me.

"That's why I want to take care of you tonight. Come on." His eyes burn into the side of my face as I stare at the door handle. *How broken would I be if I jammed the door open and jumped?*

"Nate, take me home. Please. I can't do this," I whisper.

"What's going on? Did you talk to Darrien?"

What does Darrien have to do with any of this? "Please, just take me home," I plead.

"Jules, we need to talk."

Tears spring to my eyes. I shiver and shake. He stares at me, then looks back at the road.

"Okay, let me turn around." He pauses, glancing back at me. "Juliette, are you okay?"

When he takes my exit, I sigh with relief. "I'm okay—just tired." I count the seconds til we're in front of my door. Three hundred and fifty-seven seconds ... a lifetime.

"Can I come in?"

"No, please...." I bolt out of the car, relieved to have escaped.

Once inside, I sag against the door. I peak through the blinds to be sure he's gone. Then I dig out my journal from my locked desk drawer and thumb through it. Could he have gotten ahold of this? Beneath it, I find Mani's unopened letter. My hands shake as I replace them both in the drawer and lock it. There's only one key to this desk and I keep it in a zippered compartment in my purse. Maybe he jimmied it open.

Even here, I have to deal with the same garbage I had in Port Louis and Bogota.

Fucking Barrett. I was being friendly—which is important for building team rapport. I smiled when he made a silly joke. Ten minutes later he had me cornered in the copy room, attempting to rub up against me. I was in baggy scrubs, for Christ's sake. My knee made it clear I was not interested. He turned a ghastly shade of gray and stumbled from the room, mumbling how he'd tripped and didn't mean to grab me. Yeah, right. Now the rest of the team is giving me the stink eye.

I got harassed when I first moved to Mauritius, wandering the streets of Port Louis, especially when I'd go for runs. Guys assumed I was flattered by the attention. Girls even more so. Mani's co-worker, Tamil took an interest in me despite having a serious girlfriend. They have a kid together but that didn't stop him from groping me. He made a move when we were surfing, thinking I wouldn't notice where his hands were when I got thrown off my board. He planned the entire thing, dropping in on the same wave. His girlfriend blamed me, like I'd somehow asked for it, "flaunting herself around in that bikini." *Really?* Compared to other women on the beach, I was covered more than most. And I never encouraged Tamil in any way. I knew from the get-go he was trouble.

Since Goran, I've tried to stay beneath the radar.

I hop in the shower, hoping the hot water will wash away the filth layered beneath my skin. Maybe I'll never be clean.

Despite the steaming hot shower, I shiver. I can't get warm. I throw on fleece pajamas and climb into bed after taking something for sleep. No more nightmares, please.

Chapter 43

Confusion

Nate:

Pounding at the door startles me awake. I squint at the clock. 3 a.m. Peeking through the blinds, I find Juliette on the landing, mumbling, unintelligible.

"Hey, come in. You okay?" She's drenched. "You ran here?"

I lead her inside. Her eyes dart around the room, not saying a word.

"What happened, Jules? Did he call again?"

Her teeth chatter like she's just come in from a winter storm, but her body's flushed and hot. I wait but I'm not sure she can talk right now. Her eyes bounce around like a ping-pong ball. Is this another panic attack?

Her outburst yesterday reminds me of Gavin when we were in that little village and he was convinced we'd been taken hostage.

Her pajamas are soaked. Odd, considering it's not raining. Maybe she ran through someone's sprinkler. Did she just run three miles from her place in her pajamas in the middle of the night?

"Come with me." I take her hand and bring her into the bedroom where I find towels and dry clothes. She moves like a sleepwalker. I help her change. She's a rag doll, allowing me to undress her.

I talk in a low voice, wanting to make her feel safe. She won't speak or answer any of my questions. I'm not sure she understands what I'm saying. When I try to hug her, to warm her up, she pulls away, shaking like a leaf. Instead, I wrap her in a wool blanket, tucking the ends into her hands.

I consider calling Dani, who's trained as an EMT, but remember she's going through her own difficulties now.

I tuck her into my bed and watch exhaustion take over. I need to speak with Darrien.

She wakes repeatedly, crying in her sleep, sometimes screaming, tossing and turning. Her nightmares are bad. She settles when I talk to her quietly. My voice soothes her better than anything else. Any kind of touch is out. But reciting words to songs – any song – calms her.

Could the call from Goran have been a delusion?

In the morning, I wake when I hear her moving around. She sits up in bed, looking around, wide-eyed. She notices the Cornell swim sweatshirt she's wearing. Her eyes narrow. She's no longer a zombie.

"What am I doing here? Dressed in your things?" She grips the blanket to her chest.

I scramble up from the floor. "You ran here last night. Remember?"

Her eyes flare when I sit on the edge of the bed.

"I found you on my doorstep in the middle of the night."

She doesn't look convinced. I try again. "Look, Jules, something's going on. You could be having the same kind of delusions as Gavin when he had the virus."

"You think I have the virus? What's that got to do with me waking in your bed...when I remember being at my place? How'd I get here?" She glances at the blanket and pillow laid out on the rug. Glad I didn't attempt to sleep in the same bed with her.

"I told you... you ran here last night—showed up after midnight. You don't remember?" I ask gently.

Angry eyes find mine. "I ran here? From my apartment? How do I know you're not a stalker who kidnapped me?"

I breathe in slowly, willing myself to calm. Surprisingly, she does the same.

"Juliette, do you remember my name?"

"Yeah, Nate," she snaps.

Her body is coiled like a cobra.

"Do you remember where we met?"

She gazes absently at the blankets on the floor. "The Comoros—Darrien and I were there when your team got sick. And..." Her face crumbles a bit.

"And then what?"

Silence.

And then something remarkable occurs.

Her eyes shift – deep sea green in a storm, lighten and warm, as the clouds clear. It's like she really sees me...like the first time we met when she and Darrien showed up on my doorstep in the Comoros, after I thought my friends had died. The honeyed warmth only lasts for a moment before she's lost in her head, shrinking in on herself. But it was there.

She's in there... somewhere.

Chapter 44

Puzzle Pieces

Fragments of the map of my life jumble like jigsaw pieces around my head. I see myself as a kid, running from the school bullies who picked on me. Other images: riding Fuego down the beach, his blonde mane flying; making *buenelos* in our sunny kitchen with mom, my hair tied up like hers and balancing on a wobbly stool as she held me; studying biochemistry with Ana in our walk-up apartment off Calle Septima in the heart of Bogota; flirting and dancing with Goran at the Marina Submarino. Who are these Juliettes? Can they really all be me?

"How about Goran?" Nate interrupts.

Goran? I don't want to answer that.

"What about him? He was a guy I dated. Kind of a jerk and full of himself. What's he got to do with anything?"

His eyes pierce mine. I'm giving him the wrong answers. I wrestle with the sheets and get out of bed. I need to stand up.

I'm in his office, beige and boring. Looking through fabric swatches, I'm reminded of home. One sample has the colors of sunshine and the ocean. It's been a long time and I miss my parents. I want to call them. Where the hell is my damn phone?

I'll hunt down Trudy to borrow hers, but Goran appears out of nowhere, shutting the door, locking it. He's all smiles and grabs me around the waist.

"I think you need a break. I know I do."

"You told me he hurt you. Abused you..."

I laugh. I don't know why. It's not funny. None of this is funny.

"Abused? I said that? That's a bit of an overstatement. He wasn't the nicest guy. He just liked rough sex. That's no crime."

The devil is in his eyes as he tangles his hands in my hair, pulling it from the ponytail. His other hand cups my ass, squeezing hard.

"Hey, that hurts." I squirm to get away. He holds me captive.

"I thought that's how you liked it." We've acted this out before. His eyes flare as his hand works its way under my skirt, rubbing and pinching me roughly. I close my eyes so he can't see my terror. He needs to think I want this. When my skirt becomes an obstacle, he tears it off and bends me over the desk.

STOP! I force myself to the present. The past has nothing good. Nate's eyebrows form a line, his deep blue eyes, stormy. What'd I do? It's none of his business anyway. He takes my arm, gently, like he wants to dance, lifting it.

"So this never happened? He didn't do this... this little spot where he stamped out a cigarette, or the scar on your hip where he hit you with a belt?"

His other hand finds my breast, tearing my silk blouse and lacy bra. His hands bruise and twist my skin and all the layers beneath. I cry out, unable to pretend. He covers my mouth, jamming into me from behind. My body is split in two, unable to get away. His teeth on my neck, scraping, his voice in my ear, low and threatening. When he finishes, I flop onto the desk, unable to stand. He backs away, zipping up.

I gag, choking down vomit. Shaking my head, "Where are my clothes?" I demand when I discover I'm wearing his Cornell sweats.

"Jules, you ran here last night. You were drenched. I helped you change. We put your clothes in the washer. And yes, you told me about Goran and what he did."

I can't deal with this right now. I don't know what's real and what's... "Please get my clothes. I want to go home."

He backs away, frustration rolling off him as he turns on his heel.

"Bet that felt good, huh?" He slaps my ass hard and pulls me up to him. "Now be a good girl and get yourself cleaned up." He balls up my skirt before throwing it at me. "Can't have you looking like a scarlet harlot for tonight's dinner. Wear the gold dress, with the low back. We're entertaining."

Nate returns and hands me my clothes. I stare at the pile in my arms, neatly folded, even my underwear.

I shudder, chilly, like a layer's been peeled off.

I peek at him, afraid what I'll see. Shoulders hunched, eyes tearing. And there's something else.

The weight of my layers drags me down. I slide to the floor. "What's happening?"

He crouches to where I huddle. He offers a hand and I lunge for it, pulling him down with me. I sob, hysteria bubbling like a geyser, sulfurous and rank. He curls himself around me, not saying a thing.

"I don't know what's wrong with me. I'm losing my mind."

He brushes the hair out of my face. "It's gonna be okay, Jules. We'll figure it out, together."

His breath on my neck warms me. I'm not quite in the present or the past. His arms tighten around me. I lean back into him, tucking my legs into a ball. I'm safe within his cocoon.

I don't know what to say but realize I trust him more than I've ever trusted anyone else.

"Why are you being so kind to me?" I whisper.

"Because I love you."

I bring his hand to my mouth and kiss it, shaking. "I think... I love you too." I've never said that to anyone before. But soon as I say it, I know it's true. Tears spill as I turn and kiss him with all I have, mumbling. "I love you."

He chuckles, running his hands down my back, and returns my kisses. He holds me, a smile on his lips.

"What do we do now?" I ask.

"Why don't you get dressed and we'll go to the NIH after breakfast? Darrien wants you to get tested." He twists a strand of my hair around his finger.

"He thinks I have the virus? How's that even possible?"

"I'm not sure, but let's start there." He untangles from me and pulls me to standing.

Despite the weight of things, his arms around me make me feel lighter than I have in days.

"I couldn't tell if you were good or bad. Only someone good would neatly fold my clothes after washing them for me."

Chapter 45

Test Results

Nate:

Juliette tests positive for RESV101. We're baffled by the results but at least we now have an explanation for her outbursts and paranoia.

As we leave the NIH, we bump into Dani and Gavin. They've been to see Dr. Khan, a colleague of Darrien's. Unbelievably, Dani also tests positive for the virus. We learn RESV is suspected to be sexually transmitted. This is a crazy new twist.

Another surprise is that RESV has made the headlines. What was once an obscure virus known only to a handful of people in a remote corner of the world, is now front page news, being covered by all the major networks. We find ourselves trapped at the NIH.

After a long afternoon, we're ushered out a back entrance to a quarantine facility. Juliette almost loses it when she realizes we can't go home. A medical team is dispatched to bring in Sara, so we'll be housed together until the testing and evaluations are completed. We have no idea how long they intend to confine us.

Bea and Jorge are transferred to Emory, where a team of OBs and Infectious Disease physicians monitor her pregnancy. With the world shut down, there's no travel, no work to speak of. Just hours spent on the computer or in front of the TV, to learn what's happening around the world in respect to this virus. More cases are found in Madagascar when a number of tour groups from Australia and Europe become infected. Peace Corps volunteers in the impacted countries are sent home, after lengthy medical evaluations to ensure they don't have it.

I no longer test positive for the virus, even though I must have given it to Juliette. And although Dani's breast milk dried up, it likely protected Sam from getting it, as he has RESV virus-specific antibodies, but no live virus.

The world has ground to a halt. We were supposed to go to Manitoba for the polar bear story, but not now.

After two weeks in a quarantine facility, we're sent home. We're requested to stay home while medical teams continue to monitor us. The news of the virus's death and resurrection symptoms is something out of a horror movie. Darrien and the OGRE team are heroes, working the front lines of the crisis. He's on front pages and interviewed by everyone: CNN, MSNBC, Al Jazeera, BBC, ... all the biggies.

I think Juliette regrets she's not working with the team. I feel terrible that I'm the one who gave it to her. She continues to suffer mild episodes of paranoia and confusion. She feels disconnected and it's been a long time since she's seen or spoken with her parents. One evening when she's particularly testy, I suggest she reach out to them.

Chapter 46
Calling Home

Juliette:

"Washington, D.C.? When did you leave Mauritius?" Mom's voice cracks. I picture her in the courtyard.

It's been a long time since I've been home. I see the two of us riding down the beach. Flying. There was nothing I loved more than time alone with her. Especially with the horses.

"I'm working in D.C. at the NIH."

She sucks in a breath. I see her in my mind; wavy blonde hair, eyes twinkling with mischief. I want to hug her across the line. A lump forms in my throat as I realize how much I've missed them.

"Wait a minute, let me get your dad. Greg, it's Juliette," she cries out.

His voice brings me to tears. Big, sloppy, ugly tears. Now that we're out of quarantine, it's possible to plan a visit. I was hesitant to have them come, but not anymore.

I picture my childhood home...the cheery casita in Periquo Aquao outside Santa Marta, adorned with lady's slipper vines and flamboyant thunbergia, a living tapestry growing up the side of the house. A mosaic of vibrant Talavera tile stepping stones lead to the front entrance where I'd play hopscotch with my cousins, Liliana and Sofi.

My favorite room, outside of the kitchen, was the court-yard—bursting with tropical plants: lemon-ice-colored *hibiscus manihot* and Cattleya orchids—where hummingbirds flitted flower to flower. Most nights I'd sleep in the hammock Dad hung for me. I miss sleeping under a sky full of stars.

I spent a lot of time romping the beaches and hidden coves near my house. I didn't resent solitude, despite all the time I spent alone. I craved it. I never connected with my classmates in town. With my light-colored hair and skin, I was an outsider. The girls in my class thought me weird because I didn't play with dolls or enjoy dress-up. My usual uniform was cutoffs, T-shirts, skinned knees and dirt-crusted fingernails. I was more interested in wrangling horses and building things with Dad. My tomboy nature never bothered my parents, but Mom's cousins gave her an earful. They worried I was too rough around the edges.

My best friends were Chepe and Pacho, our stable-hand's kids. They didn't mind a girl in their midst if I could keep up. With my long legs, I had no trouble. We'd catch snakes and spiders and study them in the lantern light of the old, abandoned barn. Funny to think I still do that now, only I get paid for it.

Those boys were the only ones who could outride me. Fuego, our spunky palomino, was a handful but lightning fast. If I needed to win, he was my mount, though sometimes he'd dump me in the dirt when I'd ride bareback, just to remind me who was boss. But in a saddle, I could beat even the cockiest of riders twice my age.

Coming home after long hours trapped behind a cramped wooden desk and mean kids calling me *Bruja De Ojos Verdes*, *Green-eyed Witch*, I'd grab Fuego and fly down the beach to my secret haven where the perfume of wildflowers mingled with saltwater. I'd gallop Fuego so hard we'd be drenched and winded by the time we made it to the cove. I'd lead him along the narrow path, enclosed by walls of moss-covered rocks. Sunlight filtered through the dense canopy overhead, casting dappled shadows on us. I'd tie him to a mangrove stump, strip off my clothes, and dive into the briny waters. I'd stay there until just before sunset, knowing that was all the time I had to get over whatever horror had occurred at school. Sometimes it wasn't enough. But I'd dress and hop on a tired Fuego and we'd trot home to settle into evening chores. Dad knew where to find me when I'd disappear, but he was kind enough to give me space.

My parents let me grow up outdoors with horses and wild things as companions. They didn't harass me the way my aunties and cousins would.

Now I can imagine letting them back into my life for real. Maybe I don't need to be so careful anymore.

On the day my parents arrive, we stand in the terminal, waiting. I tingle with nerves, wishing I'd gone on a run earlier.

Nate pulls me to him, settling me with just a touch. We're working on things. I'm trying to be more honest, less secretive. He's patient but has his breaking points too.

Emma did a number on him two years ago when he found her in bed with another rafting guide. It was a few weeks after they'd returned from climbing Haleakala in Hawaii and he'd planned to propose. She'd been sleeping around from the start. She claimed all the guides messed around and it was no big deal. It was for Nate. He's got a strong moral center and I'm afraid I won't live up to his expectations.

Yesterday I overheard him on the phone with his parents. His dad's raised voice railed him for being intentionally vague about the virus early on. I was at the kitchenette counter drinking coffee and eavesdropping.

"Nate, what if you'd given it to your mother? Or me? You should have told us."

I splutter, coffee shoots from my nose. His dad has no idea how it's spread. Guess that info hasn't been released.

Nate took his dad's frustration in stride. He clarified things and nodded to me, smiling when he revealed RESV's status as an STD. I looked away, trying not to laugh as I mopped my face and the counter. By the end of the conversation his dad was laughing and joking with him. Nate ended the call, promising we'd visit soon.

My parents emerge from the terminal holding hands, searching for me. When our eyes lock, I run to them. Dad's woodsy cologne wraps around me like an old scarf. I forget how safe I felt bundled in his arms as a little girl, especially after a particularly tough day. We hold each other tight, tears streaming down our faces.

Dad wears dark khakis and a maroon fleece pullover. Mom's in a long, flowy skirt, a cream-colored quilted suede jacket, and burnished leather boots. Her smile lights up the terminal. Other passengers stare—my parents could be aging movie stars.

As a gangly, awkward kid, I was jealous of their beauty and ease in how they moved through the world. Boys from middle school made lewd comments about Mom when she'd drop me at school. They'd criticize the old jalopy she drove but couldn't help but notice her looks. I blamed her for the hell I went through, certain it was her fault. Thinking back, she never dressed to impress. She lived in barn clothes—straw in her hair, manure-crusted boots, and faded jeans. The other moms were far fancier in pressed stirrup pants, fitted silk blouses, pointy heels and overly made-up faces.

Dad pulls back. "You must be Nate. It's nice to meet you. I'm Greg."

"Great to meet you, Greg. How was the flight?"

"Good. Thankfully we could fly direct from Medellin and not have to trudge through Bogota."

Mom folds Nate in a hug before saying anything. We all laugh. "I'm Marta." She backs up to appraise him. She smiles as more tears fall. Nate instinctively hugs her again and whispers something in her ear. She squeezes him.

"I meant it when I said you're welcome to stay at my apartment with Juliette. It's not a big place, but I can stay with our friends Dani and Gav," Nate offers. My apartment has a gas leak and Sara and I have evacuated for the time being.

"Nonsense, we're happy to meet you, and so far, you don't seem like a psychopath," Dad says, winking at him.

Nate snorts, laughing. "Good to know. Do you have any other luggage?"

"Nope, we travel light. We've got what we need here."

At the apartment, we find the team setting things up. Nate laughs when he sees Kenny adding fresh flowers to the table, having creatively hung some of his climbing equipment as an art installation.

Nate pulls me to him and whispers, "I think Kenny is wooing your parents on my behalf."

"There's no need. I think Mom's a little in love with you," I tease.

Chapter 47

Welcome Party

Nate:

"Hey, let me do that. I'm the film guy, right?" Jorge says, as I pull out my ancient Leica. I want to get pictures of Juliette with her parents. "Go and enjoy yourself and I'll get shots of everyone. By the way, I love this camera."

"Thanks, Jor, that'd be great. How's Bea doing? I'm glad she's here."

"A lot better. She needs to take it easy and can't dance, but we'll take this. And we found a cute house nearby."

"I'm glad you're taking the plunge. Does she have a new studio?"

"Yup. It's a bit of a renovation project, but it'll keep her busy, especially if she can't dance. And how about you two?" He nods towards Juliette who's across the room.

"Good. I'm glad she can see her parents. It's weird she hasn't seen them in so long. Thanks for being here."

"My pleasure. I'm glad things are improving for her. She looks happy. Here she comes..." Before he leaves, he lifts the camera and snaps a picture of Juliette.

She floats to me, sultry and drop-dead gorgeous. "Thank you for this." She reaches up and kisses me.

"It's great to finally meet them. You should stay at their hotel. They need time with you."

"I'll see what they want to do. And by the way, they love you. They're relieved you seem so normal."

"I don't know about normal, but as your dad put it, I'm not a psychopath—so that's something." I laugh, wrapping my arms around her.

We join her parents who are chatting with Bea. Every time Bea tries to get up, Dani waves a threatening finger.

"I hear you came from Santa Marta. I have friends with a house there. Where in the city do you live?" Bea asks.

"We're on the outskirts where we keep horses for our horse trekking business. We live near Periquo Aquao, on the coast."

Bea decides she and Jorge need to get the team down for a riding trip.

The evening flies by, and before we know it, we're taking Juliette's parents to their hotel. Juliette goes in for a few minutes to plan for the next day while I wait in the car. I'm not sure why, but she doesn't want to stay with them. She has a few days off to take them around D.C. while I prep for the upcoming Manitoba trip. I'm glad it's finally back on.

I'm listening to the new Green Day album when she opens the car door, startling me.

Her eyebrows press together when she gets in the car.

"They think I'm worthy?"

"Yes, definitely yes." She gives me a brief smile but there's more behind those eyes.

"What is it?" I ask gently, rubbing my thumb over her knuckles.

"They're pressing me about Goran."

"You never talked about this before?"

"No. I kept a lid on about all things Goran...that is, until recently."

"Recently?" In the pale moonlight, she looks spooked as she stares out the window.

"I called them a day or two ago. Only I don't remember it. Dad says I told them things—things I never talked about before. Now they want the whole story—the unabridged version."

She looks like she might break in two. I wonder what she's told them. How much do I even know?

"Maybe tell them in stages."

"Nate, things got bad. And I played a certain part in that. Telling them will only hurt them."

"How old were you when you met Goran?"

"Nineteen. But..."

"And how old was Goran?"

"Thirty-something, but I knew..."

"Jules, you were a kid. He targeted you, used you, and hurt you."

As we clean up things from the party, Juliette's lost in her head. She moves around aimlessly. I wish she could focus on being reunited with her parents. Greg and Marta are clearly ecstatic to have her closer.

Maybe I can help.

While she's in the bedroom changing, I find a sultry Cuban salsa she's played before. I'm a terrible dancer but remember how my bad moves made her laugh the last time she was overwhelmed. When the music comes on, I attempt to find the rhythm, shaking my hips spasmodically. When she peeks her head out the bedroom door, wearing a T-shirt and only a T-shirt, I grab her hand and pull her to me.

"Come on, Jules, teach me to salsa. I need help."

She frowns. "Really, Nate? I'm so tired."

"Please. Otherwise, I'll have to take these moves else-where." I emphasize my "moves," thrusting my hips.

She laughs. "Okay, but stop all this flailing. Salsa is a subtle dance, in the hips." She places her hands on my hips, forcing me to quit my gyrating. "Now you need to frame up."

I have no idea what that means. She takes my arms and lifts them from my elbows to form an arc. She places one of my hands on the flat of her back, higher up than I would have thought. I let it slide down to her derriere.

"Listen, Cassanova, none of that. This is serious." She moves my hand back to where it should be. "Shoulders back. Hold me like I'm trying to get away."

I pull her to me, our hips flush against each other. That's why this dance is so damn sexy. Hip to hip. And damn those legs of hers... She puts her hands on my hips to direct me, eyes on mine as she pulls me into the rhythm. I keep looking down, but she forces my eyes level with hers.

"Up here... You'll just stumble if you look down. You've got to *feel* the salsa." Her arm snakes around my back, guiding me as if I were the woman.

Then I start to feel it. She's right. It's a feeling—a sensation. After a few moments, her arm slides up to my shoulder and I press her to me. I don't think I can get more turned on, but each day there seems to be a new level of seduction. She backs away for a step and moves in close again.

"Juliette..."

"Shhhh, follow my lead. You asked for a lesson. I'm giving it to you."

She pushes her hips into mine and then away. I hold her close and feel the music pulsing through me, among other things. The flimsy fabric of her T-shirt and not much else is maddening. We dance, swaying into each other and then back away. I close my eyes and find the experience both terrifying and the most erotic thing I've ever done.

She steps back from me, continuing to dance. Her eyes, dark and shadowed... her body mesmerizes. I feel like I'm struck dumb, staring as she unbuttons my shirt. I hold my breath. She dances into me and turns, grinding me with her hips and ass. My resolve is spent. I spin her around and throw her over my shoulder.

"Guess dance class is over," she laughs in my ear.

"Not quite. It's my turn to lead."

Chapter 48
Truth and Reckoning

Juliette:

I wake early and leave Nate sleeping. He mumbles something, reaching for me as I slip out of bed. I'm meeting my parents for breakfast and I'm eager to show them where I work and some of the touristy things to do in town. I need to keep them busy enough that there won't be time to grill me about Goran.

"Sweetie, you know we need to talk," Mom says as we're sitting down to café au laits and omelets at the Old Georgetown Grille. She looks to Dad for support. He cocks his head, giving me his dad look.

I want to climb under the table. I didn't think they'd pull this so quickly.

"We will but let's enjoy breakfast and I'll tour you around."

Dad clears his throat. "Jules, we need to talk—now. The things you told me the other night...well—we're concerned."

"Dad, that was seven years ago. I'm not with Goran anymore. It's in the past. Let's leave it there."

He shakes his head. Mom reaches for my hand. I want to pull away but know how that will seem. I don't want to hurt them.

"Why didn't you tell us things were so bad? Why didn't you ask for help?"

Oh God, the tears are coming. I can't watch my mother fall apart right now.

"I couldn't. It wasn't safe. But I got through it, okay?"

"Did you ever talk to anyone about it?" Dad asks. His eggs are getting cold.

"Yes, I had a therapist in New Orleans. You know that. Do I look like I'm suffering? I've moved on. Things are good. Don't you like Nate?"

"Of course, we do. He's darling and clearly, in love with you. But..."

I've stopped tasting my omelet. It's sulfurous mush in my mouth. I push the plate back.

"I need to use the restroom." I don't wait for them to respond.

I stumble to the bathrooms and into a stall. My heart races. Feels like I might pass out. I practice the breathing exercises Nate did with me the night I had that first panic attack. I try to remember his gentle words grounding me. Only I don't particularly want to ground myself in this bathroom. The smells alone make me lurch from the stall toward the row of sinks. I splash water on my face.

An older woman enters. I put on lip gloss and pat my face to bring the color back into my cheeks. I catch a smile from her before she enters a stall.

Midafternoon, I drag my parents back to Nate's apartment. I want to change before dinner and my dress is at his place. Nate looks up when we come in. Dad holds Mom, who's limping. I think I wore them out.

"Nate, sorry for invading your space," Dad says.

"No trouble. Have a good day?"

"I'm gonna get changed, okay?" I hustle into the bedroom, shutting the door behind me. Their mumbled voices bleed through the walls. Mom complains about her feet. Sheez, these walls are thin.

Nate pops in after a few moments as I'm stuffing myself into a sweater dress.

"Jules, what's going on?"

I grab a pair of tall black boots and sit on the bed. "They

want to know about Goran. About this..." I pull up my sleeve to reveal the cigarette burn.

"What'd you tell them?"

"Not much." Sitting, I realize how tired I am. All this ducking and dodging is exhausting. I slide to the floor and bury my head in my hands.

He sits behind me on the bed and rubs my shoulders. It should feel good, but I squirm away.

"What do you want to do?"

"I want it all to go away..."

He comes around, crouching in front of me. "Look at me, Jules." He takes my hands. "If you were in their shoes, would you want to know?"

A sob erupts from deep inside. "Yes...and no."

"Your parents are stronger than you think. You don't need to carry this rock by yourself."

I stand, pulling him up, and stare into his concerned eyes. How can I tell him about any of this? "Nate, I did things I... Not all this mess is because of Goran. I got in way over my head."

"Do you think they deserve to know the truth?"

"I don't think they'll see me the same way." I lean against the dresser for support. I just want to sleep. No more parties. No more questions. No more diving into the past.

"You told me and I'm still here." I grab the hairbrush, needing a distraction. He takes it from me, holding onto my hand. "Talk to me, Jules."

"I told you part of it. I'm not ready to blow this up."

"Is the truth as damning as you think it is? You were nineteen and prey to an older man, a psychopath."

I shake my head, wishing he wasn't so fucking perfect. This would be easier if he were an asshole.

"Come on. Start with the beginning stuff. Little steps."

He leaves me with my parents as he heads out for a walk. *Motherfucker.*

"You lost your scholarship?" Mom asks, her voice sharp. She and Dad sit on the couch, staring at me.

"I couldn't tell you... I was ashamed. I wasn't doing well in school."

"But Juliette, you were always a good student. What happened?"

"Goran happened. And I let it happen. I got side-tracked. Stopped going to classes...and was eventually asked to leave."

They exchange a look.

"Did you live with him?" Dad asks.

"No, but he wanted me to. He, uh... I started working for him, which helped me keep the apartment with Ana."

"You worked for him?" they ask in unison.

"I kept his books. That's why I knew his businesses weren't exactly on the up and up. He convinced investors to write checks for various causes. Ironically one of his biggest charities was a battered woman's shelter."

"So, there was no woman's shelter?" Mom asks, baffled. She comes toward me.

I back away. "No, unless you count his apartment."

She gasps, reaching for me. Dad sucks in a breath. I dodge them. I can't stand to be touched.

Thinking back on it all now, I'm sickened by what I let happen. I was caught up in his lifestyle...fancy dinners out, trips to the finca, nightclub openings where he'd show me off like a prized pony, the clothes and jewelry, shopping trips to Cartagena or Medellin... I sold my soul for stuff and to be his piece of ass. How'd I let myself get so derailed? I learned to compartmentalize the other stuff – the not so good things.

"Why didn't you call us? Why didn't you ask for help?"

"Because I was stupid enough to think I didn't need help." How do I admit to my parents that I was blinded by his power and was taken with his possessiveness? In the beginning, I liked that he only had eyes for me, even if he got rough at times.

They stare at me, unsure what to say.

"Goran was in with the cartels. At least he made me believe he was. He told me how the cartel dealt with traitors. I was terrified he'd set them after me if I reported his fraud. He reminded me I was as complicit as he. I couldn't drag you into that."

They're silent for a moment, but I see the cost of my confession in their eyes.

Dad stands like he needs to pace. "Juliette, why the secrecy all these years?"

I laugh sharply, a burst of air from a pressure cooker. "Why? Why do you think? Would you have told anyone?"

The hurt in his eyes breaks me.

"I thought I could handle it. I had no idea what it would turn into. And I couldn't face you." I look at my feet, wishing I could disappear. "By the time I recognized Goran's demons, it was too late."

There's barely a breath in the room. I've sucked it all out with my admission.

"I should have stayed in Mauritius. I'm sorry I never told you, but I couldn't. Go back to Santa Marta." I grab my bag and slide out the door before they can stop me.

I still feel his hands around my throat, choking or brutalizing me. So real—it hurts like it's just happened. How could I have been so stupid?

The apartment's dark and I keep it that way. There's caution tape across the front door because of the gas leak. I slide beneath it, hoping no one will know I'm in here. I slink into the bedroom and shut the door, burying myself under the covers. My body weighs a thousand pounds. I sink into the comforter, wishing the buzzing would stop. I should pack and leave but I can't get my parents' faces out of my mind. I shiver, unable to get warm.

Someone's here. Could *he* be here? Has he been waiting for this exact moment to make his presence known? I listen to the familiar sounds of Nate walking around. He moves nothing like Goran. Goran was a leopard, light on his feet and stealthy. Light floods under the doorway.

"Juliette?" Knocking at the bedroom door.

"Nate, just go."

"Your parents want to know you're okay. I want to check on you too." He stands in the doorway.

"You can see I'm fine. Just go."

"Don't keep pushing me away. And your parents deserve to know you're safe." He edges into the room, making his way toward me.

"I'm fine. Just go. I've got nothing to give you but trouble." I shrink into a ball.

"That's not true. I don't think you want to be alone with this..." He stands at the foot of the bed.

Please don't come any closer. He reads my mind and stays put.

"Let me be here for you, Jules. If roles were reversed, would you want to help me?"

"Yes..." It comes out without any thought. "But I'm no good for you. I've done bad things..."

"I think you made some necessary choices and you paid for them. Those things don't make you a bad person. They make you resilient and smart and tough." He climbs into bed but keeps to the opposite side. "Can I come over?"

"No, this hurts too much," I sob. His eyes stay locked on mine, as he inches closer. "No, Nate... I can't do this."

"I'm not leaving."

I'm too cold to get out from under the covers. He slides over and wraps me in his arms.

My parents and Nate want me to talk to a therapist again. I didn't want to six years ago and I really don't want to now. They think my bad life choices were because Goren hurt me. He did. I'm not sure if that's what set me on my disastrous path, but I was cocky. I thought he was taken with me. I assumed I could walk over him like I did Tonio, my cadaver buddy from Los Andes.

I forget he plied me with drugs to get me to do things, things I wasn't okay with. I've pushed his sadistic predilections from memory. My mind plays tricks—making me think I wanted to do those things. But when the nightmares come and I wake, heart racing and Nate holding me together, I can't fathom being okay with any of it.

I spend the last day with my parents and make plans to join them for Christmas in Santa Marta. They've forgiven me, too easily. They're wracked with guilt over things that had nothing to do with them. I want them to stay pissed. Instead, they're overly touchy and think I need talk therapy. Nightmare. I don't deserve any of this kindness. I lied and stole and allowed things to get out of control.

I throw myself into work to numb myself. Besides leading training teams in the field, I create curricula and education modules. I work long hours or hide in my apartment. Nate thinks the virus is mucking with me. I'm not so sure. This just may be who I am.

Travel restrictions have lifted and Nate's scheduled to fly to Manitoba next week. He and Gavin spend hours talking logistics, lighting, weather conditions. His eyes light up like a little kid waiting on Santa Claus.

I'm resentful. I shouldn't be. I should be happy for him. That's what a good girlfriend would be. Instead, I think about what'll happen when he's gone. Even though I don't want to need him, I do. He's an outlet for the dark corners. When he goes away, I'll be alone with the nightmares. Not sure what I'll do when it's just me.

Chapter 49

Rough Landing
2 Weeks Later

Nate:

Manitoba was incredible. It was refreshing to get back to work, dealing with the logistics of filming in a freezing environment. And the bears were unbelievable.

Kenny's working on my apartment but it's not finished. I'm staying with Juliette until the work's complete. When we returned, Sara's sister Casey whisked her off for a sister's spa weekend at the Ritz. Juliette and I have her apartment all to ourselves. I was not inclined to let her out of bed this morning. She didn't mind. I think she missed me as I found her decked out in my sweats, smelling of my aftershave.

It was good to be working again. Juliette, too has been working hard since I left; education modules are scattered across the apartment. She freaked out this morning when I gathered them and stacked them in a corner. I need to make room for my work but I feel like I'm invading her space.

When I think she needs breathing room, I head to the gym. Later in the afternoon, I find her at home, staring at her phone, frowning. When I ask about things, she nearly bites my head off.

"Why are you pissed at me? I only want to help."

She spins on me as she grabs clothes from the chair. "I'm not pissed at you. I'm trying to live up to your expectations of what a good girlfriend should do. The thing is...I'm not. I'm selfish and stubborn and likely being investigated for my participation in Goren's illicit enterprises." She strips off her jeans and slides on running tights.

Then it hits me why she's so testy.

"What are you talking about? Is this about that certified letter?" I stand in front of the door so she'll have to go through me to leave.

Her eyes flash, molten. "What do you know about that? Did you look at it?"

I hold my ground, though my instinct is to back away and let her leave. "No. That would be snooping," I say slowly. "And I don't do that. But I saw it on the pile of things with your work papers. You want to tell me what's going on or do I have to guess?"

Her expression softens a smidge. She sighs, throwing up her arms. "Fine, but I need to get in a run."

After she's put on running shoes, she walks to me, eyes locked on mine. Guess she's taken up running since I left. She's sharper, leaner and angular. I miss the softness of her face and body. I wonder if the virus is mucking with her metabolism too. She's really skinny but I'm not about to dive into that morass just now.

I back away. "Go run, but I want to talk about this." I'm afraid to touch her. Is this still the virus or is this who she is?

She gives me a brief kiss on the cheek. It's as passionate as a root canal. "We'll talk later."

I don't see her for two hours. When she returns, she's a sweaty mess and limping. There's still a fire in her. I keep my head down, watching her out of the corner of my eye. I work on notes from Manitoba.

Later, she comes up behind me while I'm at the computer, not wearing much. Her freshly showered skin - silky against my back. She wraps herself around me. My body responds the way it always does. I wish I could separate my physical attraction from my mental and emotional need to understand her, but when she rubs against me, I can't think straight. It's a fatal flaw of the male body. I strip off her remaining clothes and take her to bed.

"Can we talk now? We can't keep pretending things are fine."

She sits on the bed, brushing out her hair. She looks up and tosses the brush on the dresser, and slips past me.

Why is she so fucking evasive? I follow reluctantly. I refuse to be her dog.

"I got a message a few days ago. The first message was left on my cell, telling me to call a number. The second was that certified letter. I'm wanted for questioning about Lukas Enterprises." She grabs the letter, handing it to me.

"It's from Homeland Security. When did you get this?"

"Three days ago. And the message was maybe five days ago."

"Have you responded to either?"

"No. I didn't know if they were real. It could be someone posing as Homeland Security."

I stare at her. "Jules, it would be difficult to fake a certified letter. I think this is the real deal. You still have the message on your phone?"

She turns away. "I deleted it. It freaked me out."

"Why don't you respond to the letter? There's a number. Give them a call and see what they want."

Her eyes get big and she shakes her head emphatically. "It could be Goran coming after me. If he's looking for me, my reaching out, well—shit. I'm not doing that."

"Did you ever press charges against him when you left?"

"Are you kidding? No. I wanted nothing more to do with him. I wanted out and that's what I did. I had no interest in stirring that hornet's nest."

"But you had proof his business dealings were illegal?" I

work to remain calm. She's getting more amped up and that's no good.

She shivers visibly. "I did some hunting in the office. I found things. Somehow he knew, 'cause he showed up and..." She turns away, her face almost green.

"What'd he do?"

She spins on me, seething. "You can't ask that." She pushes past me.

I grab her arm without thought. "Goddammit, Juliette, stop running. I don't know if I can continue this—whatever this is—if you can't trust me."

She meets my eyes for a moment and pulls her arm away. "You're right. This isn't working. I can't trust anyone right now, even you."

"Fuck you, Juliette! Why the hell did you come all this way, only to push me away? Have I ever given you a reason not to feel safe? Have I betrayed your trust?" I have the urge to grab her and shake some sense into her.

She shrinks from me, her anger dissolving into thin air. "No," she says without much conviction. "I don't want to hurt you. If Goran's really coming after me, you're in danger too."

"You don't want to hurt me?" I snarl. "It's a little late for that. You want to leave so bad...then go." I look around, realizing we're at her apartment. "Never mind. I'll go." I stomp to the front room and gather my computer and backpack. I'll get a hotel room for the next few days. Kenny will be done soon. I throw random things into random places, not my usual anal, retentive packing style.

"Nate, stop. I'm sorry."

She watches me from the doorway.

"Are you?" I glare at her.

"Yes, I am."

"There's got to be a better way through this. You know that, right?" I rock back on my heels and stare at my backpack. The thought of leaving is terrifying. She sits, reaching for me. She takes my hand and pulls me to the couch. I sink into it with her.

"I don't know how to trust people, Nate. Besides my parents, I never had anyone I could trust. It's not fair to you. Just don't know how to do this the right way."

"There is no right way. But it's hard when you hide from me. I'm not trying to fix anything, and I'm certainly not judging you. But can't we try to tackle some of this together?"

She leans her head on my shoulder. I can't get any of this straight, but my body craves her touch.

"I've fallen hard for you, Juliette. I fell hard when you hung blankets in the sun and took care of me. There's a soft side to you. You aren't the twisted sicko Goran was."

"I'm afraid this is too good to be true."

I nuzzle her neck, wanting her again. Why is sex so tied up in conflicting emotion? I think I know where this is going, but she's gotta give me something. I level her with a look. "Jules, why haven't you gone to see the therapist—the one Dani recommended?"

"Can't you stay out of my business?"

I put my arm around her shoulders and turn her to face me. "No. You don't get off that easy. Do you love me?"

Aegean eyes hold mine, nodding. "Yes."

"Then talk to me. What happened? Why would Goran want to find you now—after six years?"

The tight ball of her being begins to unravel, loosening. If we're to have any chance at all, she's going to have to trust me.

"Before I escaped, I grabbed some things from his office. He found me just after I'd stuffed the documents in my backpack. He wasn't happy to see me in his office without permission. He made sure I never made that mistake again."

She tells me more of what Goran did to her—the choking, the cigarette burn. I'm not sure she's told me all of it, but I can imagine the rest.

Taking her arm, I lift it and press my lips to the small

indent of the burn. She shivers and all I know is that I want to protect her.

My cell rings, startling us.

I'm about to let it go to voicemail when Juliette mouths for me to take it. I don't want to end our talk. We're finally getting somewhere, but maybe we need a break. She extracts herself and goes into the bathroom.

A minute ago, I was leaving her. And now I know just how abused she was. It makes sense why she doesn't want to share any of this with me.

I wander out to the balcony as Mom tells me about her upcoming art show. She's enthusiastic, she has no idea my mind is elsewhere. I congratulate her and tell her I'll try to make it. When I come back inside, Juliette's nowhere in sight. The bedroom door's closed.

I knock lightly. It's quiet. I peek my head in and find her laying on her side, her back to me. She's in a ribbed tank top. I can practically count each vertebrae, she's gotten so thin. I climb into bed and wrap my arms around her. She's taut, unyielding.

"Come with me." I take her hand and lead her into the bathroom.

She moves stiffly—I think that long run took it out of her. I fill the tub and throw in lavender bath salts. She won't look at me when I help her undress. I bring in a small speaker and play some soothing music. I light candles around the tub and climb in behind her, hoping to help her relax. The hot bath settles her. She leans back against my chest and rests while I rub her legs and arms. She doesn't say anything.

In the flickering candlelight, I see more of the scars she's worked hard to disguise. I wish I could erase these horrors.

She falls asleep. I reach for a towel, lift her from the tub, and carry her to the bed. I'm surprised she doesn't wake, dead weight. By the side of the bed, I notice the empty pill bottle.

"Juliette, wake up!" I shake her. She's breathing but I have no idea how many Ambien she's taken. I call 911.

Chapter 50

Undone

Juliette:

There's an annoying beeping by my head...not my alarm. The reek of antiseptic and bleach fills my nose. I crack open my eyes and the last hours come crashing back. I really did the unthinkable. What was I thinking?

An older, dark-haired nurse delivers a tray of food. The smell is nauseating - worse than the bleach.

"You need to eat something, sweetie, or we're going to have to tube feed you. That's no fun." She smiles, removing the plastic wrap to reveal murky soup and a Hawaiian roll. She adjusts the bed so I'm sitting.

Must be lunchtime. I nod to her and lift the spoon, hoping she'll leave me in peace. She takes her time, refilling my water tumbler, checking the monitor and IV.

"Let me know if there's anything I can bring you. Doctor Guichard will be in soon." She stays rooted, and I have no choice but to take a sip of the tasteless, lukewarm broth. I choke a spoonful down. It's revolting. If they're so worried about me eating, they should provide appetizing food - not refugee camp fare.

"Thanks," I croak. Feels like I haven't spoken in ages. She nods and walks to the door. I'm relieved to be left alone.

Now what? Will I be subject to all manner of psychological testing? A therapist? The looney bin?

I should have left when he was in Manitoba. I thought about it for a hot minute but couldn't find the courage to leave. Instead, I worked nonstop to keep the terrifying thoughts at bay. Not sleeping cured the nightmares.

Mark couldn't believe how much I accomplished. He shook his head in disbelief.

"Everything okay, Juliette?" he asked.

"I'm full of ideas and wanted to get these done while they were fresh in my mind."

He gave me a fatherly look—the one saying, *I know that's baloney, but I'll give you the benefit of the doubt...for now.*

"Get some sleep, Juliette. You look exhausted. We won't need more modules for months to come. Don't burn yourself out." He was kind but it was clear he knew more about my past than I'd ever told him.

I headed home and out for a long run. Running cured the daylight demons. Six to eight miles a day... I'm thinner now—too thin.

And then there's Nate... I keep sabotaging things. And yet, he's still here.

Thank God he's still here.

Can I do better? Can I be good for him? He deserves a good woman. He deserves uncomplicated love. He'll never have that with me, but maybe we can love each other anyway.

I close my eyes and picture us on the night when I showed up at dinner as a surprise for his birthday. I want to go back to that time.

He comes in moments later, eyes searching my face, trying to determine which Juliette he's gonna get. I want to be what he needs.

Chapter 51
Baby Steps

Nate:

Juliette had her first visit with the therapist today. I waited in the reception while they talked. She didn't say much but I think she likes Dr. Rossen. She also talks with Claire a lot - when she's overwhelmed. Claire was there for her in the early days. I'm glad they're still close.

After I've gotten food into her and she's gone to bed, I try to refocus on the Manitoba story. Too many distractions keep me from getting a good draft going.

My phone rings.

"Nate, how are you, honey?"

"Mom..."

"What's going on?"

How's she know?

I walk out to the balcony. She called that night before I found Juliette. So much has happened since then.

"I'm worried and..." My voice cracks. I'm scared and hearing Mom's voice brings me back to my childhood when she could make everything okay.

"I'm sorry, sweetie. What's going on?"

I fill her in briefly but worry I'm breaking Juliette's trust telling her these dark secrets.

"What can I do?"

I sit at the mini bistro table and close the French doors to keep the heat inside. I tell her a bit about things, keeping details sparse. I break down, feeling like a little kid again.

"Nate, can I see you after the show Saturday evening? Dad and I will drive up afterwards. I never told you, but I was assaulted when I was in college. I'd just met your dad. I have an idea what she's going through. Maybe I can help."

"What? Really?"

"It was a long time ago, but not a day goes by that I don't think about it."

"How come you never told me? Does Dad know?"

"I imagine the same reason Juliette's reluctant to talk. It's hard to discuss...and embarrassing. Your dad was there for me—in his quiet, unassuming way. He never judged me. My parents couldn't grasp how such a thing could happen and blamed me. It took a long time to realize how wrong they were. It nearly tore us apart. My advice is be patient and a good ear."

"Shit, Mom, wish I'd talked to you earlier. I've already fucked up."

"Language, Nate," she scolds, her strict Baptist upbringing shining through.

"Sorry, it's just I've already screwed this up."

"No, you haven't. You're still there. No one's perfect. Just keep showing up. You're sure it's okay if I come Saturday night after the show?"

"Yes, please come." I wipe my tears, taking a shaky breath.

"I'll call when we get in. You'll get through this, honey. From what you've told me, Juliette's a fighter. I believe she'll find her way back to you."

I sit in the cold a few moments, watching as crows and jays vie for territory on a nearby oak tree. My phone vibrates with a message from Kenny. My apartment's ready.

When I head inside, there's a knock at the door. Sara's on the doorstep, luggage in tow. Forgot she was due back today.

She drops her bag and grabs me in a hug. "Hey Nate, talk to me."

I can't speak for a moment. "It's Juliette. Uh…"

"It's okay, Gavin called. What can I do?" She leads me to the barstools at the kitchen island, pulls out a bottle of whiskey, and pours two tumblers. She eyes the closed bedroom door. "She in there?"

"Sleeping. She had her first visit with a psychiatrist this afternoon."

Sara sips her whiskey, studying me. "How'd that go? Is she okay?"

"No, not right now she isn't. But she's finally talking to someone. Think she felt responsible for the things Goran did to her."

"What can I do? Do you want me to stay with Gavin and Dani or can I help out here?"

"I don't know." I run my hands through my hair. "My mom's art show is in Philly this weekend, but there's no way I'm leaving her alone. I don't know what I'm doing."

Sara puts her drink down and looks at the bedroom door. "Let me look after Juliette while you go to your mom's show. She was good to me after Tom left. You both were. Let me be here for you guys now. I'll check on her. She needs some girl time and I can do that. Give yourself a break."

Chapter 52

Do-Si-Do

Juliette:

Sara's been on me. She won't let me hide away and pulled Bea in to get me out of my funk. I know it's not as trite as being in a funk but if I hear the word "trauma" one more time, I'm going to scream. Believe me, I know what I lived through.

The upside is I no longer solely rely on Nate. Sara makes me talk about things. Bea drags me to the studio, though I'm reluctant. I don't want to be their pet project, but after an afternoon working on choreography, I feel better. It's good to move again. I've missed this. It's something I can do without Nate, without fear or PTSD.

Dr. Rossen suggested it when I told her I used to dance. I danced in New Orleans after finding a studio where I was hired to teach ballet to little ones. Dancing helped me escape the dark corners then and it's helping now. That and the new meds. I'm less scattered and steadier throughout the day. I haven't felt this stable in a long time.

Nate called to invite me to a party Saturday night to meet his parents. His apartment is finished and he's excited to show it off. He's going to his mom's art show this evening and thankfully doesn't expect me to go. Instead, I'll spend hours in the studio with Bea. Because she's still on limited activity, I'm her dancing and choreography muse.

When I walk into Nate's apartment, I'm blown away. Walls repainted in shades of warm terra-cotta and limestone, while a collection of masks and more of his gorgeous photographs in natural wood frames dress the walls. His bike is hung artfully over a smooth gray boulder-shaped couch. Rustic wood and stone tables display his collection of exotic artifacts from world travels. His mother's pottery, once stored in a back closet, accents the desert canyon vibe of the room.

He's happy to see me— nearly spilling a decanter of whiskey when I walk in. His face flushes red when he pulls me to him. I'm embarrassed but also thrilled by his attention in front of all these people. He brings me to meet his parents.

Nate favors his mom, Chaney, with her sparkling blue eyes, wavy, dark hair, and dimpled smile. She's wearing navy chinos and a gray silk top. She has an artist's hands— rough but warm when she grasps me in a hug. His dad, Clay, is a teddy bear with graying hair and warm brown eyes, decked out in light khakis and a blue plaid flannel. He's affectionate with Nate, cuffing his shoulder and jostling him. It's clear his parents miss him, which isn't a surprise as he's an only child. I imagine his rural Appalachian upbringing wasn't all that different from mine—where extended families raise children communally—as they update him on all the goings-on with his cousins.

It's a fun night. Nate is quite the cook, making fancy Mexican meatballs in red sauce and Moroccan harissa-roasted vegetables over couscous with crusty baguettes from a local bakery. The aromas of toasted spices—cumin, coriander, fennel, and caraway—fill the apartment.

Sara brings boxes of Georgetown Cupcakes for dessert. Kenny's partner Kyle is also here, having brought a plate of boulder-shaped cheese puffs made from scratch. Turns out he's a pastry chef. He and Kenny are crazy about each other.

Later, after Nate's parents retire to the guest room, he brings me into his bedroom and I'm stunned again. Kenny's outdone himself; I take in the Bedouin tented room, with panels of fabric draped from the ceiling and colorful Moroccan lanterns hung around the bed...a perfect place for seduction.

"How...are your scars?" he asks hesitantly as he rubs circles into my hip. We snuggle in bed as sunlight streams through the window.

"They're healing...slowly." I kiss his chest and move up to his neck. "I'm sorry I scared you. I didn't mean to hurt you."

"Shh, I know that. I'm glad you're here," he says into my hair after pulling me back to his chest. His lips nibble my ear, arms around me.

I'm home.

"That bed was great. We slept like rocks, which I guess is fitting," Chaney says, laughing.

She has a great laugh. She's in old work overalls and a paint-stained shirt, a hair tie attempting to tame feral curls. She's a lot like Nate. Clay comes out of the guest bedroom, ribbing Nate as he walks by. It's sweet to see them together. His dad's a lot less gruff than I imagined after hearing some heated exchanges between them on the phone. He gives me a peck on the cheek and then looks around.

"Nate, where do you have an apron?"

Nate laughs. "I'm afraid I don't have one. Are you Mom's sous chef this morning?"

"Why yes I am. I'll make do. Juliette, I may need your assistance."

"Happy to help. What do you need?"

"Music - to accompany my chopping."

"I know just the thing." I connect my playlist to Nate's stereo. I have a collection of bluegrass and folk music I think they'll appreciate.

The doorbell rings and Sara walks in with my overnight bag.

"Join us. My parents are making breakfast," Nate offers.

"Oh, no, I can't. I just wanted to bring this to Juliette." She hugs me, whispering, "Everything good?"

"Yes, all good." I take the bag from her. "Thanks for bringing this. Stay. There's coffee and Chaney's making roasted veggie frittata."

"That's right, and we have enough to feed an army. Please join us."

"That would be great. I don't want to work anyway." She grins at Nate.

"Be right back. Going to hop in the shower quickly, if that's okay."

"It's got another twenty minutes, sweetie. Take your time," Chaney tells me, running her hand down my cheek just like my mom would do. "Sara, honey, come get coffee."

Standing under the steaming hot water, I feel like my old self again—the old self I'd forgotten existed; the one before Goran...before Javier... I can imagine myself with these people. My parents will love Chaney and Clay. I just hope this isn't too good to be true.

"Time for us to be on our way. Thank you for letting us crash and putting up with our snoring. It'll be a couple weeks until we see you in Kentucky," Chaney says, picking up the car keys. They've invited me to join them for Thanksgiving.

"I hear you're quite the dancer, so be prepared. We Fishers like to pull up the rugs and get our square dance on." Clay leads me in a do-si-do.

Nate laughs, watching us. "This is a new side to my parents. I don't ever recall do-si-do-ing as a child."

"When you were a baby, we did. As you got older, you

slowed us down. We had to keep an eye on you as you were prone to falling out of trees."

"One time."

"At least a couple trips to the emergency room. That's okay. Nobody's counting."

Nate rolls his eyes, smiling, and grabs their bags.

Chaney has tears in her eyes. I hug her, not wanting them to leave.

"It's just two weeks. We'll be down before you know it."

She kisses my cheek, then uses her thumb to rub the lipstick off. "We can't wait to see you both. We'll make apple butter and play cards."

Clay grabs Nate. "Maybe some cow-tipping and moonshine tours." He winks at me. "Son, this was great." He chokes up too, clinging to us.

Nate and I watch as they pull out of the lot.

"They're wonderful, and God, they love you something fierce."

He smiles, wrapping me in his arms. "They loved you. I haven't seen my dad that easygoing in a long time."

"I'm glad I met them. I was a little terrified."

"Terrified?"

I look down. "I was worried they'd think I was a bad influence because of my past. I don't know... I let it get into my head that I wasn't good enough for you."

He lifts my chin. "You're incredible, Juliette. My parents loved you. And..."

I don't let him finish.

Chapter 53

Country Roads

We drive to Kentucky for Thanksgiving. It's damp and chilly but beautiful. I miss home. When we enter the Daniel Boone National Forest, I'm brought back to my childhood of running the creeks with Tom and Hobe, twins I grew up with. I wonder where they are these days.

Thanksgiving morning, Juliette cooks a Colombian breakfast—arepas con huevos, corn cakes stuffed with eggs. I'm sent to find fresh tomatoes, avocados, and jalapenos for the spicy aji that accompanies it. She also makes frijoles antioqueños to add to our Thanksgiving dinner. She enjoys bossing me around the kitchen. I'm her sous chef and try to figure out what she wants as she insists on directing me in Spanish. My parents watch us with cups of hot spiced cider, laughing.

One morning, when my parents have gone to the farmer's market, I find Juliette in Mom's ceramics studio. Mom introduced her to the art of throwing pots and she's an eager student.

"Here you are. Whatcha making there?"

Juliette's decked out in ripped jeans and a long flannel shirt. Her hair is tied back with a red bandana and she's concentrating hard, trying to keep the gray blob of clay from spinning out of control.

"I really don't know. But this is very relaxing. Have you ever thrown a pot?"

"As a kid she had me out here a lot. I never got very good at it. But I loved watching her work. She'd be lost in her world and could do miraculous things to make the clay yield to her will." Around the room are examples of my childish attempts, which Mom kept for nostalgia.

"I noticed these primitive works and thought they might belong to you," she says, laughing.

I straddle her from behind, putting my hands over hers. Even though this is a scene from some cheesy movie, I want to do this with her. I nuzzle her neck, taking in her heady scent of clay and honeysuckle.

"Whoa, okay—so are we acting out that scene in *Ghost*?" she jokes.

"Uh-huh," I grunt in her ear. The cool, wet clay and her proximity make me not care about cheesy movie remakes.

She leans back into me and turns her head to kiss me. "I hope your mom doesn't walk in on us."

"She and Dad headed into town to hit the farmer's market. I think we're safe. May need to get one of these in my apartment. Whaddaya think?"

She doesn't respond as she rubs her clay-covered fingers up my arms. I move my hands to her stomach, under her shirt. She sucks in a breath as I touch bare skin.

"We're gonna make a mess of your mom's studio," she worries.

"Shh, we'll clean it later." I unbutton her shirt and trace the edge of her bra with my clay-crusted fingers. I move my hands to her hips and lift her to standing, turning off the spinning wheel.

I pull her jeans over her hips and lay her on my mom's drafting table. I take her there, on the drafting board. We're not quiet and I'm glad my parents live in the middle of nowhere.

Juliette's hair is a matted mess afterward. I laugh as I lead her to an outdoor spigot to clean up before tracking the mess all over the house. We shiver as we wash each other. I love being naked outside with her, even in the cold. We head into the house to warm up and find clean clothes.

"We better get out there and tidy up the studio before they return." Juliette worries about making a bad impression on my parents. She doesn't realize she can do no wrong, even engaging in a seduction scene in Mom's studio.

Back in the studio, Juliette finds the clump of clay she'd been working on. It's not salvageable. I show her where to stow it.

My parents return later that afternoon with gorgeous pumpkins and a crate of apples. Juliette learns the art of making old-fashioned apple and pumpkin butter. Mom would have loved a daughter.

"How would you feel about going on a little hike today?" I ask.

She eyes me, suspicious. "Sure. What's in the backpack?"

"Oh, a little picnic and some ropes. I may do a little climbing if there's a good spot. I'm not luring you out for some scary climbing expedition, I promise."

"Let me get my hiking boots and another layer."

It's chilly, although it'll warm up once we're hiking. I smile because she's going to trust me.

I drive to one of my favorite spots—Blanton State Forest in Harlan County, on the south face of Pine Mountain. It's a thirty-five-minute drive. Juliette stares out the window at the ancient Appalachians. This piece of woods is one of the rare spots to find old-growth deciduous forest. I haven't been on the trail in years but hope to find my way. I don't want to get lost with a nervous Juliette. Thankfully the trails are well marked.

As we climb, the sun emerges, warming us. Despite the forty-degree temps, I shed layers. I love the feeling of moving through this familiar landscape, weaving through tulip poplars, American beech, white oak, hemlocks, and sugar maples.

In various shades of brown and rust, everything is beautiful in a desolate way. Leaves crunch underfoot. Without a leafy canopy overhead, we see a variety of birds: woodpeckers, finches, and sparrows flitting through the treetops.

Juliette takes pictures of interesting flora and fauna. She concentrates on getting good angles for her photos. This is a great way for her to lose her fear of hiking in the woods again. Up ahead are some rare plant communities in acid seeps and mixed mesophytic deciduous forest. I know she'll be wowed by these plants, even though winter isn't the best time to see them. The advantage of winter is we have this stunning forest to ourselves—just the sounds of our own breath, birds, and wind moving through the trees.

After climbing past Knobby Rock and up toward Sand Cave and the Maze, I lead her into Watts Creek and Big Branch watersheds. We've hiked a couple hours and I find a nice overlook to pull out the blanket and picnic.

"Nate, this is stunning. I want to come back in the summer. It must be magnificent."

Shading her eyes from the sun overhead, she gazes across the mountain tops. She's flushed from hiking and radiant. I drop my pack, pull out a blanket, and set out the picnic: small containers of mixed nuts, olives and cheeses, dried sausages and fruit, sliced apples and pears, and fresh apple butter.

She smiles when she sees all the goodies. "How did you manage to get that all packed into your tiny rucksack?"

"I've learned to pack efficiently over the years." I turn to her, blinded by the sun for a moment. I catch a glint of her stunning eyes, which gives me the resolve I need. I bend down on one knee as I pull out a small, black velvet box from my pocket with shaky hands and sweaty palms.

"Juliette, I can't imagine spending my life with anyone else. I want to grow old with you and I want to wake to see your beautiful eyes every morning. Will you marry me?"

She drops to her knees. "Yes, oh, yes!" She pulls me to her.

"Wait, please open this." In my rush to propose, I forgot to open the ring box. I wrestle it open, feeling foolish.

She backs up, laughing and crying. She stares at the delicate sapphire and diamond ring. I take it out of the box and, with shaky hands, slide it on her finger. I stop and hold her hand, staring at the delicate ring for a moment.

"Wait, when did you...?"

"It was my great-grandmother's. It's been in the family for years and Mom showed it to me when we first showed up here."

"Oh, Nate, this is the most beautiful ring I've ever seen. I..." The sapphires set in rose gold twist around her finger like branches with tiny leaves. The precious stones are unique—bicolored, giving them a greenish tint that matches Juliette's eyes nearly exactly.

"I hope you like it."

She's speechless, eyes wet. We hold each other, taking in the golden and russet trees, feeling the bite of the breeze. I sear this moment into my brain.

Hours later, we make it back to the house. My parents must have known my plans when I suggested Juliette go on a hike. Mom bounds out of the house as we pull up. She struggles to behave normally, then runs to Juliette, spinning her around, laughing and crying all at once.

"It fits? I'm guessing you said yes?" She's covered in flour and coats Juliette in a layer. They dance around, clinging to each other in the setting sun.

That evening as we lay in bed, Juliette props herself up on my chest. "I thought you were going to climb when were out there."

"I was, but I wanted to see how you felt about the possibility. I had the gear with me. I was so nervous about proposing, I couldn't think of anything else. After you said yes, well, I didn't want to spend a moment away from you."

She stares at me. "You were that nervous? Really? I mean..."

I nod as words escape me.

"This was my best day ever," she says, tears in her eyes.

I pull her down and kiss her. I'll never tire of this.

She props up again, silky hair tickling my face. "I'm going on the record right now. I will climb with you. If you can trust me enough to ask for my hand, then I'll do the same."

"I'd love that, but you don't have to. I love you, Juliette, and want to spend the rest of my life with you, whether you climb with me or not. You had me when you pulled that cheap bottle of Jack Daniels from your fridge in Bethesda."

Chapter 54
Prom Night

"Did I miss the costume memo for movie night or have we shown up for prom? Dani, we're underdressed." Gavin touches Nate's slicked-back hair, making a face.

The others stand on the doorstep, taking in Nate's black poly tuxedo jacket over a pink ruffled shirt and hot pink bow tie. I hide in the bedroom, peeking through the cracked door, waiting for my cue.

"I wanted an excuse to get you over here...to celebrate."

I dance out of the bedroom in a hot pink tulle and taffeta number with a matching bridal veil cascading over seriously teased-up hair. Bea's jaw drops when she sees me and there are looks of honest confusion from everyone else. Guess my disguise works.

Everyone stares as I shimmy over. When Kyle and Kenny follow with a tray of champagne, and I'm close enough to identify, our friends bust out laughing.

"She said yes!"

Gavin grabs Nate in a hug. "Congratulations! Can't believe you kept this quiet. Really thought you had a mental break and brought home..." he pauses, "someone else."

My bloodred lips and pasty white face, highlighted with dramatic bright blue eyeshadow and thick black eyeliner, fooled everyone—even Nate, I think. Not to mention I put on some weight when we were in Kentucky. Chaney's cooking helped.

"No, it's Juliette. Finally got up the nerve when we were in Kentucky over Thanksgiving."

Jorge asks if he proposed with a cherry-flavored Ring Pop. I'd have said yes to that too.

"Very funny. It's my great-grandmother's ring."

I stumble in my hot pink pumps, grimacing. They're torture. Dani, Sara, and Bea grab me, and get entangled in the puffy dress.

"Jules, this is perfect. Let's see this ring. You're quite the chameleon," Sara says.

Tears in her eyes, Bea holds my hand. "It's beautiful... I'm afraid it's prettier than you, right now. Where did you find this remarkable number? You've inspired a new dance number."

"I hit the resale stores in Adams Morgan. When I found this creation, I couldn't resist. A girl doesn't feel truly bridal until she puts on one of these numbers. Think I'm getting a rash," I say, scratching.

When I returned with our outfits, I made Nate try on his heinous tuxedo to be sure it fit. I made a few tweaks and encouraged him to slick back his hair with gel. I refused to let him see my outfit, telling him the groom mustn't see his bride ahead of time.

I laugh, twirling around, hellish shoes be damned in my hot pink monstrosity. I haven't felt this carefree in weeks.

Nate spent the day cooking a traditional Comorian tuna pilau using fresh whole spices: cardamom, cloves, and cinnamon sticks. I baked fresh naan and made an arugula salad with blood orange vinaigrette. Everyone eats with gusto, even eight-month-old Sam.

Kicking off our shoes, Bea plays DJ as we drag the furniture out of the way to dance. I boogie to Dani, who's holding Sam, his bright blue eyes taking in the commotion. Dani hands him to me and I feel the weight of him as he grips me with tiny hands. He's adorable. A surge of love and longing hits like a Mack truck. Nate joins us and we dance.

Later, Kyle surprises us with an engagement cake—part tropical island and part boulder with a mini Nate and Juliette wrapped around each other in climbing ropes. The room goes silent when he brings it out.

"I guess we know where we're getting our wedding cake," Nate says, giving Kyle a hug. "Just wow—this is incredible. How'd you whip this up so quickly?"

Kyle grabs Kenny's hand, smiling. "Can't reveal my tricks of the trade. I'm glad you like it. It turned out better than expected. I worried I'd show up with a gray rock lump of a cake, but got inspired when I started working on the tropical island side of things."

Chapter 55
Afterburn

Nate:

After an evening of dancing and toasting, people peel away. We collapse, putting our feet on the new coffee table. Juliette's hot pink gown poufs everywhere. She could be an exotic sea creature hiding in elaborate coral. I snap a candid as she smiles, leaning her head back. Her teased hair shoots out all over her head, and red lipstick is smudged across her face. I pull up the tulle of her skirt searching for skin. I run my fingers up her leg. She tries to unbutton my shirt, but I push her hand down.

"It's my turn to undress you. Although I'm not sure where to begin with this."

Her propped-up feet are red with blisters. I sit on the coffee table, pick up her right foot, and begin massaging. She perks up when I rub with warm massage oil. I hope this isn't a *no-go*. She relaxes as I continue. With more pressure, I work out kinks from her arches and toes, moving upward, slathering her legs in oil.

Think I drank too much last night. Head thick. I glance at my Bridezilla, dead to the world. The pillow's smeared with red lipstick and black mascara. I nearly slip and fall when my oily feet touch the floor. Time for a shower, although I'm hesitant to wash it all away.

As I come out of the bathroom, a knock at the door gets my attention.

Two suited individuals flashing official badges stand there. A stocky man with dark blonde hair and piercing blue eyes in a crisp black suit stands on my stoop. His partner is a fifty-something woman, also wearing a dark suit, with short blonde hair.

I close the door behind me. I have an inkling who they may be.

"Nate Fisher?"

"Who's asking? And who are you?"

"I'm Agent Hastings. And this is Agent Stype. We're with the investigative branch of Homeland Security."

I glance at their badges and confirm their names match the ones they've just given me.

"Can you confirm that you are Nate Fisher?" Agent Hastings plays "Bad Cop" while his partner gives me an easy smile. Why do I feel like I'm on the set of *Law and Order*?

"What's this about?"

Agent Stype clears her throat. "Mr. Fisher—or may I call you Nate? We're looking for Miss Juliette Fernandez. We believe you're familiar with her. Can you confirm that?"

I nearly argue but realize the fruitlessness of that gesture. I pray Juliette is sound asleep and unaware what's happening here.

"Yes, I know Juliette, but I don't know why you think she's here." I keep my eyes on their faces. Eye contact's important.

"We have a few questions. It'll be less public if we can come in for a few minutes." Agent Stype is flirty. She's attractive, I'll give her that. But I have no desire to tango with her.

"Do you have a warrant?"

The agents exchange a surprised look. No, I'm not letting them waltz in.

"No. We'd like to speak with Miss Fernandez. We've reached out but she hasn't responded. Her cooperation would be greatly appreciated and will certainly help her case."

"What case?" pops out of my mouth before I think.

The agents smile.

"We're not at liberty to speak without Miss Fernandez present. If she's here, we can clear up any confusion."

I shake my head. "If I see her, I'll pass along your message. Thank you." I attempt to slide through my door, closing it quietly.

Agent Stype stuffs her card in my hand before I escape into the apartment.

Shit, what was that all about? Maybe Juliette's fears about Goran's illegal enterprises catching up with her aren't so off-base. She must not have responded to that certified letter. And now they know to show up here. Not good. Did they go to her place first? I should call Sara.

I go back to the bedroom but Juliette's not there. She must be in the bathroom. The shower is running. I'll leave her in peace. We can talk when she comes out.

I pull out the French press and get coffee brewing. I see Juliette's pink tutu where I tossed it last night. Her pink stilettos lay in a heap by the coffee table. I pick things up when I hear my phone buzzing on the kitchen island.

It's a text. From Juliette.

Sorry Nate. I love you.

I stumble to the bathroom, hoping I'm misreading things. The shower's running but no Juliette. Just an open bathroom window. *What the fuck?*

When I call, it goes to voicemail. I call Sara. She's hungover and not aware of the urgency in my voice. No one's heard from Juliette. I should call her parents but don't want to send them into a tailspin just yet.

I have one other idea. I grab my wallet—it's thick with something. My heart sinks when I find her engagement ring stuffed inside. *This can't be happening.*

I drive to her apartment, where I find Sara blurry but more

coherent. My distress sobers her.

"Where is she?"

I shake my head. "I don't know. Two Homeland Security officers showed up at my doorstep this morning." I pull out the ring.

"She gave that back? What the fuck?" Sara hugs me. There's nothing to say to make any of this better.

I've got to find her. She can't disappear now. Not after everything we've been through.

I tell Sara where I think Juliette might be. "Will you come with me? She might be willing to talk to you."

"Of course."

Chapter 56

Running

Juliette:

The studio is empty and freezing. Not sure Bea's paid to have the electricity turned on. There's running water, though. Just no heat. I need to wash my face. I can't disappear looking like a crazed clown from some carny act. I've got next to nothing with me aside from my purse, this phone, and Nate's sweats. I don't even have underwear, I left so fast. I managed to throw on my old trainers before hopping out the window.

Whoever those two people were—they cannot find me. They'll lead Goran right to me and that cannot happen. I've worked too hard and been too careful to let them bring that wolf to my door.

Maybe I'll go back to Mauritius. I could stay with Mani. He'd take me in, even if I haven't seen him in months. I finally read his note a few days ago. Not sure what compelled me but he wrote he'd been in love with me since we first met and started surfing together.

Love? Really? I mean, we had fun together—but how can he claim that? I don't understand men sometimes.

Claire and Darrien will also take me in, although I don't think I can face Darrien after all he's done for me. And Mark... he doesn't deserve this kind of treachery.

No time for regrets or what-ifs. I've gotta figure out what comes next.

I wipe the ridiculous makeup off with a rag I've found in

the bathroom. As I'm rounding a corner, I bump into... *Shit, how'd he find me so quickly?*

"Nate? You've got to leave."

He puts his hands up, backing away. "Juliette, are you really running again? Will that make any of this any better?"

I put the rag down. "It's too hard, Nate. I can't talk to you..."

I look around.... nothing here, just dusty floorboards, a ballet bar that needs assembling, and a long mirror. I avoid our reflections, afraid what I'll see.

"Juliette!" His voice startles me. "Look at me. Do you love me?"

Too much pain and conflict between us.

He grabs my arm. His touch, a lightning strike, nearly knocks me off my feet. I don't want to run, even though I should. I *want* to hang on for all I'm worth, but those people from Homeland Security—they're the threat. He has no idea.

I yank my arm away. "No, I don't love you," I say through gritted teeth, not meeting his eyes.

"Say it to my face. Look me in the eyes and say it." He takes my hands, again.

When he pulls me in, our bodies flush, I liquify— molecules blending and bleeding together. I need to hold fast. Be unrelenting... But when he rubs my back and breathes into my hair, my scaffolding warps, bending.

"Jules, why do you think this is your only choice?" Our bodies stay locked together as he whispers into my neck. His fingers tangled in my hair, make me shiver.

I want him, I do. I want this life... but...

The front door swings open and two uniformed agents appear.

I rear back. "I thought I could trust you. Why are you doing this?" I cry.

"I didn't know they followed me..." he stammers.

I see red as I ball my hand into a fist and sock him with

everything I have. He stumbles back as I lunge at him again. Burly arms grab me around the shoulders, and pull me back. Yelling and hysteria fill my ears as I grapple with the stocky agent. I collapse after expending every ounce of energy. When I stop flailing to catch my breath, all goes quiet.

"Juliette, we only need to speak a few minutes. Please hear us out. It would be better if you cooperated. You're not under arrest or in trouble..."

"I will be if I talk to you," I snap. "I can't tell you a thing. Get the fuck out! You have no right to be here."

Nate climbs to his feet, a wary eye on me. He should be wary.

The agents exchange a glance.

" Mr. Lukas's business enterprises have been seized, including the ones under your name. This may come back to haunt you if you don't work with us," the blonde woman says.

"Jules, come on. Don't do this. They can help you."

His voice enrages me. I spin towards him as he scrambles back.

"Not. Another. Word."

And then, Sara walks in. The sight of her drains all my fury. I deflate like a balloon. She scoops me up and guides me to a back room.

I'm exhausted. Sara sits with me, holding my hands, icing my bruised knuckles with a towel. She reminds me of Claire, who I nicknamed Clairevoyant. Sara's not so different.

I want to run when the female agent walks in, but Sara holds me in place.

"Talk to her. Find out what's going on. You don't want to keep running."

When she says this, I'm able to listen. When Nate says them, I go ballistic.

"Let me update you on things. Then you decide if you want to assist us."

The agent tells me about the raid on Lukas Enterprises.

He's been under investigation for the past five years over tax evasion and fraud. She tells me a subsidiary of the company is in my name. If I agree to tell them what I know, it'll be better for me when they investigate my participation in his schemes.

They have no idea I have the documents I do... proof of Goran's shell companies set up to look like charities, taking in millions in donations. I'm amazed he got away with it for so long. But he had well-heeled investors with connections who didn't mind the unscrupulous nature of his work. They enjoyed the steep profits.

The agent leaves me to think about things. I have until Thursday to decide.

Sara and I return to the apartment. It's lost its allure as every room reminds me of Nate. I can't shake him.

"What's going on, Jules? Are you guys still engaged?" Sara stands over me, hands on her hips.

It's two days since I lost my mind. We're at our apartment and I'm struggling to work. Scattered scraps of training materials cover the dining table and I'm in the midst of the mess, with my head in my hands.

I can't look at her. "Um, I don't know."

"You don't know? What does that mean?"

"I gave back the ring, that's what it means." I'm pissed but still the tears flow.

"You haven't talked to him since that night. Is this what you want?" Sara sits next to me at the table.

"No...I just... I don't know how to undo what I've done," I sob.

She puts her arms around me. "Jules, it's okay. It's Nate—he's no Goran. He loves you. You two have something incredible. Right now, things are hard. But you'll figure it out. Have you talked to him?"

"No, I came here to get my head on straight. It's not working. I can't get anything done. I can't sleep. I keep picturing him after I hit him. I mean, who does that? A crazy person. I'm a crazy person. I can't keep my mind in one place. I'm no good for him," I sob into her shoulder.

"That's nonsense. You spoke to Darrien, yes?" She pushes me back and levels me with a look. "Your new meds may be impacting things. Nate knows that too. He loves you. Promise me you won't give up. He hasn't."

"I don't know what to do."

"Yes, you do. But I'll help. I may even have an idea." She gives me a conspiratorial smile.

Chapter 57
The Climb

Nate:

I spend nights tossing and turning, unable to erase Juliette's rage from my mind. So much secrecy and she ran. Again. What am I doing? I need to let her go. It's too hard.

I catch a glimpse of myself in the bathroom mirror.... my eye's an impressive shade of purple, rimmed in green. It aches. It's the first time I've been punched in the face. And by the woman I think I'm in love with? This is nuts.

Darrien offered an interesting update and, although it could explain Juliette's bizarre behavior, I can't live like this. It's another side effect of the treatment against the virus, especially when combined with her new anti-anxiety meds. Even if that's true, what if this is who she truly is – unhinged and untrusting? I need to forget about her.

Gavin brings dinner the next day. I pretend to work, staring at a blank computer screen. I have no desire to do anything. I hate the pity on his face. Even he skirts around talking about Juliette. After he leaves, I make a plan. Time to leave this pity-party. I need to focus on something else - a rock-climbing trip. That's how I got over Emma. Maybe this will work for Juliette too.

I haven't climbed since I met Juliette. I need to get back to it.

2 Days Later...

"Geez, Nate, it looks like you're getting ready to hit the Himalayas." Gavin lets himself into my apartment. I should get my key back. He stands in the doorway watching me.

"No, I'm going to New River this weekend."

"How's the Manitoba story coming?" Gavin eyes my closed computer.

"Liar. You're checking on me." I continue the pull-ups, ignoring him.

"Yup, so how're you doing? Heard from Juliette?" He stares at me.

I stop to catch my breath. "No. I think that chapter is over." I switch to wide-arm pull-ups, sweat dripping.

"What does that mean?"

"It means I'm done trying to make things work. Time to move on." I continue my pull-ups and ignore his looming presence. I feel the frown on his face.

"I think you're missing her more than you want to admit."

I stop and glare at him. "Yeah, I miss her. Is that what you want me to say? I do." *God, I want to punch something.*

"Have you called her?"

"What? No. Gavin, just leave it alone." I drop to the floor and start fingertip push-ups.

"Any good places to stay nearby at the Gorge? Cabins or a lodge?"

What's he up to?

"You mean at New River? I usually car camp. Why?"

"It might be fun to come out, even if I don't climb. I can hike around while you climb. Might be nice to get out of the city for a few days."

"Suit yourself. I was just going to car camp."

"I'll look into it. Winter's low season, so we get a good deal."

I don't look up when he leaves as I start my crunches and Russian twists using a thirty-pound weight.

I pick up Gavin at an ungodly hour and we make it to the gorge around 10 a.m. We don't talk much on the long drive as I keep the radio blasting. At the gorge he agrees to do some preliminary climbs with me. I'm glad for his company, despite my shitty mood. He's patient and follows my lead as we begin the climb. We're unusually quiet - just the sounds of our efforts moving up the rock. We go slow and I help him climb up some easy pitches for the first hour. Eventually the pitches get more technical and he's not comfortable going higher.

"You keep going. I'm going to hang here and admire the view.".

"You sure? I can rappel down with you and hit another pitch—so you're not stuck here."

"No, don't want you climbing alone. Go up a few more—just be back in an hour or so. Cool?"

"Okay, but yell up if you need me to come back. I won't be gone long."

"No worries, it's a nice view."

Chapter 58
On the Ledge

I can't believe I agreed to this.

Dani has me outfitted. She shows me how to move up the rock face. She's patient and knows her stuff.

Now that I'm focused on keeping my hands on the rock and where to place my feet, I can't think about much else.

What if this harebrained idea doesn't work? What if he hates me and throws me off the ledge? I deserve it.

Focus. Can't think about that right now. I need to deal with what's right in front of me...a smooth granite slab and ropes and Dani's voice in my ear.

After a few moves, Gavin stands above me, grinning.

"Howdy, stranger, fancy meeting you here. How was it?" he whispers, hugging me when I clamber onto the ledge. My heart's thumping through my chest.

"Wish I didn't find this so terrifying. Aren't you dizzy up here?"

"Plant yourself against the rock and you'll be fine. He'll be down soon. You okay?"

Am I okay? I'm not sure, but they don't need to hear that. They got me up here. They want us to reunite. But I may have pushed Nate too far. He may not be able to do this with me again.

I don't know what I'll do if he rejects me—especially up here.

"Think so."

"Dani's gonna help me down. Here's the ring."

I gasp when he pulls the ring box from his pocket. "What? How do you have that?"

"I snuck it from his apartment when we were packing up yesterday. He'd be surprised to find you with the ring on, don't you think?"

I shake my head. "I can't take that, Gavin...unless he offers it to me. I can't..." This was a bad idea. I start shaking, unable to think straight. What the hell am I doing?

He puts an arm around me. "Hey, it's okay. I'll put it back when we get to town. Don't worry about it." He looks up suddenly when we feel the rope overhead moving.

"We gotta go. Jules, you sure you're okay up here for a few minutes?"

I don't have time to think, which is a good thing.

"Yeah, be careful getting down. Don't rush." I don't want anyone to fall. I've wreaked enough havoc.

After they leave, I take a few deep breaths. My heart drums loud enough that my body vibrates.

Gavin took the ring from Nate's apartment. At least he didn't incinerate the thing after I left it behind. He's coming down. I find a spot on the ledge to make myself less visible. I creep around – shit it's narrow up here. I find a low shrub and crouch behind it as I watch him make his way down to the ledge.

"Gavin? Shit, Gavin, where are you?"

I stand up. He looks confused. I'm clearly not Gavin.

"Wait, Juliette? What are you doing here?"

I stand so he can see me better. My knees are wobbly and my heart thumps in my chest. He's not look happy to see me. "Hey."

He shakes his head. I wonder if he thinks he's having a hallucination. Maybe he thinks I pushed Gavin off.

"It's really me," I say.

"How did you get here?" It's hard to read his expression, with his helmet low over his eyes. His stance is taut. Is he pissed?

"Sorry, I didn't mean to interrupt your climb. I just..." I look over the side. Big mistake. I stumble back, shaking.

"Juliette, hey...." He's at my side in a flash and takes my hand. "Easy, you're okay."

No, I'm not okay. *Why the Hell am I here?* This is terrifying. I pant like I've run a marathon.

"Breathe with me. You're okay." He gives me a smile – a small one. I shove my back against the cliff wall.

"I shouldn't be here. This is a cheap trick to get you to take me back... and that's not fair." I vomit at him, then turn to the side and really vomit. He grips my waist to keep me from falling.

"Easy, Jules... Breathe slowly... Here." He hands me a canteen. I rinse out my mouth, and crouch down, wishing for the dizziness to subside.

My head clears after a moment and I look up into his concerned face. God, he's beautiful. Especially when he's worried. I remember that about him in the Comoros.

"Are you okay?"

I nod, and then shake my head, as tears stream down my face. "I'm sorry for what I did... for all of it," I blubber. "I'm a mess and you should stay clear of me." He wraps his arms around me as I sob, shaking, snot running everywhere. "Oh shit, sorry. I need to get these back to Dani."

"Dani's here?" He looks around and it dawns on him what I'm doing here. "Of course, she is. God, those two." He laughs, lightness brightening his face. I have an urge to kiss him but no, I don't deserve that privilege.

"Nate, I've been an idiot. Please, can we try again? I can't sleep. I can't eat. I can't work. I miss you." He grabs me and kisses me – a kiss that reaches the deepest recesses of my being. My knees would buckle if I weren't already crouched down.

He pulls back a moment, staring into my eyes. "Jules, I swore I wouldn't do this – I wouldn't give you another chance. But I'm a glutton. I've got no resolve when it comes to you." He drags his hand up my back and pulls me to standing. "How did you get up here anyway? Dani? For real? You climbed up here even though you're afraid of heights?"

"Yeah, idiotic. But yes. How else can I show you what you mean to me?" I shiver, feeling panicky again.

"Well, you're gutsy alright, and batshit crazy." He hugs me again and I press myself into his solidness. I need him.

"Think you can handle repelling down, so we're no longer dangling off this ledge?"

Teeth chattering, "I thought you'd never ask." He takes my hand and holds it to his chest.

"I won't leave you up here. I'm just going to show you how to rappel. It's easier if you watch first. Can you do that?"

A part of me doesn't want to let go. But I nod, wiping my face.

I brush his hair away from his purple eye and kiss it gently. "I'm sorry about that. I'm sorry about all of this."

It's easier than I expect. He demonstrates and climbs back up, so I can try. We rappel down to the next pitch and I'm ecstatic. He smiles at my reaction. We continue down and make our way to find Gavin and the rest of the crew gathered with an impromptu picnic.

Dani hugs me. "Was he surprised to find you up there?" She looks at Nate, grinning.

"Dani, I should have known. I like the rock-climbing garb."

"Least I got to put my REI skills to good use," she laughs.

Gavin walks over, smiling. He's relieved to see us together again. "Surprised?"

"You guys know how to keep me on my toes."

Bea and Jorge are here too.

"Okay, rock stud, I want you to teach me how to do that too," Bea says in all seriousness, hands on her hips with her baby belly pooching out.

"I'd be happy to, but Jorge here, isn't enthused about me taking his pregnant wife up a rock face right now."

Jorge frowns. "Sorry, Bea, in a few months, after our precious child is born, *then* you can come out here with Nate," he tries to appease her.

Bea rolls her eyes and leans into Nate, "Come on...he doesn't need to know."

"Don't put me in the middle of this marital squabble. Let's stick to dancing. 'Kay?"

She kisses Nate on the cheek. "Then you're going to have to learn to salsa properly if you're gonna stay with this spectacular woman."

We gather around a festive spread of goodies everyone has pulled together, eating and laughing. It's a relief to have Nate at my side again. He seems to feel the same way, finding any excuse to touch me. We're like elephants, needing physical contact to secure our bond.

Chapter 59
Off the Ledge

Nate:

This morning I woke thinking I'd need to move on without her. Now she's here, next to me. I'm a little whiplashed.

Gavin nudges me and pulls me aside. "So, I took something from your apartment yesterday and I have it with me." He drags me behind a cluster of trees and pulls the ring box out of his pocket. "Thought you might need this later."

"Wait, you took that? Shit, I had a heart attack when I couldn't find it anywhere. Gavin, you're killing me." I open the box and suck in a breath when I see the ring nestled inside.

Gavin claps me on the back. "Sorry, man, thought I'd take matters into my own hands. Hope you're not mad."

"No, I'm relieved to see it again. Just glad I didn't lose it. Maybe I can give it to her this evening."

Gavin smiles. "We all have cabins not far from here—and you and Jules have your own. We figured you'd want some privacy this evening. Dani and Sara put together an ambiance pack for you guys. It's in a blue bag, in the back of your car."

I hug him, touched they've gone to such lengths for us. "You guys are the best."

"That's right. We are the best—and don't forget it...especially when we press you to babysit Sam so Dani and I can have a date night."

"You're on. We'd love that."

Juliette walks toward us, carrying Sam, who plays with her

hair, giggling. She has a steely look in her eye.

I tuck the ring in my jacket.

"What are you two plotting over here?" she asks.

"Nothing, and what would you like to do this afternoon?"

"I want to climb more. With you."

"Really? Thought you found it terrifying?"

"I do, but I want to climb with you. I want you to teach me. Please." She hands Sam to Gavin who watches us, smirking.

"Okay, just don't tell Bea."

We start slowly. She needs to acclimate to the height and feel of the rock.

I want this first climb to be amazing.

As we're about to start, she turns to me. "I haven't been easy and you've been nothing but patient. I'm sorry for the things I yelled at you." She runs her hands over my face and down my neck. "I'm sorry for doubting us."

I kiss her bruised knuckles. "It's okay. But let's work as a team. I don't like fighting and I really don't like being on the receiving end of your rage...you've got a mean left hook."

She looks down, ashamed, but when she raises her eyes, I see new determination.

"You're right—we need to be a team. I love you." She puts her arms around my neck and kisses me, melting all the hurt and loss I'd been feeling these last few days.

"Let's climb some rocks so I don't try and find other ways to burn off this energy." I turn her around, smacking her gorgeous backside. I hand her a helmet and lead her up the rock face, one pitch at a time.

The climbing she did with Dani showed her how to move up the wall—how to use ledges and wall cracks to maneuver. She's a natural and I'm impressed with her natural agility and grace. I see the dancer in her. We get to a pitch and she looks at what comes next. I find a few mid-level pitches that require her to consider the route. She has good instincts. I can't wait to take her to a boulder lounge to see what she can do. She's strong and, although she doesn't have the finger strength I do, she's good at moving her body efficiently.

We make it to the top of the canyon and hold each other as we take in the view. The sun begins its slide into the western horizon.

"I think you may have left this behind the other day." I take the ring out and slide it on her finger. I lift her hand and kiss it.

"I love it, Nate. I really love it."

I love how the bicolored sapphires match her eyes. Somewhere in the universe, my great-grandmother is smiling.

I hold her close. "Just promise me you won't give up on us. When you feel scared or uncertain, find me. Talk to me. Okay?"

She nods, tears slipping down her cheeks. "I promise."

"Jules, you're a natural out here. I don't know how you feel about climbing now, but you have good instincts and body control."

She squeezes my ass. "Really? Good body control? We'll see how long that lasts." She presses her hips to mine.

"Hmm, as much as I'd like to take you right here, right now, I'm not sure there's enough room on this ledge. But I do have a spectacular place in mind for another climb where there *is* enough space and a view you won't soon forget."

"This is all the view I need right now," she murmurs into my neck.

Chapter 60
Rock and Roll

Juliette:

We belay down and after an hour find ourselves on the ground. I'm giddy from the experience. Climbing with Nate is incredible. I had no idea he could move so fluidly. He's a gorgeous climber.

I have a hard time containing myself when we're on solid ground, but know we need to stow gear. I come up behind him after I've gotten the last of the ropes and harnesses put away. I wrap my arms around him, taking in his musky scent—sweat and the faint hint of cedar and pine aftershave. I slide my hands under his shirt, stretching my fingers across taut muscles. He sucks in a breath.

"God, I'm not sure how to resist you," he groans.

"Then don't."

He turns and throws me over his shoulder.

"Hey," I gasp.

He carries me to a little enclave just to the side of the rock we'd been climbing. He stands me up against the rock and tugs off my pants and underwear. He massages my butt. I'm sore, but I want him. Within minutes we're having sex standing against a hard rock face. It's not soft and sweet. I feel the sharp rock against my backside. There's a lot of pent-up energy between us. Despite the rock digging into my upper thigh, I don't care. I deserve whatever he's feeling.

He slows a minute, realizing I'm watching him. He slows,

going more gently, but I need hard sex now too. I want his power—our power—together.

We practically collapse in a heap when we're through. Every muscle quivers.

No one's here. Everything is brown and dry around us—the leaves, the trees, the ground, even the rock...except the two of us. We're flushed and sweaty. I crouch down to catch my breath. My pants tangled at my ankles, I trip and Nate catches me. He's in the same predicament. I look at his beautiful face and push his hair out of his eyes. He needs a haircut. He bends down and helps me pull my pants up.

"Shit, Jules, I'm sorry about that." He points to the rock gouges on my backside.

"What are you talking about?"

He reaches back and prods the sore spot gently.

"Ouch."

"We'll need to clean that up when we get to the cabin."

" You can doctor me later, deal?" I sit gingerly as the cuts sting on the drive back.

I fall asleep on the way. I wake when he carries me from the car and lays me on a couch. I'm out of it—exhausted.

Someone tugs off my pants and rolls me to one side. More words but I can't understand. I jolt as a horrific sting jars me awake. He holds my leg down. I'm in the cement room, waiting....

"Hey, it's me. I'm not going to hurt you."

Yeah, that's what you always say. I don't move a muscle.. Maybe he won't see me. He rubs my back, talking softly, trying to trick me.

"Juliette, it's me. I want to clean this."

I stay silent.

"Juliette, look at me. It's me. Really." He works to turn me around. I don't want to face him. His hands are soft on my face, caressing.

I peek open my eyes...

It's Nate. It's my Nate.

I shake and cry, an utter mess. God, how is he going to put up with me?

He holds me, hugging, whispering in my ear. I stop fighting.

I'm okay.

I'm okay.

I'm okay.

Nate runs his hands over my hair gently. Goran only touched me gently in the early days. After the first hit, he'd grab my hair in anger or when raping me.

"Jules, I want to clean up that gash to keep it from getting infected. Can you stand so I can see better?"

I nod. If I stand, I can see him.

"It's going to hurt, I'm sorry."

I'm prepared now. "I'm ready." I brace myself.

He takes his time and is gentle. He warns me before putting on the betadine.

"Why don't you shower and I'll wrap it afterwards."

The hot water feels good, but I hurt. I'm having a hard time knowing where I am—am I safe? Or am I delusional? I come out wrapped in a towel and notice the rose-petalled bed. It brings me back. I leave the land of limbo and laugh.

"Did you do this, Casanova?"

He wraps his arms around me like a security blanket. "Uh, no, I wish I could take credit. Our dear friends have worked to be sure the ambiance is just right. They've also filled the fridge. I'm pulling out some snacks. You must be hungry after our workout." He kisses my neck.

"Yeah, I could eat. Let me get dressed first."

He kisses me and my towel falls away. I want him again. "Hmm, let's see if we can manage this where you don't get injured."

He leads me to the petal-strewn bed and stares as I lay down, surrounded by the fragrant roses. Daylight dims as night closes in. The cabin is cozy and warm and just as he shrugs out of his clothes, there's a loud knocking at the door.

"Shit, is it that late?"

He looks at his watch. "Damn. My love, I'm afraid we need to dress and be presentable for those hooligans out there. Feel up to it? Or should I send them away?"

I pull him down for a lingering kiss. "Maybe we pretend we're not here." I push him back and grin. Then I think of Sara and the others who've worked hard to help us.

He sees my indecision. "Yeah, we gotta let them in. If it weren't for them, I'd be car camping alone, feeling sorry for myself."

Chapter 61

Christmas

Nate:

I finish editing the polar bear migration piece and it's being picked up by *Outside Magazine*. They want it for their cover story for the new year. They've also accepted our narwhal and beluga piece and may combine them for an Arctic exposé. When we get magazine covers, lots of job offers come in, which is good and bad. At least we get to pick our next projects.

Juliette's talked to the Homeland Security agents again and shared the documents she took from Goran's office. Goran's still MIA but his businesses have been shut down and, with her help, they may be able to get him locked up for a good long time.

Christmas is next week. Juliette and I decide to divide and conquer. It's been over eight years since she's been back to Santa Marta and she's anxious to spend time with her family. I'll drive to Kentucky to spend Christmas with my parents, then fly to Santa Marta to meet Juliette for her birthday and New Year's.

I drop her at the airport and leave from there to drive home. The highways are slick and icy.

When I arrive in the evening, snow's on the ground and the house is decorated with twinkling lights and a large Douglas fir. The house smells of cinnamon and cranberries and stewed chicken—my favorite.

"Sorry we won't see Juliette this time around. It's good to

see you, though," Dad says as he hugs me.

"Good to be home. You pulled out all the stops. Love the decorations and lights. It smells like Christmas in here."

The newly renovated house has a large central fireplace and they added a large picture window that looks out onto the surrounding forest. It's cozy and rustic. Mom's stunning ceramics dress up different corners of the room.

"Hungry, sweetie? I made stewed chicken with cornbread. Glass of wine or mulled cider?"

"I knew I smelled your stewed chicken. I've been craving it. And a glass of wine sounds perfect—red, please."

Dad pours a glass and leads me to a comfy chair by the fire. "Warm up a spell before dinner. You have your next assignment scheduled? And congrats on the *Outside* cover. Just terrific!"

"Thanks. We're stoked about that. Jorge and Sara's photos and film really nailed it for us. And yes, we've got our next gig. We're headed to the Mexican border near El Paso to look at the migrant crisis." I sip my wine, losing myself in the flickering light of the fire.

"When'll that be?" Dad asks.

"Early January sometime."

"Please be safe down there," Mom says as she stands over my shoulder.

"I will." I stare into the fire, missing Juliette. I wonder if she's gotten to her house yet.

The smell of chicken smothered in garlic and wine brings me out of my melancholy. I look up when they bring the food to the table.

"That smells incredible. I haven't had this in ages." I kiss Mom on the cheek.

She smiles and pulls my face to hers. "I know you miss her. We all do." I nod and smile. "Now let's eat this delicious food before it gets cold."

"Yes, ma'am."

It's good to be home, seeing my parents relaxed. I tell them about climbing with Juliette.

"So, she's a natural, huh? She may give you a run for your money," Dad says between mouthfuls of stew. He hands me the basket of steaming cornbread.

"You're right about that. She climbed one of the intermediate pitches with me on her first try—without breaking a sweat. She was great and I think she had fun." I bite into a hunk of spicy cornbread, butter melting down my chin. I feel like a little kid.

"I'm glad she can share that with you. Have you talked about wedding dates yet?" Mom asks, pointing to where I've got food on my face. Yup, I'm eight years old again.

"Uh, not yet. I need to look at my work schedule. I have an idea but need to float it by her first."

"Don't keep us in suspense. Come on, spill," Dad chides. He puts his fork down, waiting.

Truthfully, I want to know how they feel about it.

"I thought we might get married at her parents' place in Colombia and do a riding trip with everyone. And then I'd like to whisk her away somewhere for a honeymoon. How would you guys feel about that?"

My parents grin at each other.

"Oh, honey, I love the idea—a destination wedding. I'm sure her parents will be thrilled. Any idea when?" Mom passes the salad.

"June or July. Bea's due in April. I hope she'll be recovered enough to join us. Knowing her, she'll be dancing around right after delivery. She'd kill me if we didn't wait 'til Baby Garcia's born. She's been trying to get me to take her rock climbing while six months pregnant."

They both laugh.

"I bet. Poor Jorge. How's he handling impending fatherhood?"

"He's excited, but nervous. He and Bea babysit Sam a lot, for the practice."

Mom and Dad are relieved there is a plan.

Before I leave to fly to Santa Marta, Mom presents me with a gift for Juliette—a small ceramic vase the color of her eyes, an intense olive- and emerald-green combo. Juliette will love it.

As I'm leaving the pottery shed, I notice a clump of clay Mom's been glazing. The colors are gorgeous but I wonder why she'd spend the effort to glaze this chunk of clay. And then I remember. I laugh as I make my way out of the shed.

Two days later, I catch a flight to Santa Marta by way of Medellin.

Chapter 62
Romeo and Riptides

Juliette:

I arrive at the airport late. Nate stands outside the terminal, looking lost. I watch him a minute before running to him. He's in a crisp white button-down and khaki shorts, legs pale and muscled. He's gotten a haircut—still wavy but tamer. I hop out of the car and run to meet him.

"God, I've missed you." He swings me around. "Santa Marta looks good on you. You are definitely a girl of the tropics."

I'm embarrassed by his attention, but thrilled he still finds me beautiful. "Come on, we've got so much to do." I grab his hand and lead him to the car.

"Nice wheels." He grins when he sees the cute blue convertible. "We're gonna have fun."

I kiss him. When he grabs for me, I push him away. "Uh-uh, not 'til later, Romeo. We've got things to see and relatives who want to meet you. You're going to have to keep your pants on for a while. My Aunt Fiona and Uncle Stefano from Medellin are coming in today. I haven't seen them in seven years."

He pouts. "You better give me a little time alone with you, or I may not be able to contain myself. I missed you," he says huskily. I love when his voice drops like that.

"I will—actually, there's a little spot I'll show you where we can play."

"Hmm, play?" He pulls up the white cotton skirt of my sundress, and runs his fingers up my thigh.

The Caribbean Sea sparkles aqua blue as a warm breeze tosses our hair around. I try not to drive off the road with his hand fastened to my leg. I look behind me and make a crazy U-turn in the road and head to the spot.

"Whoa, where are you taking me?"

"You'll see." I lay my hand on his chest, wiggling my fingers between the buttons of his shirt.

"Whoa there, hands on the wheel."

I laugh and pull into the overlook along the coastal highway. I planned to bring him here later, but his proximity makes it hard to think. He's a drug and I need a fix. When I turn off the car, his hand wanders up under the hem of my dress. We're alone out here. Once we're at the house, there won't be much privacy.

I surprise him by straddling him in one deft move. I run my tongue along his cheek to his ear. He groans, pushing me back.

"Jules, we gotta find someplace less public than this." His hands knead my butt and hips.

"Follow me." I undo his seatbelt and give him another kiss as I hop out of the car. I lead him down a path where a massive boulder sits, hidden behind an outbuilding. I lay down as the wind kicks up my dress, rendering me indecent. My sultry pose draws him to me.

He takes my leg and kisses my knee, moving up—slowly, an inch at a time. I run my hands through his tousled hair as he strips off my thong. He takes me with his teeth and tongue as the salty breeze whips around. I'm a bottle rocket, about to explode. He takes his time, not allowing me relief. When I can't stand it a minute more, I grab him by the shirt, nearly tearing off the buttons. He mounts me there, forgetting Dani's earlier advice. Don't care.

"I shouldn't crave your touch so much," I say as we lay,

spent on the boulder, listening to the waves crash around us. He's on his side, watching me, stretched out on my back, arms flung over my head. I take in his chiseled face and chest, his open shirt dancing in the breeze.

"It's hard to look at you laying there and not want to go again."

I sit up, smiling. "We can come back, but I've got other cool hideaway spots where we can do this again, with less risk of being seen." I hop off and go looking for my underwear. "Shit, they've blown away." They're cartwheeling down the beach.

He laughs. "Guess I'll have easy access now. How's your backside, by the way?" He pulls up my dress to check out my scar from our earlier sexcapade.

I slap his hand away. "Hey, it's bad enough I'm going back without underwear. Behave yourself."

"Just admiring your assets." He gives me a playful slap. I grab his hand. His touch is electrifying.

We return to the car and head for the casita. He keeps a hand on my thigh, teasing me.

My parents run out to meet us and engulf Nate in a hug when we pull up.

"Was your flight delayed?" Dad asks. Nate turns beet-red.

I'm buzzing with the wind-tousled image of Nate taking me on that boulder. I zip off to my bedroom for another pair of panties. When I come back, I find Dad hugging Nate with tears in his eyes.

"Dad, are you okay?"

He doesn't say anything but pulls me into the hug. "I'm so happy for you two. I'll leave you in peace. Aunt Fiona will be here soon. She and Stefano arrived earlier but jetted out to pick up goodies for dinner tonight. They're ecstatic to see you—both of you." He leaves us, wiping his eyes as he backs away.

"What was that all about?"

"He asked about our wedding plans. I should have spoken to you first, but I mentioned I thought it might be nice to do it right here."

"Nate, really? But...what about your parents and family? Isn't this kind of far for them?"

"It's not a bad flight. Look, we can talk about it later, but I think it's very doable, if it's something you'd like."

I kiss him and run my hands through his wind-tousled hair. "I'd love that. And I know it would mean the world to my family."

He pulls me to him and realizes I've found another pair of panties. He snaps the elastic band and frowns.

"Shame." He squeezes my backside.

I laugh. "Hey, I need to be respectable for the relatives."

I lead him to the central courtyard, where my Uncle Stefano and Aunt Fiona are chatting with Marta and Greg.

"We drove by the overlook and found a couple going at it. Those two were hot for each other..." Fiona giggles and looks up to see me. "Oh God, Juliette..." Her face turns cherry-red.

Uncle Stefano folds me in a hug, chuckling. "Sweet Juliette, it's wonderful to see you after so many years. You're radiant. And you must be Nate, or should we call you Romeo?" he laughs, turning to shake Nate's hand.

"Nate will do. Thanks."

He's such a good sport when my family gives him all kinds of grief.

Fiona pulls him into a hug, laughing. "I'm sorry for...err...I don't even know...but I'm thrilled to finally meet you. Marta and Greg haven't stopped talking about you since visiting Juliette in D.C."

"Well, it's great to meet you too," Nate says, smiling.

Guess we'd been too caught up in our bouldering to notice we were on display. Poor Nate—his ears are almost purple.

Mom and Dad bring in a tray of fresh sangria. We find seats around the courtyard and drink our sangria while telling stories. I catch Fiona and Stefano staring —I'm not the same girl they knew seven years ago.

We head to the stables, where we spend the afternoon grooming and tacking up a pair of horses. Nate knows his way around a horse. He talks as he brushes them and picks their hooves. The horses are usually skittish around folks who aren't used to them, but they're calm and enjoy his attention.

He rides Canela—a sturdy little chestnut. She's quiet and gentle. I'm on Bache - who's a little more fiery. We mount up and ride out to the beach. I keep us at a walk for a bit to be sure Nate's okay. A large wave crashes nearby and Bache decides it's time to play. He breaks into a canter, bucking here and there. He's spunky but not out of control. I bring him back to a bouncy trot. Canela picks up on his energy and wants to play. Nate gives me a nervous look but goes with it. Then he encourages her into a canter.

He turns to me. "Race ya."

I know Bache will not stand for being left behind. I hope we don't kill ourselves. We fly down the beach, the horses at a gallop, bounding in and out of the waves. Bache doesn't do anything stupid. After a wild run, I pull back to a trot. The wind howls, making it impossible to speak. I lead us along the shore to the little cove where I plan to bring Nate later. It's my childhood hideaway and a place we can be alone. I dismount and Nate follows my lead. We guide the horses to the inland river where they can drink.

"You never told me you were a jockey in a former life."

Nate smiles. "I can't tell you all my secrets."

That afternoon, I take him back to the cove. The inland river is completely secluded and deep enough for a swim. This was my very own secret jungle garden. I had an active imagination and would run around with the boys, who wanted to be pirates or bandidos. I always had this place to be my true self, wild and uninhibited. I'd collect bugs and watch as the animals came at dusk to drink.

It's strange returning after so many years. I'm not that reckless girl anymore. Or am I?

I love watching Nate swim naked in the lagoon. He's a seal, slick and graceful and a beautiful swimmer.

After our naked swim, we put on suits and head to the Caribbean side of the cove. Before I say anything, Nate sets out to sea. I'd forgotten to warn him about the riptides. He turns to beckon me out. I stare in horror as I see what's about to happen.

"Nate, it's a rip current. Come back!"

He can't hear me over the wind and waves crashing. I jump up and down, gesturing madly for him to swim out of it, to go parallel. I see his fear when he recognizes what I've known for three interminable seconds.

He swims hard parallel to the shore. This is a strong one. People drown here. I look around for anyone with a boat or canoe—anything to help. I'm terrified he'll wear out fighting the current. There's no one in sight.

I watch, transfixed by the horror unfolding in front of me. He's slowing down.

God, please, fight for me…fight for us…don't give up. I can't tell if he's slowing because he's exhausted or it's just the motion of the current he's in. He's so far away, and yet, just there. I can't get to him. He's drowning and I'm going to be left on this beach, alone.

He swims, slowly, methodically. I yell, to encourage him to keep swimming. He has to make it back to me. He eventually gets out of the current, but he's far from shore. He can still drown out there. He floats on his back for a rest, but realizes he's getting sucked back into the current. He starts swimming hard again. I look to see where he'll come ashore and run to meet him. He muscles his way up the beach, coughing and gasping. I fall next to him, grabbing him.

"God, Nate, I almost lost you. Shit, are you okay?"

He doesn't speak. He spits up saltwater while I rub his back. I lean into him until he's only heaving, out of breath.

And then it hits me...

"You nearly died out there. Fuck, Nate! What were you thinking? Why would you take the risk?"

He won't look at me. A tidal wave of fury engulfs me.

"Why would you do that to me?"

When he glances at me, shame is written all over him.

I've seen my life go from complete joy to utter desolation in a matter of minutes. I storm off down the beach, leaving him behind.

"Jules, where's Nate? What's going on?" Dad's outside, cleaning the grill.

"Down on the beach where he nearly drowned...that fucker. What's he trying to prove anyway?" I stomp back to the bedroom and slam the door.

I wanted to kill him. Now I feel terrible. Dad found him on the beach where I left him. He brought him back and now Nate is slumped on the bed, green and miserable.

I run cool water in the shower. "Come here, let's get that saltwater washed off so the aloe can do its job."

He finally looks at me, resembling a drowned puppy. "Jules, I'm sorry. It happened so fast. I'd never do anything to hurt you or scare you."

When I touch his burnt skin, he gasps. "Shhh, it's okay. I know that. I was having a moment. I get those from time to time." I smile at him.

He looks lost. His eyes are more stunning with his sun-baked skin. I kiss him, then pull him into the shower. The cold water is bracing and we both shriek. He clings to me.

After the chilly shower, I pull out soft, fluffy towels and wrap him up.

"Sit still. You're going to need aloe to soothe that burn." I gently massage the gel into his shoulders and back. He winces but relaxes as the aloe does its job. I push him back on the bed so I can apply it to his chest and stomach, which are also bright red.

He reaches for me, despite looking utterly exhausted. He pulls off my towel and drags me on top of him. The light comes back to his eyes. "How come you're not fried? Your skin is golden. I'm a lobster. It's not fair."

"I wear sunblock every day. Did you do any such thing?"

He looks away in mock shame.

"Uh-huh, so this is your doing. I will not have you turn into a crusty lobster. You get a pass this time," I scold.

"Or what?"

Chapter 63
Sancocho and Blossomcrowns

Nate:

I thought she might hit me when she realized I was no longer in trouble. Thank God Greg came to my rescue. I should be mad she abandoned me out there, but I'm not. I'm touched she was so angry at the thought of losing me. She could still buck and run— but I don't think so, not anymore. We've entered a new stage. It feels steady and like the worst has passed. A week before Christmas, she assisted Interpol and Homeland Security. Goran's been caught and extradited to Sweden to face charges. The documents she stole from his office sealed his fate.

God, I love her—even her wild temper. She's as fiery as the horses she rides. This morning she had two horses in the cross ties—no saddles. Just groomed and ready to go. She wants to practice barebacking so we can ride away together on horseback after the wedding ceremony. She's been thrumming with energy since yesterday's mishap. Now she sits astride a lively 1,500-pound sleek black beast, hopping on with grace...from the ground. I'm in over my head.

Seeing her here, with her parents and cousins, I realize she hasn't had this support since leaving Bogota. When we return to D.C., things will be even better now that we're not worried about Goran or the rest of it.

At lunch, Marta pulls steaming bowls from the open-hearth oven.

"Sancocho," Juliette informs me. "It's a traditional Colombian soup with chicken and potatoes."

Earthy and hearty, it's perfect after working up an appetite. Juliette grabs condiments—aji: hot chile sauce, cream, and capers. They serve the soup in large charcoal pottery bowls. Fiona grabs a basket of yucca and cheese rolls, called buñuelos. I could live here forever.

As we dine in the sunny courtyard, a colorful hummingbird flits on one of the flowering vines - a tiny, sparkling jewel.

Juliette smiles. "That's a Santa Marta blossomcrown. They're common but exquisite to watch."

It nips from flower to flower, completely unbothered by our presence.

After lunch, we walk on the beach to stretch our legs.

"So, you like it here?" she asks, grabbing my hand as the breeze tosses her hair about.

"It's stunning. You must have missed it." I pick up a seashell. It's pearly white, nearly blending in with the sugary sand.

"I can't believe it's been over seven years since I was home. Nice to be here now, knowing my past is finally behind me." She wades deeper. If she weren't dressed in crisp linen shorts, I'd drag her in, but after yesterday's debacle, that might not be well-received. This stretch is close to where I nearly drowned.

"What do you think about next June or July to tie the knot?" I ask.

She wades back toward me, squeezing my hand. "I was thinking the same thing. Just need to check with Mark—we should invite him anyway."

"Great idea. I'd like to invite Darrien and Claire too."

"We should also invite Campbell and Charlie and I'm going to ask Dani, Sara, and Bea to be my bridesmaids. I'd love to have Kenny and Kyle too, if they can swing it." Her eyes sparkle in excitement.

"Sounds like we're starting a guest list. Let's compile our

lists and see where we are in terms of numbers. Any good hotels we can reserve for out-of-town guests?"

She smiles. "My Tio Pablo owns a resort down the beach from here and may be able to put people up for a reasonable fare. June is low season, as it'll be chilly."

I pull her to me.

She blinks up at me. "Let's swim this afternoon. Suits optional and no riptides."

Chapter 64
Shifting Sands

Juliette:

As we're hosing down the horses the next afternoon, my parents find us in the barn.

"Nate, your mom called. Why don't you give her a call?"

"Sure, anything wrong?"

Mom tries to hold back tears as she pulls him into a hug. "It's your dad. He's in the hospital. He's had a heart attack."

The ground shifts beneath my feet.

Nate goes gray. "Oh shit, is he..."

"He's alive," Dad says quickly, putting a hand on Nate's shoulder. "Go call."

I take the hose from him and he runs back to the house.

"Jules, you should fly back with him. I looked into getting your tickets changed. You can fly out this afternoon," Dad offers.

I nod, speechless. I grab them in a hug. I can't imagine losing either one of them.

"Go be with him. We'll finish up here."

At the house, I hear Nate on the phone with his mom. He paces the room as I stand outside the door.

When he hangs up, I put my arms around him. "My parents got our tickets changed. We leave this afternoon."

He pulls me tighter to him, crying into my shoulder. I've never seen him this undone. "Thanks."

I rub his back, feeling the tension in his muscles. His cell phone buzzes.

"I'll start packing. It's going to be okay." I reach up and kiss him, looking into his bloodshot eyes.

He squeezes me. "Thanks, Jules."

That afternoon, we fly to Medellin and from there to Houston and on to Lexington.

It's just past midnight when we arrive. I forgot how cold Kentucky can be. It's icy and I'm frozen through as I don't have much with me. Nate grabs me a sweater from the front closet and puts it over my shoulders.

We find Chaney sleeping in a chair. The house is frigid as the fire has died. Nate stokes it back to life while I go to Chaney. She rouses when I put a hand on her shoulder.

"I can't believe you made it so quickly." She gets up to hugs us. "You two look like you came from the islands. Juliette, thank you for coming."

"I'm so sorry about Clay. How is he?"

"He's okay. They're transporting him to Lexington tomorrow. I should have just met you there tomorrow instead of driving all this way tonight."

"That's okay. Mom, we'll take my car tomorrow and get a room at a nearby hotel. When's the surgery?"

"It's scheduled for later tomorrow. They don't want to wait too long. Are you hungry?" She looks exhausted but would cook us a meal if we asked.

"No, we're fine. Chaney, let's get you to bed. You need to sleep." I take her arm and lead her up the stairs. Nate locks the house and brings up our bags. I tuck Chaney into bed and bring her a glass of water.

Once she's settled, I find Nate in his room.

"Thanks for helping her. She's gotta be a mess."

"I can't imagine what she's going through. It's a good idea to get her a hotel in Lexington. I didn't realize they wouldn't be able to take care of him nearby."

We drive into Lexington the next morning to meet the helicopter. Nate's upset to see his dad so gray and pale and visibly older. We spend the morning at the hospital as his dad gets checked in. His surgery is scheduled for later in the afternoon. While Nate and his mom meet with the cardiologist, I pick up lunch. Afterward, Nate tells me the cardiologist is optimistic the bypass will take pressure off his dad's heart.

It's a tense afternoon and evening. I go on food runs and encourage Nate and his mom to nap. Later that evening, the surgeon tells us the procedure went well and Clay is expected to make a full recovery. Nate and Chaney cling to each other. I convince them to come back to the hotel to get some sleep. We're sharing a suite because we don't want Chaney to be alone.

I spend the next few days picking up meals and running errands. I talk to Mark and plan to return to work in a day. Nate wants to stay with his mom until his dad is released from the hospital in the next five to seven days. He wants to be sure she can handle Clay's home care as he'lll be recovering over the next two to four weeks.

When I get home, I'm exhausted. But I'm grateful I could be there for Nate and Chaney to them. It felt good to be needed and Chaney was appreciative. She gave me a long hug before I left for the airport. She told me I was the daughter she always wished for, making us both cry.

Part III

Four Months Later

Chapter 65
Wedding Plans

Nate:

Bea gave birth to a beautiful baby girl on April sixth—Carolina Margarita Garcia. She's a sparkling combination of her parents with a mop of dark, curly hair and penetrating, deep brown eyes. She's a pistol, giggly and happy or dead serious, copying Bea's scowl when the occasion calls for it.

Sam is a toddling one-year-old with chubby little legs who keeps his parents on their toes. Juliette and I spend many a Friday night babysitting. Juliette's a natural with the kiddos.

I worry about my parents, as they're getting older. Dad's doing better. I sent him a stationary bike, which he loves. He rides daily and doesn't mind the heart-healthy meals Mom's cooking. I'm bringing them a pair of sturdy mountain bikes they can ride on the back roads near home. When I video chat with them, I'm amazed how great they both look.

I think about Mom and her fear of losing Dad. That's the downside to loving someone the way I love Juliette—the paralyzing fear it could disappear, in an instant. I understand Juliette's reaction to my near-drowning. When I needed her most, she was there for me. And every morning I wake next to her, I count my blessings.

Wedding plans are progressing. Juliette's uncle will host the out-of-town guests at his resort down the beach from Juliette's parents' place. I've reached out to Bea for dancing classes. Juliette can pull off anything on the dance floor but

I want to wow her—or at least not make a fool of myself. In exchange for dancing sessions, I've promised Bea we'll do a climbing trip in the weeks after the wedding.

Now to decide where to whisk Juliette off for a honeymoon. She's convinced we're delaying a few months, but plan to take her to Glacier Bay in Alaska for ten days or a cabana in the Bahamas. Sara's agreed to pack her a bag once I get tickets bought. Dani's got me doing extra climbing classes for beginners as an REI consultant. With the extra money, I can afford to splurge a bit on the honeymoon.

Chapter 66.
Bachelorette Party

Juliette:

While at work one evening, I get a message that someone's in the reception waiting to speak with me. My heart beats eratically, hoping it has nothing to do with Goran. I find Sara, who tells me I'm requested outside. I nearly refuse, but Mark appears, telling me I should leave for the afternoon. Dani's waiting in the car. As we drive along, she and Sara glance at each other, smiling. I have an idea what they're up to.

Bea answers the door clad in a peacock-blue cha-cha number. She hands me a hilarious white and gold tutu, complete with a fairy wand and tiara. I planned to spend a quiet evening at home—was even looking forward to it—but that's not happening.

After changing, I find Claire, although I almost don't recognize her in an enormous feather-festooned headpiece.

I can't imagine how I'd have gotten through this past year without these women.

I'm handed a glass of watermelon sangria and the ladies line up in formation. Pink's "Get the Party Started" booms from the speakers and Bea leads the flash mob.

Later, appetizers are brought out - that must be Kyle creations—a pasta and sausage dish resembling mini Nates and Juliettes tied up in climbing ropes and a crudité platter with a tropical palm made from carrot and green pepper. There are fresh tuna and blistered cherry kebabs with fiery habanero salsa. And the watermelon sangria goes down a little too easily. I've been stressed over wedding plans and trying to keep up at work. Tonight, I'm letting go.

The next morning, I'm surprised with breakfast in bed, brought in by mom and Chaney. I practically burst into tears when I see them. Everyone comes in with TV trays, courtesy of Kenny, and we enjoy omelets, biscuits, and fresh fruit and hot coffee. Claire has arranged for us to hit the Voda Spa and Wellness studio for a day of pampering and respite. We get facials, massages, and mani-pedis throughout the day, interspersed with dance lessons, as Bea wants us to perform a flash mob at the wedding to surprise the guys. The women have already been working on their moves—I just need to catch up.

"Okay, Jules, this is the final stage of your bachelorette party. Tonight, we're going out. We've got shower gifts for you."

I look at their expectant faces—beautiful, made up and ready to hit the town. They're worried I'm not up for this. Truthfully, the thought of taking this party out into public makes me nervous, but they've worked hard to make this weekend special—I don't want to disappoint them.

Chapter 67

Pre-Nuptial Dance

Nate:

"Bienvenidos mis amigos. Tenemos una celebración esta noche."

I hear *celebracion esta noche* and realize I'm in trouble. I shoot a look at Gavin, who struggles to keep a straight face.... unsuccessfully. We're at a table at a swank Latin dance club Kenny has ties to. The guys have brought me here as part of my bachelor party weekend.

"Would Señorita Juliette Fernandez and Señor Nate Fisher please make their way to the stage?"

What? She's here? I look around, but the place is packed. I can't see anything but masses of bodies. I don't move from my seat.

"I understand there may be reluctance to come up, but please—this is a part of tonight's show. Don't make me stand up here alone. Freddie? Kenny? Will you please escort our guests up here?"

I'm mortified. Kenny walks up as I try to melt into my chair. He takes my arm and pulls me up. "Come on, Nate. Believe me, you'll want to see Juliette. Nothing to be afraid of - you're among friends." He laughs and I smile nervously, following him up to the stage.

"Ah, you must be Nate. Bienvenidos - soo glad you could join us. Now, where is your ravishing bride? She didn't buck and run?"

Juliette's led to the stage. She *is* ravishing. I've never seen her look so sexy—golden hair flowing over sexy shoulders. She's wearing a black leather vest over skinny jeans. Jesus…

"Check out this guy's expression. Amore - mis amigos. And you must be Juliette."

Everyone claps. She looks up, smiling. She's dazzling but nervous. The announcer asks us some questions, but I can't think straight. And I can't tear my eyes from her. I'm worried because she's like a deer in the headlights. We reach for each other at the same time. The band plays and all I want to do is to hold her.

"I see you two are ready for a pre-nuptial dance—and my guess is this isn't your first one."

The audience roars in appreciation. I pull her to me.

"This song is for you. *Felicitaciones!*"

We begin slow, and I feel her settle into the rhythm. "You look incredible," I whisper.

"So do you." She sways into me.

The music builds and Juliette does her dance magic. I work to keep up; Bea's lessons have helped. I anticipate the moves and know we're doing a rhumba. I step around so she can show off what she does best.

She pulls back, catching my eye. "You hiding something from me? Like a fling with a dancing girl?"

I forget we're in this very public place when I kiss her. The crowd responds appreciatively. The band continues, a livelier number. The band leader calls up the rest of the bridal party. Gavin and Jorge tackle me. The girls swing Juliette around, laughing. Kenny and Kyle join us and we dance for hours. We're invited backstage to hang out with the band and they offer us tickets to one of their shows later in the year as a wedding gift.

As we come out of the club, drunk and feeling no pain, a large black limo waits.

Gavin leads us to the car. "Surprise! Your folks wanted to treat you to a stay at the Ritz. Enjoy. We'll see you tomorrow."

I look around at our friends, grateful we're all here together.

Sara pulls me aside. "You'll find suitcases in your room, waiting with all you need. Have fun!"

We hug everyone and climb into the limo. I have a hard time keeping my hands to myself as we make our way to the hotel.

"I never took you to be a black leather kind of girl, but that top is incredible on you."

When we open the hotel room door, we're stunned.

"My God, how'd they do this?"

The room is awash in candlelight. Next to the bed are matching white suitcases, labeled *His* and *Hers*. A huge red STOP sign sits on the nightstand, with a note attached.

"Looks like our friends are commanding us tonight," she laughs.

"Hmm, we better follow their directions or we may have a hostile wedding party on our hands."

Dearest Lovebirds,

Before you whip off your clothes in a night of unprecedented lust and hedonism, we've put together a love package - customized - just for you. Everyone knows the sex gets stale after you tie the knot. We want to be sure you have a few more nights of hot and heavy before the inevitable. Take your respective suitcases and you'll find your next instructions. You won't be disappointed...

I go to my suitcase and read the note.

"Wow, they've orchestrated tonight." We laugh.

"No detail left to the imagination."

I come up behind her and finger the buttons on her leather vest, wanting to undress her.

She pushes me off, pouting. "I've got my instructions. You know I'm a rule follower."

"Really? That's not my recollection, considering all the places…"

She puts a finger to my lips and pushes me back by the hips. "Back off."

Shit, really?

She retreats to the bathroom with her suitcase.

When I open my case, a huge, expandable spring-loaded penis jumps out. The case is full of kinky sex toys and a heinous metallic blue G-string. There's a note telling me blue's my color. *Sorry, Gavin, not doing it.* In the bag I find a pair of boxers covered in lipstick kisses. These I can manage. I pull my jeans on over them. I want her to undress me.

Juliette emerges from the bathroom in a short, slinky gold robe. Her hair is tied loosely at the nape of her neck. Something sparkles beneath the robe. "Why are you still dressed?"

I fling the G-string around my finger. She laughs and approaches me, wagging her finger.

"You're not following directions." When she comes closer, jasmine and almonds float in the air. The sounds of guitar—something Spanish, classical maybe captivates.. She sways ever so subtly to the music.

When I reach for her, she pushes my hands down. She moves behind me, wrapping her arms around me. I suck in a breath. She's silky soft. Her hands splay across my chest and stomach. I can't breathe..She moves in front of me, unbuttoning my shirt, swaying to Spanish guitar. It's maddening - like the time we spent at the Museum of Natural History. God, she was such a tease. She holds my gaze then drops her eyes to my mouth. Still a tease. She pulls off my shirt, kissing my collarbone. She slaps my hand way when I attempt to grab her. The music builds as she unbuckles my belt.

"Jules," I rasp. "I'm not going to last."

"You'll last, practice that rock-climbing breathing. In and out…in and out…"

"In and out…not helping," I grumble.

She's a nymph—a wicked sea nymph. She slides my jeans down, noticing the lipstick boxers. She smiles and moves behind me again. There's a swoosh of fabric. Her skin, coated in sensual, bewitching oil rubs against me. The silk of whatever she's wearing and her oil-slicked skin drives me to distraction. I try to turn, but she won't let me. Her hips thrust into mine as her hands move over my chest. When she moves in front of me, I'm not prepared.

She's in a gold lace teddy - her body shimmers with glitter.

"You weren't kidding when you said you had a make-over today." I push her back a moment to gape at her golden beauty in the flickering candlelight. "God, you're magnificent. I could devour you." I nuzzle her neck and grab her. I pick her up and bring her to the giant king-size bed and lay her down. I stare, unable to help myself. "You're too beautiful to touch."

She grabs me, pulling me down on top of her. When she's naked, I notice the body glitter artfully applied. It starts at her ankle, circling upwards, twisting around her knee and up the back of her thigh and to her hip. The trail continues across smooth stomach to encircle her left breast, up to her throat, finally trailing back to her navel.

I take her leg where the glitter trail starts—on the inside of her foot—kissing slowly, moving upward, following. I like this treasure hunt. She tastes of almonds and wildflowers.

I'm not sure I'll make it all the way without a detour.

Chapter 68
Love and Forgiveness

Juliette:

Nate flies down with his parents a few days before the wedding. His parents and grandparents stay at a friend's house down the beach from our casita. The rest of the wedding party is at Tio Pablo's resort. Wedding jitters are real, but I ride daily to keep my nerves in check.

Nate is ensconced away with his groomsmen. I catch an occasional glimpse of him running on the beach, wishing I could join him. Dani and Bea arrived this morning. Carolina, Bea's baby girl, is darling. My cousins share babysitting duties, arguing over Sam and Carolina. Mom and Fiona and Aunt Gigi keep us fed and watered. I make sure Bea gets out on a horse one morning so she can experience a ride down the beach, as I've promised.

So, this is it...no going back. I wasn't sure I had the strength, but I realized how quickly I could lose it all when Nate was stuck in that riptide. That was my wake-up call. That and my mother's voice in my head. She cornered me the day after the incident and, in her tough-mother fashion, showed me a light I wasn't keen to see.

"Jules, do you love Nate?"

I was offended by the question. I stared at her, frowning. "Of course, why?"

She leveled me with her *mom* look. She stood in a flowy skirt with the wind whipping her hair around her head like a halo. "You guys have been through a lot—especially being so young. That's all. Sometimes things get messy, even when you love someone. I want to be sure you love Nate the way he loves you."

That pissed me off.

"I do love Nate—maybe not in the same way he loves me... Am I supposed to love him exactly how he loves me?"

Mom smiled, looking past me. Mother Nature knew my mood—whitecaps churned in the shallows as thunder rumbled in the distance.

"No... and that's a fair point. You can only love someone the way you do. But it's important to see them as they are, and not for who you need them to be."

That stopped me. I tried to let her words sink in. All these years since fleeing Goran, I've deflected. I forgot how to let things seep in. Her words that day soaked in like a sponge.

"It's okay, Jules. No one is perfect. Not Nate. Not you. Not me. None of us. We're all trying our best. You were hard on Nate when he got caught in that riptide. Why?"

I felt trapped, but when I looked into her beautiful aqua eyes, there was no judgment...just a question. She's always been level-headed; accepting, but brutally honest.

She wasn't the mama bear I wanted as a kid. She let me figure things out, even the hard way. When I had an altercation with some kid, she made me handle it.

I didn't want to think about my selfish response to Nate's near-drowning. At the time, I could only think of my loss— what it would mean if he were truly gone. I felt rage...blinding, terrible rage. And I blamed him, making it his fault for allowing me to feel so desperate.

I met her eyes as tears slid down my cheeks. No use putting on armor with her. She knew my soft spots.

"I couldn't imagine life without him. When I saw how close I came to that, well...I was furious. I blamed him for taking the risk. It wasn't right. And I'm sorry."

"Have you told him that?"

I looked down. "No."

Her arms wrapped around me, pulling me in close. She was warm and smelled of cassava flour and garlic. "It's okay, sweetie. You have time to let him know you. Be with him. Love him but also grant him forgiveness. Acknowledge when you do something that warrants an apology. Saying you're sorry isn't weakness. Letting him in to your inner world is import-ant. It's vital to a healthy relationship. Let him be there for you. But you also need to be there for him. It goes both ways." She kissed my forehead and released me, wandering back into the kitchen.

I remember her talks when I was a kid, when I'd feel the world was against me. She was a sage spirit imparting wisdom from some other world—a world I didn't wholly inhabit or quite grasp. She'd float like a vision, dancing almost, her words a prayer or an intonation of something deeper. I learned resil-ience from her.

Chapter 69

Peaches and Roses
Santa Marta, June 13, 2004

Nate:

I meet Gavin and the others in the foyer of the resort. Kenny makes sure my bow tie is straight and my white linen suit is stain-free. The rest of my groomsmen are dashing in blue seersucker, even with pale bare feet. I thought Juliette was nutty when she told me she wanted to wed barefoot. Now I understand the appeal, my toes sinking into the warm sand.

The sun begins its dramatic descent. Gavin leads me to the front of the wildflower-draped altar. He kids me to keep me from getting too much in my head. Jorge, Darrien, Campbell, and Kenny start escorting guests. A pair of classical guitars plays as guests proceed to their seats. No one wears shoes - naked toes sinking into silky sand. The music is just loud enough to hear over the waves lapping behind us. My eyes fill with tears when I see my parents ushered in by Campbell.

Gavin leans over. "Do you have the ring?"

Shit. Then I remember the ring will come with little Sidique. *Keep it together.*

Juliette's parents are ushered in. I give Marta a wink and a thumbs-up. Next come the beautiful bridesmaids carrying tropical bouquets. Then the comic relief—Juliette's little cousins bounce down the aisle, throwing flower petals, adding to the lush flower petal carpet crushed into the pearly white sand. Following them is a very serious Sidique, balancing a small navy silk pillow holding our rings. He carries it as if it's a tray of crystal goblets. Then the dramatic change in music; from two guitars to a small orchestra of flutes and violins. It's time.

I look down, waiting, almost with impatience. I don't want to rush this—but God, I want to see her. I notice her naked feet first - gliding over the flower-petaled carpet. She clings to her father's arm. Greg smiles and leans into her, I imagine giving her words of encouragement. She smiles. Her chest rises with the breath she's just taken.

Her eyes meet mine and I'm the only person out here. The wind kicks up and, as she gets closer, I see her arresting eyes under the intricate lace veil, reminding me of a Spanish mantilla. The dress is gorgeous and shows off her beautiful shape. The color is a warm ivory, complimenting her sun-kissed skin.

Gavin nudges me. He knows I'm gaga.

I can't breathe when she stands in front of me. Greg lifts her veil and gives her a kiss. He says, "I love you, my darling Juliette. This is just the beginning." He smiles as he passes her to me. She gasps and grips my arm like her life depends on it.

I steal a glance at my parents. They cling to each other, tears running down their cheeks. I can't lose it. I can't lose it. *Keep it together.* I shouldn't have looked.

Juliette - right here - in front of me. She's breathtaking. I'm not sure what we're supposed to do, even though we rehearsed this earlier. It's all flown out the window. I stare into her eyes and wait for what's to come. I feel her settling and she takes a breath.

The wedding officiate, Padre Ramirez, a family friend who's known her most of her life, clears his throat. "Ladies and gentlemen, we are gathered here today to witness the..."

I listen to his every word. This is momentous and I don't want to miss any of it. Juliette gazes at me but looks lost in her head. I squeeze her hands. I want her here for this. She returns my squeeze and manages a small smile. After more remarks, I feel her loosening up.

We've boldly written our own vows. I loved the idea until this exact moment. *Shit, what if I forget?* Before I know it, I take the ring from Sidique's pillow and slide it onto her finger. Somehow my mind knows what to do.

"Juliette, I can't believe this day has come. We've walked over fiery coals and swum through shark-infested waters to get here. But we made it. I never imagined loving anyone as much. I promise to be here for you in sickness and health, in good times and bad, and through the challenges that life throws us. We've weathered storms already and although those storms may only be the beginning, I'm ready to strap on my life jacket, as long as you're next to me." I try to keep my wits so I can finish. My voice shakes. I don't care. Juliette trembles too, Aegean eyes, watery.

I fight on. "Juliette, my promise to you is that I will take you for all you are, for all you become, and for all you want to be. You're my life partner. I'll be there for you when you need me and even when you don't. I want to wake to see your beautiful face each morning and to feel your breath on my cheek as you fall asleep. When I look into your fathomless eyes, I see myself, and although it's terrifying, it's the most exhilarated I've ever felt. I will always love you; this is my solemn vow." I'm so relieved to have gotten through it, I forget myself and draw her hand to my mouth and kiss it.

She smiles, tears streaking down her cheeks, then looks down, mustering her nerve. She bends down to where Sidique holds the pillow and takes my ring. She slides it onto my finger after nearly dropping it, her hands shaking.

"Nate, I'm not sure how to stand so close without wanting to run off with you." She laughs, going off script.

"Not today, you don't," Gavin says, putting a restraining hand on my shoulder.

"You've brought me more joy in the past year. It's nearly a year since we first met—all those miles away in the Comoros.

I had no idea where that would lead. I remember your face when Darrien told you we were with a group called OGRE—I thought you might buck and run then. You didn't. All I know is I love you. I know love can get lost in the busyness of life, but I vow that I'll give you my love in good times and bad, in sickness and health, and even when I want to throttle you. If the start of our relationship is any indication of what's to come, we won't be bored. I vow I'll work to be a strong life partner. I'll try to trust you with my heart and soul and the dark places that exist within me. I will always love you." She pulls me to her spontaneously and kisses me.

Everyone claps and hoots.

Padre Ramirez laughs as he says, "Uh, Juliette and Nate, uh, please release one another so I can pronounce you husband and wife." He puts a hand on my shoulder. I back up, grinning. "Okay, I now pronounce you husband and wife. Nate, *now* you may kiss your bride."

I pull her to me and kiss her, feeling it from the top of my head to the tips of my toes. I can't hear the noise going on around us, just wind and waves, reminding me how alive I am at this very moment.

"Ladies and gentlemen, may I now present Mr. and Mrs. Nathan Fisher."

I pick her up and swing her around. I lean in, and whisper, "Jules, you are the most beautiful bride I've ever seen."

As we stand gazing at each other, I feel Gavin lean into me. "Congratulations—you did it!" I hug him, surrounded by the others. Juliette is engulfed by her bridesmaids in their coral-hued gowns.

A huge gray horse is led over. I'd forgotten about this next part. *Shit, don't fall. Don't fall,* I repeat to myself.

Dani unhooks her veil and train. Someone kindly brings over a mounting block, painted white, covered in flowers. Juliette hops on with ease. I follow, hoping I look as athletic. I mount and wrap my hands around her waist. I nuzzle her neck and she turns to kiss me. The clicks of cameras echo around us. I imagine we look spectacular up here.

Someone grabs my leg. Gavin's grinning up at me. "Be careful up there. Don't fall!"

I laugh as the mighty beast starts moving. Juliette's kicked him and we're trotting off quietly. I know the horse would like to run off, but Juliette keeps him quiet. I hang on, hoping she knows I'm not a rodeo rider. Soon we gallop down the beach. His canter is smooth. I wrap my legs tightly around his belly, hoping I'm not telling him to speed up. As we get closer to the waves crashing on the beach, the horse gets playful. He's having fun and Juliette's letting him. I hang on, thankful for strong legs and good balance. After a little frolicking in the waves, Juliette pulls him back to a trot.

Another group of photographers will meet us when we make it to Tio Pablo's resort. Juliette's in no rush to get there. When we're walking, I release my grip on her.

"We did it!" I kiss her neck. She surprises me by turning on the horse and whipping her legs around so she's facing me. "Whoa, where'd you learn that trick?"

She hands me the reins. *Shit, what if he...*

She laughs. "I've been practicing some stunts. We won't get much time alone, so this may be it until later tonight. I love you, Nate. I meant every word. I promise I'll open myself to you. And, more importantly, I'll be there when you need me...the way I should have when you nearly drowned."

I run my fingers down her exquisite face, catching soft tears as they slide down her cheeks.

"I won't hide my scars anymore," she whispers. "I never thought I'd get to have this. Thank you for loving me."

I pull her to me as she wraps her arms and legs around me. We kiss as the sky reflects the colors of peaches and roses from the setting sun, just as it had, nearly a year ago when I woke on that roof in the Comoros. We watch together, as the sun melts into the horizon.

The End

Postscript

Below are recipes mentioned in the story. Some recipes are from earlier versions of the story but some of those scenes were cut in the editing process. I still love the recipes I've included. Visit my website Wildflower Press to link to recipes. Bon Appetit.
                                                    —*Cathy Schieffelin*

Recipes:

1. Broiled Lobster Tail with Vanilla – foreignfork.com

2. Mataba – crushed cassava in coconut milk – peacecorps.gov/educators/recipe-madaba

3. Grilled Yucca with Garlic Mojo – livingsweetmoments.com

4. Green Papaya Salad – recipetineats.com

5. Tuna Pilau – taste.com.au

6. Mauritian Chicken Stew* – thefoodiesavenue.com

7. Coconut Fish Curry with Vegetables – jernejkitchen.com

8. Albondigas in Red Chile Sauce – Mexican meatballs* – bonappetit.com

9. Harissa Roasted Veggies* – somethingnutritiousblog.com

10. Miso glazed Salmon with green tea rice – finecooking.com

11. Arugula salad with Blood Orange vinaigrette* – emerils.com

12. Garlic Naan* – cafedelites.com

Jamilla's Grilled Tuna with Harissa

Ingredients:

4 - 8 oz tuna steaks
Salt to taste
1/2 tsp black pepper
1/2 tsp cumin
1/2tsp paprika
1 Tsp olive oil

Harissa Sauce:

4 diced fresh Roma tomatoes
1 or 2 tsp Harissa spice mix
1 tsp ground coriander
1 tsp ground Caraway seeds
3 cloves of garlic, chopped
4 Tbsp olive oil

Grilled Tuna:

1. Season the Tuna with salt, pepper, paprika and cumin. Rub tuna steaks with olive oil. Grill the tuna each side on preheated grill for 5-8 minutes, depending on your preferred temperature.

For the sauce:

1. Heat the olive oil in a skillet on medium heat. Add the garlic. Sautee for 1 minute.

2. Add the tomatoes, sauté for 10 minutes. Add tomato paste, harissa, spices and 1/2 cup of water. Simmer for 10 minutes.

Arrange the tuna on a platter with 4 lemon wedges. Serve the sauce on the side.

–Recipe Courtesy of Jamilla Sbaa of Jamilla's Café,
New Orleans, LA

The Call Music Playlist

This is a global mix of music I found inspiring while writing *The Call*. Arabic, Afro-Caribbean, West African, Colombian, Appalachian and more. All music can be found on Apple Music

1. The Adhan (Call to Prayer) – Yusuf Islam

2. Bwana – Baco

3. Huzalwa – Chebli Msaidie

4. Amarain – Amr Diab

5. Sidi H'bibi – Jalal Hamdaoui

6. Saharouny El Leil – Ragheb Alama

7. Dindin – Putamayo and Kimi Djabate

8. Wassiye – Habib Koite and Keletigui Diabate

9. Kothbiro – Ayub Ogada

10. KaWone Mayo – Baaba Maal and Mansour Seck

11. N'ba – Habib Koite

12. Batoumambe – Habibe Koite and Keletigui Diabate

13. Si Tu Vieux – Baaba Maal and Mumford and Sons

14. There Will Be Time – Baaba Maal and Mumford and Sons

15. Sodade – Cesaria Evora and Bongo

16. Miss Perfumado – Cesaria Evora

17. Pegate – Ricky Martin

18. Two Step – Dave Matthews Band

Acknowledgments

My sincere thanks to so many who supported me on this writing journey...

Page Beary for reading every version of this story, even on your tiny cell phone over the past three years. Your friendship and encouragement mean everything to me.

The Thursday Night Writer's Workshop Crew held in the Crow's Nest of the landlocked Mid-city Yacht Club captained by wordsmith and motivator (Do Better Cathy!) Stephen Rea.

Asata Radcliffe, developmental editor at Atmosphere Press—for your wisdom, gentle guidance and expertise. I'm deeply indebted and grateful.

Mona Musser, Monique McCall, Shanda and MJ Brown, Laura Moise, Caroline Finegan, Amy Porche and Troy Moon—for your friendship, card games, walks, workouts and great meals.

The Red Tent Book Club—for great reads, delicious meals and memorable conversations.

Moncef and Jamilla Sbaa of Jamilla's Café on Maple St. for fabulous food, friendship and Grilled Tuna with Harissa recipe. I'll be back soon—save me a lamb tagine and bottle of Bordeaux...

Peace Corps Comoros volunteers and Comorian friends who are never far from my mind. I dream of waking to the call to prayer and nights spent camped on the beach waiting sea turtles.

Santa Francisca Romana colleagues and friends in Bogota. Sancocho and Taganga sunrises—nothing better. And a shot of aguardiente to keep the words flowing...

The Frontier Nursing Service and community of Hyden, Kentucky. My time at FNS was instrumental in Nate's origin story and so many other stories I'm compelled to write.

Nothing better than misty mountain mornings...and Cassie's Circle Pie.

Thanks to Jon and Hildy Massy for years of horsey adventures and family holidays at beautiful Logis Lagniappe. We wouldn't have Clifford if it weren't for you.

Thanks to my brother Richard Croft for his support and willingness to take my calls at all hours of the night. You inspire my writing and are ten times the writer I'll ever be. Tag, your turn!

Thank you to my beautiful sisters: Mari, Aynne, Deborah, Diane and Denise for staying connected in a very disconnected world. I'm grateful for you. Bonds of family can't be broken.

Thank you to my children: Anna, Caroline and Sam for indulging my writing life and allowing me to disappear for days at a time to Folsom. I'm proud of you and love you to the moon and back.

Finally, thank you John, my very own infectious disease expert who helped make this crazy, made-up virus somewhat plausible. I'm deeply grateful for your encouragement, sage advice, Little Feat playlist and ridiculous sense of humor. You keep me laughing. All my love.

About Atmosphere Press

Founded in 2015, Atmosphere Press was built on the principles of Honesty, Transparency, Professionalism, Kindness, and Making Your Book Awesome. As an ethical and author-friendly hybrid press, we stay true to that founding mission today.

If you're a reader, enter our giveaway for a free book here:

SCAN TO ENTER
BOOK GIVEAWAY

If you're a writer, submit your manuscript for consideration here:

SCAN TO SUBMIT
MANUSCRIPT

And always feel free to visit Atmosphere Press and our authors online at atmospherepress.com. See you there soon!

About the Author

CATHY SCHIEFFELIN is an avid reader and writer. A love of nature and years of adventure and travel contribute to her daily writing life. Her work has been published in *Adanna Literary Journal*, *Halfway Down the Stairs* and *Microfiction Monday Magazine*. *The Call* is her first novel. She lives in New Orleans with her husband, three children and pack of mongrels.

www.ingramcontent.com/pod-product-compliance
Lightning Source LLC
Chambersburg PA
CBHW021344150726
47989CB00005B/2099